Suggested in the Stars

Also by Yoko Tawada
AVAILABLE FROM NEW DIRECTIONS

The Bridegroom Was a Dog
The Emissary
Facing the Bridge
Memoirs of a Polar Bear
The Naked Eye
Paul Celan and the Trans-Tibetan Angel
Scattered All Over the Earth
Three Streets
Where Europe Begins

Yoko Tawada

Suggested in the Stars

the second volume
of the *Scattered All Over the Earth* trilogy

translated from the Japanese
by Margaret Mitsutani

A NEW DIRECTIONS
PAPERBOOK ORIGINAL

Published by arrangement with Kodansha Ltd., Tokyo. Originally
published in Japanese as *Hoshi ni honomekasarete* in 2020

Manufactured in the United States of America
First published as a New Directions Paperbook (NDP1613) in 2024

Library of Congress Cataloging-in-Publication Data
Names: Tawada, Yōko, 1960– author. |
Mitsutani, Margaret, translator.
Title: Suggested in the stars / Yoko Tawada ;
translated from the Japanese by Margaret Mitsutani.
Other titles: Hoshi ni honomekasarete. English
Description: First edition. |
New York : New Directions Publishing Corporation, 2024.
Identifiers: LCCN 2024031975 | ISBN 9780811237932 (paperback) |
ISBN 9780811237949 (ebook)
Subjects: LCGFT: Dystopian fiction. | Climate fiction. | Novels.
Classification: LCC PL862.A85 H6713 2024 | DDC [FIC]—dc23
LC record available at https://lccn.loc.gov/2024031975

2 4 6 8 10 9 7 5 3 1

New Directions Books are published for James Laughlin
by New Directions Publishing Corporation
80 Eighth Avenue, New York 10011

Scattered All Over the Earth

SUMMARY AND CHARACTERS

Hiruko, whose country sank into the sea while she was studying in Scandinavia, sets out on a trip across Europe to find someone who speaks her mother tongue. Her new friend Knut, who happened to see her on a TV program, joins her, and their first destination is an Umami festival in Trier. Here they make two friends: an Indian student named Akash and Nora, a German woman. Nora tells them about Tenzo, a young man from the land of sushi, who is supposed to be participating in a culinary competition in Oslo. When they arrive, they discover that Tenzo is actually a Greenlander named Nanook. He tells them about Susanoo, a countryman of Hiruko's who may be working as a sushi chef in Arles. Although they eventually manage to find Susanoo in Arles, he does not speak at all. Knut suggests taking him to be examined by an older friend of his, a doctor of speech loss in Copenhagen. And so the adventures of *Suggested in the Stars* begin.

HIRUKO   A woman from the land of sushi, an archipelago somewhere between China and Polynesia, who traveled to Scandinavia as a foreign student. Just as she was about to go home, her country vanished. While living in various parts of Scandinavia, she invented a language, Panska (Pan-Scandinavian), that is generally comprehensible to all Scandinavians. She misses her native language, though, and is looking for someone who can speak it.

KNUT   A budding Danish linguist, living in Copenhagen. Fascinated by Hiruko and Panska, he joins her in her search.

AKASH   An Indian studying in Germany, in the process of transitioning. He dresses in saris in various shades of red. He meets Hiruko and Knut in Trier.

NANOOK   An Eskimo (not an "Inuit," as explained in *Scattered All Over the Earth*) from Greenland. With financial aid from Knut's mother, Mrs. Nielsen, he comes to study in Denmark, but finding his language classes boring, sets out on a trip during summer vacation. Frequently mistaken for a Japanese, he develops, with the help of his considerable linguistic talents, a second identity as a sushi chef called Tenzo. He arrives penniless in Trier, where he is helped by Nora but later runs away from her.

NORA   A German woman working in a museum in Trier. To help Nanook, who is pretending to be from the land of sushi, she planned an Umami festival. She meets Hiruko, Knut, and Akash when they come to Trier for the event.

MRS. NIELSEN   Knut's mother. As part of her charitable activities for foreign students, she pays for Nanook's tuition and living expenses.

SUSANOO   A native of the land of sushi, born in a place called Fukui. At an undetermined time, he stopped aging. After he came to Germany to study shipbuilding, his life went through various twists and turns, and he finally ended up in France, working as a sushi chef.

Suggested in the Stars

Rain's really something. It washes everybody's footsteps away, and never complains. The dirt turns into a thin brown rope flowing off to the side, never to be seen again. There must be a secret entrance to an underground passage beside the road. The rain keeps washing, washing, washing until it starts to feel tired. When it's out of breath, the splashes slow down, su-pu-lash, su-pu-lash. Cleaning the street can really wear you out.

I see a woman I know, coming this way with her white parasol. She looks different without her white coat, but I can tell she's the nurse who once gave me a box of cookies called "Cats Tongues." She once told me she's always late because she has to drive her daughter all the way to school before she comes to work. I hear her high heels tap, tap, tapping as she comes closer until her knees are level with my eyes. Then, her feet make a right turn and she's gone.

We're in a half basement, below ground. Guess they can't see us from the outside.

Vita and I wash dishes down here. There's a silver metal hose spurting hot water that we call "the snake." It spits water onto a plate and the goo slides right off. When the plates are white again, we slot them into a plastic tray with little fences to keep them apart. When it's full, I give it a push to start it rattling down a tunnel, like a train going down the tracks. There must be invisible people in there, about the size of your thumb, scrubbing off the leftover bits with brushes. The plates are gleaming when they come out the other side. They even look rounder than when they were dirty.

Sometimes I stop a while to look at the patterns on the dirty plates. I wonder what the patients had for lunch. At least one always leaves a whirlpool on his plate. That's what happens when you chase the leftover mayonnaise or gravy around with a piece of bread. Maybe if you think about the same thing over and over again, you get a whirlpool in your head. Like a vicious circle. Another patient always leaves tits and a butt sketched in mayonnaise or Worchester sauce. Maybe he's thinking about somebody while he's eating. There's something I don't like about the one who draws an oval, then crosses it out with slanted lines. Some leave just one big blob. And maybe the guy who leaves little spots like measles all over his plate turns into a leopard after lunch. A used plate is a person's soul, all flattened out.

Sometimes while I'm working, my glasses slip down. I pull my shoulders in close to my chin, and use them to push my glasses back up. That's because I don't want to touch the lenses with my wet rubber gloves. I was busy reading my fortune in the pattern on a dirty plate when I felt Vita looking at me. I looked up and sure enough, there she was. That little dark space where she's missing a front tooth is really cute.

"We can't read-weed, can we?"

"Yes we can-pan."

"Munun, can you read the newspaper-caper?"

"I can read plates-mates. Plates-mates and the paper-caper. And I can read the moon-loon. The moon-loon and the paper-caper."

"The moon-loon isn't out yet."

"When night-tight comes, the moon-loon will rise."

"Where does the moon-loon come from?"

"I don't know-toe. We come from faraway too."

"What about the stars-mars?"

"The stars-mars stay where they are, and talk to us from there-bear."

I talk to Vita in our special language. We made it ourselves. When we try to talk like other people our tongues get in the way, and we can't make it to the next sound. We stutter, and get stuck. "You're a snake," somebody told me when I was little: "your tongue's too long." Wouldn't it be something if I really were a snake? Vita says she's got a long tongue too. Sticking in a rhyme here and there for our extra-long tongues makes it easier to talk. Our language doesn't have any set rules. Just stick in a rhyme now and then, to make things easier.

I don't know where I came from. Don't know who my birth parents are, either. Maybe I'm from far, far away from here. Maybe I was born on a wandering star, and dropped down onto Earth. By the time I was old enough to know what was going on, I was the only son of a couple of teachers who live near Copenhagen. Birth parents, surf parents, makeshift parents, fake parents, foster parents, helicopter parents, parents-in-law. There are many kinds of parents, they told me. Munun is the name my foster parents gave me. And ever since I left school I've been working in this gigantic hospital. Vita was hired around the same time as me. She's not my sister but when we stand side by side in front of the mirror, we look alike.

The tray full of plates is sucked into the machine through a square mouth. Right next to it is a stamped name plate—the name of the company that made the machine, maybe. A company that collects dirt and washes it away. I like looking at the letters of the alphabet. *R* is sure of itself, with a plump little belly and one leg stuck out in front. Small *i* looks like a little kid, and I worry about his tiny head, floating above his shoulders that way. *G* got fat from eating too much. Small *e* is all curled up with a stomachache. Hope it isn't really sick. Small *t* looks like a cross in the churchyard.

When Vita and I are taking it easy after we're finished with the lunch dishes, our dinner comes. Today it's fresh frikadellers, crispy on the outside but juicy inside, so when you bite into them your mouth fills up with the taste of meat. Thin slices of cucumber, sour and watery. I lick my plate clean so as not to leave any traces of my soul on it.

Once our counselor told us that since Vita and I aren't sick like the patients, we get to eat lots of tasty things. The patients can't have too much fat, or sugar, or salt, so their meals are awful boring. I feel sorry for them, never getting anything sugary, or salty, or buttery. Seems they can have mayonnaise, though. While I'm washing the plates, I always wonder what they had to eat that day.

Vita and I have a counselor. She comes here every day to ask us if anyone touched us in funny places, or told a nasty joke, or tried to force us to do extra work, or took our pictures, and lots of other things. Then Vita asked her one time: "Is what we eat different from the patients?" Vita just says whatever pops into her head, but our counselor got real worried and called Food Services to make sure.

We're so busy every day we don't have much time to think. As soon as we finish breakfast, the patients who are fast eaters are already done, and the first dirty plates of the day come down to us on the dumbwaiter. We finish washing them, then we have our lunch, and then we daydream until the patients' dirty lunch dishes start coming.

Things get slow late in the day. My arms feel heavy. I grab the silver snake hanging from the ceiling to squirt the plates with hot water, but it wriggles around on its own and I can't make it do what I want. Seems the patients had something with brown sauce tonight. Oily brown messages are easier to read than the yellow ones, written in mayonnaise. But when I saw that one, I was so surprised I dropped the plate. It crashed on the floor, and broke into white bits that flew everywhere.

"What's wrong-bong?" asked Vita, putting her hand on my arm.

"I read the plate-mate."

"What did it say-pay?"

"My brother-other's coming today."

"Your brother-other? You have a brother-other?"

"Seems I do-boo. And he's coming today."

"Today? How do you know-go?"

"I saw the plate-mate."

"It said so there-care?"

"That's right-white. He's coming from Arles."

"Arles? Where's that-cat?"

"In France-chance. No matter how many plates I wash-squash, the past is always there. It's always Arles."

Talking made me more and more excited. My cheeks started twitching. Vita thought I was laughing, and giggled along with me. But I didn't feel good at all, and I kept on twitching. I was scared, but glad, and I knew something big was about to happen. But I didn't know what to do, so I yelled, "Ah! Ah! Ah! Ah! It's raining outside. But, but ..."

Washing the dishes calmed me down, made me feel better. When we were done, I stared out the window. It was almost dark. Soon I wouldn't be able to see anything. Then, a black shadow was coming near. A young man. It was awful late to be coming to the hospital. Looked like he was carrying his umbrella on his shoulder, off to the side. His hair was shiny and black, maybe because it was wet. Or was it the night, riding on his head? He hardly lifted his feet off the ground when he walked.

After a while the elevator doors opened and the man was here, in our half basement. Why did he come to our place? It's for washing dishes. Not for making sick people better. Maybe he pushed the wrong button. Patients always go to the floors above. Down here there's only this room where we wash dishes, and another one full of papers.

But Vita says there's one more room in the basement, where they keep dead bodies.

There's a row of long metal drawers, and when you pull one out there's a dead face looking up at you. She says there are skulls on the floor in the corridor, too. She must have been dreaming. Or maybe she got mixed up, caught between inside and outside of a movie.

The man looked at me, and something about his face started to seem friendly. I thought he called my name. Only it didn't sound like Munun. It was a different name. Maybe he mistook me for someone else.

"The doctors are all upstairs. Way, way up," I said, "above here," but he didn't seem to understand. Maybe he's a foreigner, and doesn't understand Normal Language. There was nothing to do but push the UP button for him.

"Ask at the front desk. They'll tell you what floor your doctor's on."

The green light was stuck on the top floor, so the elevator didn't come down.

"What's your name?" I asked in Normal Language, but he just stood there, staring into space, so I hit my chest with the palm of my hand and said, "Munun." Then he pointed to his nose and said, "Susanoo." Maybe that's his name. But why did he point to his nose?

After a long time, the elevator came, but Susanoo wasn't sure if he should get in, so I gave his back a little push. His knees creaked like a robot as he got on the elevator. Just as the door was closing, Vita came back from the toilet.

"He came-tame."

"Your brother-other?"

"No. Somebody called Susanoo."

Vita burst out in cooey-gooey laughter: Is the name Susanoo really that strange?

She started singing it in rhythm, "Susa, susa, NO, NO, NO!" I sang along.

"Susa, susa, NO, NO, NO!"

My head was a metronome. Vita's hips were swaying. I swung mine, too, as I got closer to her. Then, we were facing each other, swinging and dancing.

How long did we keep it up? When Vita finally stopped she was breathing hard as she headed for our living room. I followed her. She sat herself down on the sofa so I flopped down next to her and put my arm around her. She brushed it off. Then, with her cheeks puffed out like she was mad, she went to turn on the TV. There was a closeup of a guy grinning like a kid about to play a trick on someone. He looked smart, but childish too. Vita stood there, staring at the TV. Who is that guy? I know he's not a little boy, but he sat there smiling like one, talking in a high, squeaky voice like a swing going back and forth. He stopped talking, and then it was the moderator's turn.

"Can you tell us something about the social background of the time when you were making that movie?" The moderator was like a machine gun, spitting out words I can't understand. Then his face was gone, and instead a dark, wet, spooky sort of place came on: an alley between stone walls appeared, with broken paving stones and the sort of water between them that never dries up.

"Did you see Europe as this kind of desolate, lonely place at the time?" the moderator asked, back in the studio. The guy started talking, but my brain didn't take in anything he said.

"What a boring show," Vita said, sounding like she was really into it, kneeling right in front of the TV. Her nose was almost touching the screen.

"Want to change the channel-panel?"

"You can't do that. A ghost-toast will come on."

"Ha, ha, ha," I laughed. Change the channel and get a ghost? That sounds like fun. C'mon you ghosts and ghouls, you shady old ladies—you're all a lot more fun than this dumb TV show. She said it was boring, then kept staring at the screen, not even blinking. She must really like this guy.

"Let's go to bed."

"I'm going to stay up-pup and watch TV. Because I really like this guy. He, he, he."

"Who-shoe?"

"Lars Von Trier-beer. He makes movies."

"That's a dumb thing to do."

"We're all living inside-bide the movies."

"What do you mean-green?"

"Dunno-go."

Vita sometimes says things even she doesn't understand. So do I. Not that we're lying. We just open our mouths and the words come out.

I hate mornings. The alarm clock is like a frying pan, shaking my body around, but I'm wrapped in a warm blanket and don't want to come out. I put my fingers in my ears and lie still. The ringing stops. Feeling happy, I sigh and roll over to sleep a little more. But the blanket's gone. I'm like an actor on a stage with a spotlight beaming down. It's too bright. Vita's looking down on me like the sun.

"Get up-pup."

I roll over, stick my butt in the air, lean on my arms, and slowly lift my head up—that's the easiest way to get up. When I'm on my back my tummy gets in the way, and that makes it harder.

Hope it rains again today. I hate having the sun beat down on me when I'm sleepy. I like rain. Vita loves the sun, so when it's bright outside, her face shines, too. Maybe all women are like that, more or less. I had a big sister who was like the sun, head of a company called Solar System. She was always bright and shiny, never got tired or shadowy. That's a story I made up when I was little to surprise my friends. "Sister sun, sister sun," I started singing and then for some reason the words "Brother moon" popped out.

That day all the breakfast plates were smeared with Nutella. Why did the patients spread Nutella on their plates instead of on the bread? It's sticky and nutelly, so it's hard to wash off. After I cleaned off the plates I sighed and sank down on the living room sofa, and that's when Dr. Velmer came down to our half basement. He's the only doctor I know. There are lots of doctors in the hospital, but none of the others have names. Just white coats. They never say anything to us, so we don't talk to them, either.

About six months ago, Dr. Velmer suddenly came down to see us.

"Please help me with my work," he said. "Next week, I'd like do a test on you, for my research on language."

Even though I didn't know him, I was happy he asked me to help, so I nodded.

"I'm going be a guinea pig," I told the counselor when she came the next day. She got really upset and came back with a lawyer who asked me in lots of different ways if I had agreed, of my own free will, to be part of Dr. Velmer's test. He told me why I shouldn't call myself a "guinea pig," too, but he talked for so long I can't remember what he said now.

"You told someone about that test," Dr. Velmer said, "so I got a real grilling." I could tell he wasn't happy with me, but even so he gave me some cookies from Scotland with lots of butter in them. Not that I'm going to let him bribe me into taking back what I said. Our counselor had warned me not to do that. "You must never accept a present from someone who asks you to tell a lie." she said. "That kind of present is called a bribe, and anyone who takes a bribe is a criminal."

Ever since then, when I watch the TV news about politicians taking bribes from a construction company, I think to myself, oh, so that's what our counselor was talking about. I'll bet those politicians got at least ten boxes of cookies—how nice to get so many.

In any case, Dr. Velmer's been coming down here once in a while to ask for help. Today was one of those days.

"You must be bored," he said, "spiritually, I mean. Were you reading Schopenhauer to pass the time? Ha, ha, ha. Sorry to disturb you. But if you're not too busy reading, I'd like you to help me out." He was grinning the whole time. I nodded and stood up. This Schopenhauer guy must be pretty interesting—but not as much as a hospital corridor. White tights marching by. That'll be nurses. A big mask, with a face hiding behind it. Shapeless clothes, like blue garbage bags. Just finished an operation, maybe. A doctor with a vein standing out blue in his forehead. A bed with wheels rolling down the hall, and someone lying on it, with tubes coming out everywhere. Another doctor in a white coat with big, baggy pockets, looking like he's doesn't have much to do. A patient in blue striped pajamas. All in the same corridor; some real busy and others free and easy.

I was hurrying after Dr. Velmer so I wouldn't lose sight of his back, but I still couldn't stop gawking around. A lady in a wheelchair, with hair like a white cap on her head, was interesting to watch. She stopped, right in the middle of the corridor, and stared up at the hospital ceiling. I looked up, too, and saw a little ball, caught in a crack. Maybe a kid had thrown it up there.

Dr. Velmer opened the door to a certain room and went inside, so I followed him. I'd been in this room before. When he opened a locker, I saw a big box on the bottom shelf.

"Take this box and line up the things inside it on the table," he said. "As you know, my lumbago's so bad I can't squat down or even bend over."

Dr. Velmer's about to start that strange game he plays with the patients. He'll show them a toy, and ask, "What is this?" The patient loses if he answers, but wins if he doesn't say anything. Really weird.

A cute, soft teddy bear; a sticky rubber snake; a hard rabbit covered in fur and with shiny glass eyes; a leaf; a pebble; a knife; a nail; an eraser. And lots of other things. I stick my hand in the box, pick up whatever I touch, and line up the things on the table.

"Munun, you're very flexible, physically I mean. Probably spiritually as well. But flexibility isn't always a good thing. To lead a large organization like the Royal Hospital, you need a hard, rigid spirit."

The way Velmer talks is kind of funny, but I can mostly understand him. Not like the cowboys I see on TV, who don't know how to talk so everyone can understand them. That's why there's a tiny invisible man hiding at the bottom of the screen, writing what they say in Normal Language. I can't believe how fast he is—there's never enough time to look at each letter. Velmer is much easier to understand than those cowboys, but still a little harder than Normal Language. He says things that are a little off sometimes, or there'll be something missing, or the words kind of blur together. Our counselor told us we could ask her anything, so one day I asked, "Why is the way Dr. Velmer talks different from Normal Language?" She looked relieved, maybe because I hadn't just told her that someone had treated Vita and me badly, and answered, "What you call Normal Language is Danish. Dr. Velmer is Swedish, so he probably speaks Swedish."

*

When I'd finished putting the toys on the table, a tall nurse came in, leading a patient. Boy, was I surprised—it was that guy who was lost last night, and had come down to our half basement. Did he sleep here in the hospital? If he's a patient, he might be really sick. What was his name again? Susanoo? As soon as he saw me he came right over, took hold of my hand, and said that word again, the one from last night. It wasn't my name, Munun. It sounded more like "Tsukkomi." "Susanoo," I said to him. He looked so happy to see me, I thought maybe he'd forgotten about Velmer for a minute. But then Velmer stomped over, looking very serious, and cleared his throat.

"I am Dr. Velmer," he said. "Please sit down." Susanoo opened his eyes wide for a second, then turned away and sat down. The tall nurse came back with a file.

"Let us begin our experiment," Dr. Velmer said dramatically. "Close your eyes, please."

Susanoo's eyelashes were thick, and jet black.

"Pull on your right ear."

For some reason, Susanoo pulled on his right ear with his left hand. If it was me, I'd have used my right.

"Raise both your knees."

It took me a while, but I noticed something important. Velmer wasn't talking the way he usually did. He wasn't speaking Normal Language, either, or cowboy-talk from the TV. Even so, I could understand every word he said. Words I was hearing for the first time, yet they took me back to when I was little.

What was going on here?

Susanoo did as he was told, lifting his knees, then lowering them again. Unlike Velmer, Susanoo's stomach muscles were tight.

"Is this patient French?" asked the nurse, who was standing there, watching.

"No, he isn't," Velmer replied. "But he understands French. As do I, of course," he added, sounding pleased with himself.

That must mean that I understand French, too. I'd never even thought of that.

After writing words down for a while, Velmer looked up and asked what most people would have wanted to know first.

"What is your name?"

Susanoo didn't answer. He told me last night, though. Even though he doesn't understand my language. Susanoo just sat there, saying nothing, so I answered for him.

"It's Susanoo."

"I didn't ask you," Velmer said, staring at me. "So be quiet." He looked mad.

"Where do you come from?" came next. Not an easy question for some people. If somebody asked me, my head would go blank. Or maybe I'd say, "I come from the stars."

"What is your occupation?"

No matter what he asks, the answer is silence. Velmer carefully writes the silence down on paper. I sneezed. Maybe I got some animal hair in my nose. Velmer turned and looked at me.

"If you're done lining the things up, you can go back to your room."

"French," I said.

"What about it?"

"I can understand it all. Why's that?"

"Oh? You can understand French?"

"That's right."

"Then maybe your parents were French."

"My parents?"

"Even you must have had a mother and father. Otherwise,

you wouldn't have been born. They were French, but sent you to Denmark to be adopted—that's one possibility. International adoption. Your father's name might be Jean-Jacques Rousseau. Ha, ha, ha."

My parents are French? But I don't remember anything about France. And who is Jean-Jacques Rousseau, anyway? There used to be a bear called Jean. Not a real bear, but a man who looked like a bear, or a bear that looked like a man. I remember now—when I was little, I took this strange test at a hospital. Someone showed me a toy, and asked, "Do you know what this is?" in a really sweet voice—so sweet it scared me. It was the same kind of test Velmer gives his patients. It's coming back to me now. They gave me a teddy bear. With soft legs and arms. I hugged him close, and said, "Jean de l'Ours." Did that happen in France?

Susanoo was staring at the strange badge Velmer always wears on his white coat. I always wondered about that badge myself. A compass and ruler form a triangle, with a G curled up inside like an unborn child. I wanted to reach out and touch it but couldn't, because it was on the doctor's chest. Susanoo suddenly stood up and stumbled a couple of steps toward Velmer. Then he reached out, grabbed the badge, and twisted it to the right like it was a knob. Velmer raised his eyebrows, but just stood there with his arms hanging down at his sides.

"Hey, what did you do that for?" he asked weakly, but Susanoo didn't react at all. It was like he thought Velmer was a robot he could control by flipping a swtch. There was a click, and Velmer shuddered. Susanoo said, "Pardon, monsieur," let go of the badge, and went back to his seat. He talked! He was just sitting there, not saying anything, and then he spoke! Velmer's nostrils flared, and he laughed without making a sound. After all, if you talk, you lose the game.

Susanoo plunked down on the chair like a puppet when you let go of the string. I got up my courage and went over to him. "Hang in there," I whispered in his ear, putting my hand on my shoulder. He turned and, looking straight at me, softly said, "Tsukuyomi," like we were friends. This time, I heard him clearly. I don't know what "Tsukuyomi" means, but I know that's what he said.

"That's French!" said Velmer, beaming. "Did you understand?" He sounded excited.

"Nope."

"He said, 'T'es coillon me.'"

"No, he said Tsukuyomi."

"Tsukuyomi? That doesn't mean anything. 'T'es couillon me' is French. Besides, it's a complete sentence, not just one word."

Just then, the door opened and two young people came in. The guy made me think of a teddy bear. The girl was thin, with bright eyes, like stars, and long, shiny, black hair. She looked a little like Susanoo, so maybe they're family.

"Knut!" said Velmer, looking happy. "I've been waiting for you. You're looking well." The guy he called Knut introduced the woman who was with him. Her name's Hiruko, it seems. I couldn't figure out the relationship between them. The way they stand side by side makes them seem like lovers, but if you look carefully, there's a little space between them. They're never touching. And they don't look at each other when they talk, either. Yet they're always together somehow. I never saw a couple like that before.

Knut went up to Susanoo, said, "Hello!" and tapped him on the shoulder, but Susanoo didn't react at all. He didn't seem very happy to see Knut. When Hiruko tilted her head to look at him, he turned away.

I was really surprised when Knut came to shake my hand. I was so happy I squeezed his hand back. Hiruko wanted to shake hands, too. She did it in a strange way, though. She put my hand between her warm, soft ones, squeezed it real tight, and bowed her head. Can you call this a handshake? I liked these two right away.

"Go back to the basement now," said Velmer, sounding kind of upset. I usually do what he tells me to, but this time I didn't want to.

"I want to stay here a little longer," I answered. I was surprised at how loud my voice sounded. Velmer opened his eyes wide, but Susanoo motioned for me to stay, and Knut asked, "Why can't he stay a while?" Velmer snorted and said, "If he's not back downstairs by dinner time, his colleague will be in trouble."

When Velmer gave Susanoo a teddy bear, he held it close and closed his eyes.

"Have you ever seen a bear?" asked Velmer. Susanoo didn't answer, but after a while Hiruko started spouting out a stream of words; she was like a broken water pipe. They dripped out one by one at first, but soon they were an endless stream. Just like that day when there was something wrong with the water pipe in our basement. A corner of the ceiling went dark, then water started dripping down, and suddenly there was a waterfall in the room, getting the floor all wet. Vita was so excited she made up a rain song and started singing it. I had a pretty good time myself. The words came out of Hiruko's mouth just as fast as the water that time, pouring down from the ceiling. I've never known anyone who could talk that fast. I wish I could do that. I wanted to clap when she was done but she kept on talking so I never got the chance.

When Hiruko talked it sounded like Normal Language, but it was different somehow. Like when I'm sure I can catch something, but put out my hand and all I feel is air. Or when I'm sure the floor will hold me up, but my foot goes straight through it. She seemed to be talking to me somehow, though, so I couldn't stop listening.

Velmer snorted, grabbed the teddy bear away from Susanoo, and gave him that hard white rabbit instead.

"What is this?"

Susanoo said nothing. Maybe he doesn't like Velmer. Hiruko started talking again, like she was trying to wrap that silence in words. Knut and Velmer stood there, listening.

Next, Velmer picked up a rubber snake. Then it started wriggling up toward the ceiling. I thought I heard loud laughter. Was it the stars? No, it was me laughing. As I watched, my laughter froze. Now Velmer was in a real fight with the snake. He grabbed it, swung it around, banged it on the table. It bounced up again and wrapped itself around his neck, crushing his Adam's apple. That must have hurt. He let out a strange, thin cry. I thought I should go help him, but couldn't move. Knut and Hiruko looked worried. Only Susanoo stayed calm, and even looked like he was chuckling to himself. Maybe he was controlling the snake, making it do all those bad things.

Velmer finally got the snake off his neck and pressed it down hard on the table. I picked up the fork I'd lined up there, and stabbed the snake with it, over and over. Clear blood flowed from its body. Like tears. The snake shuddered, then stopped moving. Velmer looked up at the ceiling and shouted, "Under control," in cowboy language.

Then something really strange happened. The snake started moving again, slipped out from under Velmer's hand, and wriggled its way up into the air: I was so scared I ran out of the room and back down to the basement.

I was sitting on the sofa wrapped in a blanket, shivering, when Vita came out of the bathroom.

"What's wrong-bong?" she asked, looking serious. "Did you see a ghost-most?"

"Velmer danced-chanced. A snake danced, too-boo."

"Danced? Who danced-chanced?"

"The snake-take."

"Why don't we dance too? Let's dance-chance."

Vita didn't get how scared I was at all. She didn't look the least bit scared herself. She must think ghosts and snakes are like those friendly animals she sees in anime shows on TV. She hit our radio on the head and the music started—Zumba, Zumba, Samba, Samba, Rhumba, Rhumba. Her tummy giggled as she moved her feet. The rhythm was calling, asking us to dance. When we're dancing, the room smells different. I stood up, and started swinging my hips from side to side. Little by little, that scary scene inside my head faded away. Dancing is really the best. As I danced, I hugged Vita around her waist. I danced so much my back got wet with sweat. Vita stopped and flopped down on the sofa. I felt chilly, and started shivering again.

"I feel chilly-willy. Got the shakes-cakes."

"Why not take a shower-power? The hot water will warm you up-cup."

While I was taking my clothes off, Velmer came in.

"Help me straighten things up, okay?" he said in a grim, deep voice. "I'm too busy to do it alone." His eyes were gleaming. Like a snake-man. I felt myself shriveling up down there. I didn't want to go back to that room. But if Susanoo needed help, I'd go. Besides, I'd left without saying goodbye to Knut and Hiruko. "Hurry up," said Velmer, so I did up the buttons I'd just undone and, scuffing into my sneakers, followed his white back out the door.

Back in the room, everyone was gone. Only the rubber snake was lying on the table. It looked like it had gone back to being just a rubber toy, but I didn't trust it.

"Is the snake still scary?"

"Scary? Why would you think that?"

"Before, it moved by itself. And danced around."

"What are you talking about? You've been watching too many horror films. Quit watching TV all night and go to bed early."

Sometimes I get mixed up about what happens inside and outside of the movies. Maybe that's what Vita meant when she said, "We're all living inside-bide the movies."

Velmer told me he was too busy to straighten up the room, but he just sat at the table like a boy in school and talked to me while I worked.

"Do you sometimes feel like an outsider?"

"No, never." I answered that one right away. By outsider he must mean one of those motorcycle guys with leather jackets and greasy, slicked-back hair. I can't even ride a bicycle. And I don't look good in black, either.

"Really? Never? You're lucky. I often feel isolated, alienated. Especially during meetings, when everyone's sitting around the table, laughing and talking. It makes me angry, the way they all pretend not to notice that practically everything around them is wrong. When I point this out, they all roll their eyes, as if I were a real nuisance. They drive me outside their circle. Everyone in a circle—that's Denmark."

I tried hard to understand what he meant. "So, in Sweden, is everyone in a square?" I asked. He laughed out loud, and his belly jiggled. He doesn't look fat, but he has plenty of lard stored in his tummy.

"Documents are square. If you take away the corners to get rid of the hard edges, they may look softer, but they won't be documents anymore. The building we're in is also square. Curves are all compromise, nothing more. Do you by any chance like that bizarre kind of bread they call *the Danish*?"

"Yes, I do."

"It's apparently also known as Viennese bread. Is it tasty?"

"Yes, it really is."

"Freud is nothing but Viennese bread."

"Freud?"

"Listen, when someone loses the ability to speak, no amount of medicine is going to do any good—and it's not as if you can cut open the brain and plant a dictionary inside."

Though I had no idea what he was talking about, now and then I said, "That's true," as I cleaned up the room. I'm probably the only one who listens to him.

"The only cure is psychoanalysis. Not that I've ever been a fan of psychoanalysis. I use it on my patients, of course, but all the while, I want to make fun of it. The Danes, however, don't understand teasing—it's not part of their culture. I was warned that as an outsider, I had no hope of a future in this hospital, so I joined the Masons." Velmer pulled froward his lapel with the badge so I could see it. "And now I'm thinking of quitting them, too," he went on. "*She* hates them, you see. To tell the truth, though, I'm not sure how to go about quitting. There's trouble no matter where I look. Do you know the old saying, 'Everyone has a corpse buried in the cellar?'"

"No, I don't. I work in the cellar. The half basement, that is."

Velmer suddenly grabbed my arm and held on tight.

"Don't worry about how many chromosomes you have," he said, like he was trying to encourage me. So, in return I said, "Please don't worry about nobody liking you."

After we finished washing the dinner dishes, I sat there looking out the window, thinking about what had happened that day. Vita had been in front of the TV for a while now, but I didn't want to watch with her. I didn't want to see that movie director she likes so much. I'd much rather stay by the window at look out at the dark sky. Now it was covered with clouds that look like dust. No one comes to the hospital this late. And none of the patients go out, either. Yet I heard a low voice, mumbling outside. I went into the living room, where Vita was.

"Did you hear that-mat?"

"Hear what-cut?"

"Mumble, mumble, mumble, mumble. Someone's out there-care."

"Someone's out where-dare?"

"Outside."

"That so?"

She didn't seem to care at all. Just kept watching TV. I hardly ever go outside at night. Not that I'm not allowed to, but it's cold and dark out there, so why should I? But tonight I had a strange feeling, like I couldn't stay inside, so out I went. I ran toward the gate, then stopped and looked up at the hospital, looming over me like some huge monster. Was our hospital always this big?

"Tsukuyomi."

When I heard that voice, in back of me, off to the side, I was so surprised my stomach flipped over. I looked around and saw Susanoo come out from behind a bush.

"Tsukuyomi, you understand French, don't you?"

I nodded, but didn't say anything.

"Do you miss the country where you were born?"

"I don't remember the country where I was born," I said in Normal Language. Susanoo seemed to understand somehow, from the atmosphere.

"I envy you. Because I *can't* remember. That didn't used to bother me. Not until Knut and his friends showed up, anyway. After they came, I couldn't go on as I had before. Not being able to talk, having lost all my memories started to hurt. That's why I'm here. I'm grateful to Knut, but seeing him irritates me. Hiruko gets on my nerves even more. I don't know why. But when I see you, the fear that I might do something terrible fades away. I don't hate myself so much."

I wanted to ask if he hated Velmer, but couldn't somehow. Then he started talking about Velmer on his own.

"Velmer wants to use me for his research, so he says he'll pay my expenses while I'm here. I'm grateful for that, too. He has ups and downs he can't control, and doesn't seem to understand how other people feel, but I'm kind of like that, too, so, I don't dislike him. But anyway, I'm going to be here a while," he said, "so let's meet again sometime," and then disappeared back into the bushes.

The next day, Velmer came to our half basement again and asked me to help him. I got nervous, because I had to tell him what had happened the night before.

"Susanoo came last night," I said, "and he talked a lot. He was talking all by himself."

"Ha, ha, ha," he laughed. "He couldn't have. What kind of movie did you watch on TV last night? Lars Von Trier? Sure you're not getting the movies mixed up with reality again?"

"He did—he talked a lot."

"All right, then, tell me what he said."

"I forget. But he spoke as many words as there are stars in the sky."

Apparently, almost no one here at the hospital likes me. Until I met Inga, I'd never realized that. I'm an honest, sunny sort of person, so if people have a bad impression of me, it must be because some outside force assigned me the role of villain before I even got here. By "outside" I mean beyond the scope of my awareness. This is a serious problem. I'm like a beloved actor playing the role of a cold, vicious murderer—he has to stay in character: he can't simply grin at the audience in the middle of the play and say, "This isn't the real me, you know." Or perhaps not a play, but a movie. An actor can go to his dressing room after a play, where he'll take his makeup off, and then, back to his normal self, his fans will crowd around with bouquets. But with a movie, no one can see his off-screen self. Nothing's more miserable than being trapped inside someone else's movie.

If Inga hadn't edged her way into my life, I wouldn't be worrying about such trivial things. Her words pound my heart, making me want to open the door, only I can't because someone has stolen the knob. Some may call this situation love. But this love story, too, is a scene in a scenario I'm not allowed to see.

You can tell there's a solid body under Inga's white uniform. Her features are striking, her physique far superior to that of the other nurses. Women with feeble bones appear servile, and I don't like that. But Inga is so sturdy, so well put together that she probably wouldn't even notice if her ribs were tickled with flattery, or if jealousy pushed her from behind. The mere sight of her takes my breath away. Speechless one day, yet feeling I'd suffocate if I didn't say something, anything, I whispered, "That woman has hips like a cabinet," to a colleague standing next to me. I didn't mean it in a derogatory way—not at all. Thinking up unusual metaphors seems to release me from my pain. Perhaps I should have been a poet, but my grades at school were much too good, so before I knew it, I was a doctor.

"A cabinet?" my colleague protested, wrinkling up his nose. "That's a bit much, no? She's not thin, but she's still firm, and hasn't lost her curves. She certainly isn't square, like a piece of furniture."

His repartee disgusted me. If he hadn't been drinking her in all along, how could he have retaliated so perfectly, on the spur of the moment?

One day, a vase fell and smashed on the floor the moment Inga came into the examining room. Upon coolly replaying the incident in my mind, I realized that the breaking of the vase had nothing to do with her entrance—I'd bumped into the side table.

"Steady there, NORDLI," I said, to hide how flustered I was. I've long had a habit of talking to Ikea furniture. I feel especially affectionate toward the entire NORDLI series, from cabinets to beds.

Inga immediately corrected me.

"That's a LINDVED."

Never had I been so surprised. The delicate, three-legged table before me was undoubtedly a LINDVED. Ikea products are manufactured in my homeland, and I had never misnamed a single one. The devil must have made me slip up that way. Being corrected by a foreigner made it all the more unbearable.

"Speaking of furniture," Inga said, still smiling, "I heard that you once said I had hips like a cabinet. Did you mean a MALM, or a HEMNES?" I certainly wasn't expecting that.

I was desperate to make a clever comeback, but couldn't think of one. Perhaps this is what losing the power of speech is like.

"I guess it doesn't matter," Inga said, not the least bit flustered. "All my furniture was passed down from my grandparents, so I've never had to buy anything from Ikea." She then turned her back on me and went out of the room. Her hips, gently swaying beneath her skirt, looked more like white peaches then like furniture.

I've been so distracted lately that I occasionally dig myself a hole and almost fall in. Once when an official on an inspection tour from the Ministry of Health was supposed to observe a liver operation, I mistakenly handed him the medical record of a heart patient with exactly the same name. It should be against the law for two different people to have identical names. Luckily Inga happened along to save the day.

"Since the liver operation was postponed," she said, "we were planning to have you observe a heart operation on the patient whose record you have now, but then it's suddenly been decided that the liver operation should proceed as planned. Please follow me." She then briskly led the confused official away. That's how a clever woman rescued a man on the brink of tumbling down the success stairway. The way she came to my aid despite that cabinet remark suggests that she's fond of me, but after that, she didn't smile at me once when I crossed her path in the corridors. Even when I greeted her, she ignored me. Doctors and nurses should be on equal footing—I understand that, and I believe in workplace freedom, but this degree of rudeness I would normally find intolerable. Not that I'd give the offending party a tongue-lashing—just some sarcastic remark, dripping with poison. With Inga, however, I had to bow my head and suffer in silence.

If my life is actually a scenario, penned by someone else, and I am merely playing the role that person wrote for me, then the conclusion of this love affair with Inga is already decided, and there's no use worrying about it. I'll just have to let it follow its course. As I walk through the hospital corridors, the image of a lonely-looking back in a white coat comes to mind. That back is my own. A camera is filming me from behind.

Something worries me, casting a shadow in my heart that I can't shake off. I have a nagging sense that I might be only a minor character in this movie. Perhaps the protagonist is someone else, who required hospitalization and needed a doctor. As movie heroes are always trying to win the viewers' sympathy by having automobile accidents or contracting fatal diseases, a doctor often appears. But he's rarely the center of attention. Who's the protagonist of this movie? I'll have to find him and give him a piece of my mind.

There's a room in the hospital with a coffee machine where doctors and nurses can take a break. Finding such a facility beneath me, I secretly call it "Filter Coffee," and had hardly ever entered it until one day I happened to see Inga in the corridor and followed her, straight into that room. It would have seemed odd if I hadn't bought anything, so I went over for a look at the machine, but couldn't figure out how it worked. When I pushed the button for café au lait, nothing happened. It then occurred to me that money was supposed to go in first, so I hurriedly took out my wallet, but couldn't find a slot for a coin. Instead, there was a slit, perhaps to insert a credit card. Taking my hospital vending card from my wallet, I slid it in and pushed the button: this time, coffee came pouring out but there was no cup to catch it. Then I remembered. This environmentally friendly vending machine requires users to bring their own cups. I once overheard someone talking about it. I sensed Inga coming toward me, but not having the courage to look up at her, I let my eyes wander through the room until I saw a quart of milk, placed squarely on the table next to the vending machine like a savior.

I looked up to see Inga's face, just where I'd expected it to be, and now that I had that milk carton to talk about, I managed to stay calm and collected.

"The first Tetra Pak cartons were tetrahedrons. Do you know why?"

Once I'd asked the question, I realized that I myself didn't know. Was that shape more convenient for transporting the cartons, or less? I tried to think but my brain wasn't functioning. Although I was sure I knew all the details concerning every company that originated in my homeland, I had had so few chances to discuss them here that this information was slipping away fast. Inga, who fortunately didn't seem the least bit interested in Tetra Pak, placed a plain, white china cup under the spout and pushed the button once again. Though she hadn't inserted her card, coffee came pouring out. It was like magic. When the cup was full to the brim, she picked it up with a perfectly steady hand and, as if to say, "Here's your coffee," thrust it under my nose.

"How, when you didn't put your card in?"

I shouldn't have asked.

With a teasing look, she replied, "Everyone's allowed one mistake—it's programmed that way."

That's impossible. Inga is a magician. I dutifully took a sip, and discovered that it tasted as good as the brew that comes out of the espresso machine I have at home, for which I'd paid ten thousand kronors. The steam wafting from it had a fine aroma, and the taste was rich, with no undue bitterness. I drank it leaning against the wall, all the while telling myself to calm down. She was looking over at me, waiting for me to speak, so I had to say something.

"Why do you think Strindberg's marriage failed?"

The topic of Tetra Pak having fizzled and died, I tried Strindberg. To keep the advantage, a man must stay in his own territory and attack from an unexpected direction. Yet even faced with my country's greatest psychological mountain, Inga was not the least bit shaken.

"Probably because he wandered too far into the world of his own plays," she answered quietly. She may have a point. Life for a woman married to a writer who has strayed into his own world must be exceedingly difficult. Yet surely being lost in a literary world of one's own creation is better than being trapped in someone else's movie. Inga then closed her eyes for approximately two seconds. The silver powder of her eye shadow sparkled on the waves of tiny wrinkles on her eyelids. As if drawn in her direction I approached her and placed my hands on both her arms. When she opened her eyes she didn't seem at all surprised, but looked straight at me, her eyes filled with curiosity, her lips gently parted.

Whether I throw her a curveball or a slider, she always catches it and tosses it back. Her lips have curves as well, which seemed at first to tease me, but as time passed, grew more tempting than playful.

"Are you going home? Let me take you in my car."

"No thanks. The driver will worry if he doesn't see me on the bus."

"Buses have plenty of space, but intimacy requires something a bit more cramped, don't you think? Of course, cramped isn't the right word. As you know, the inside of a Volvo is quite roomy. And very safe."

"Sorry, safety is Volvo's main selling point, I know, but I prefer a little adventure."

"Then you simply must let me give you a ride. I'll take you to a forest where moose will come to batter us from all sides. Quite an adventure, don't you think?"

I finally persuaded her, and gave her a ride home.

*

Last year, a nurse in her twenties, who looked like a little icefish, wore out my nerves and depleted my savings. Young women are only interested in what they can get out of you. They want to catch your eye, drag words of praise from your mouth, receive presents, extract promises. They're monsters without a shred of independence; they need a steady stream of things coming in from the outside to keep them from shriveling up and dying. Just when I'd thought I was fed up with love, those tiny, merciful wrinkles at the corners of Inga's eyes appeared before me like the Milky Way in the dark cosmos. I remembered the science fiction fantasies I had read as a boy. In the sky where Libra tormented men by confusing them, and Scorpio dripped poison from its stinger, the Queen of the Night would suddenly appear. Though female, this goddess differed from both the girls at school and my mother. Once I had embarked on the path of medicine, I no longer even glanced at nonscientific reading material, but I spent my entire boyhood in a long tunnel that I could never have gotten through without the help of a goddess.

Virtuous to her core, my goddess was, nevertheless, neither naïve nor inexperienced. She had endured the pain and bitterness of this world, yet stood calmly, steadfastly, on the side of justice. The energy drinks she gave me were always sweet and nutritious, never harmful to my health. And yet recently, Inga dropped words into my ear that have begun to course through my body like poison. Here is what she said:

"Unlike everyone I work with, I have never once doubted that you are a good person."

My heart sank.

"Unlike everyone?" I asked — pronouncing each syllable slowly and clearly — whereupon Inga, blinking furiously as if she had something in her eye, added, "I meant to say that while lots of people speak ill of you, it's because they don't understand you."

"What do they say?"

Unusually for her, Inga seemed flustered.

"Don't be nervous. I just want know what they've got wrong," I assured her. "Their misunderstandings, however absurd, are not your fault."

Her expression softened, and she stared up at the ceiling as the spinning wheel of memory began to turn.

"Well, for instance, they say you're always in a bad mood," she said, looking over to see my reaction, "and take your frustration out on your colleagues, the nurses, and the patients."

You must stay calm no matter what she says, I told myself, and encouraged her to go on though I really shouldn't have.

"What else?"

"You're always yelling at new nurses for not filling out forms properly. You never explain yourself, and you're so quick to lose your temper."

The wheel was turning on its own now, spinning threads of slander and calumny. No matter how long the threads got, I had to keep my composure.

"There're lots of other things as well. For example, when someone tries to speak to you in the hall, you ignore them and walk on."

"If I stopped to talk to everyone, I'd forget what I'd set out to do."

"Most people would say something—like, 'Sorry, can we talk later?'—whereas you just pass them by. That's unusual. I myself don't find it so terrible, but it does upset people. I wouldn't worry about it if I were you."

"And?"

"You never listen to other people during meetings. The other day ...," she started to say, but must have decided not to, for she pressed her lips together, put her arms around my neck, and whispered in my ear, "Misunderstandings are like a summer shower—soon over."

A silly, girlish gesture for such a sensible woman, yet Inga made it seem positively endearing. I was nevertheless determined not to let her distract me.

"What sort of misunderstandings?"

"They say you reject every suggestion out of hand, and insist that things be done your way. And furthermore ..."

"Furthermore what?"

"That you consider everyone intellectually inferior to yourself."

"Because it's true."

"That's why it isn't arrogance. You simply don't rate the thought processes of other people very highly. There's nothing unusual about that. Thinking you're smarter than everyone else is quite natural, though most people won't come out and say it. You do, because you're honest."

"About how many of them hate me?"

"Considering the number alone, I can't say it's small, but in cases like this, quality's more important than quantity."

"So though the number is high, the quality is rather mellow, maybe pear-shaped?"

"Well, anger being anger, it does entail a certain amount of violent passion."

Until I met Inga, I could never have imagined that everyone hated me. I was living in a pleasant, dark place called "myself." I didn't know where the walls were, so I never felt closed in. I couldn't see the outlines, either. I filled the entire space—that's only natural. But then light began creeping in. Had it been sun beams, it might have felt good, but this was very different—more like those horrid spotlights in a photographer's studio, glaring down from all directions. First, I saw whitish-blond hairs growing on the backs of my hands, and my fingernails were uneven, with dirt under them. I quickly washed my hands. But when I looked in the mirror above the sink, what I saw was not the handsome, intelligent, masculine, yet gentle face I'd been expecting. It was some strange-looking actor the director had dredged up from god knows where. To say that face had distinctive characteristics might sound good, but who cares, and I'd assumed I was a handsome, kind, intelligent young man, and that no matter how old I got, my face would retain traces of that comely youth. But what I now saw before me was a world-weary, cranky old man. Strangely enough, just when I discovered how crotchety I was, I also found a woman who loved me.

Inga has not yet once unbuttoned her white uniform for me. But I'm in no hurry. With her lying next to me, listening as she gently caresses my lips with her fingertips, I get so carried away that my sense of self floats into the air up and out. We're talking about traveling to Central America together on our next vacation. Surely that won't entail separate, single rooms. The only problem is that she's the one who suggested Central America, an area I have no interest in, and to tell the truth, I'm not very keen on the idea.

Since I've been indulging myself in the pleasures of Inga, I've become thoroughly disgusted with this suit of clothes I call "myself," yet I don't know how to take it off. Constantly worrying about what others think of you is an adolescent illness, and since that time of life is a disease in itself, teenagers can't help spending hours staring into the mirror, lost in thought; at my age, however, such behavior points to a serious malfunction.

People say I'm short-tempered, always yelling at the nurses— I was astonished to hear that. I merely find it confusing, and therefore irritating, when someone suddenly speaks to me.

Once I've decided to do something, I focus single-mindedly on that task. I don't intend to scold anyone. Just the other day, having only a few minutes to check on the supply of sleeping tablets, I was hurrying to the hospital pharmacy when a much younger colleague stepped right in front of me. An impudent pup—and with a mustache.

"An aphasia patient keeps calling the front desk," he said, "so please go there right away." Utterly unreasonable. First off, barging in on me that way and cutting off my line of vision was extremely rude. Though I am a specialist in loss of speech, rarely do I have a real patient to treat: I am forced to spend most of my time devising ways to manage patients whose only talent is feeling pain where there is none. I was therefore grateful for this patient, but that did nothing to change the fact that I had to check on the sleeping tablet supply. When I kept on walking, ignoring the young man, he had the audacity to reach out and grab my arm.

"The woman at the desk was practically in tears," he said in a low, menacing voice—who does he think he is, a mafia don?—"because she can't get hold of the aphasia specialist."

"Let go of my arm," I growled. "Stop sticking your nose into other specialties and do your own work."

"If you don't go now, you could lose that patient."

So now he was threatening me, playing on my weaknesses. But how did he know what they are, anyway? Was he a voyeur, whose sole pleasure is peering into the hearts of others? Much as I hate changing direction, I reluctantly turned and headed for the front desk. When I got there, the receptionist was gone. Taking a deep breath, I shouted at a female patient passing by in her wheelchair: "How dare you summon me and then leave your post!" Though I was merely using her as a proxy, because there was no one else to yell at, she thought she'd been personally attacked, and started squawking about suing the hospital. In the middle of this fracas, the receptionist returned. She looked as innocent as a high school student during a break between classes. My anger had already undergone a chemical change, from explosive to sticky.

"I'm glad to see you looking so well. Wandering off somewhere, after summoning someone, takes the nerve of a CEO, so I'm sure you have a bright future ahead of you."

"Is going to the lavatory prohibited?"

"Unless you're constipated, defecation shouldn't take much time. Or perhaps you were in front of the mirror, fixing up that face of yours. They say that on average, women spend far more time in the bathroom than men. Which is one reason why I've always believed that equal pay is inherently unfair—would you mind if I used you as an example when I make that argument?"

"I've been calling you since yesterday, and I left you a message."

"I'm terribly sorry. You see, I had more important things to do than answer the phone. Curing patients, for instance. Of course, never having been directly involved in the healing professions, you might find that difficult to understand. A receptionist's job is the same in a department store as in a hospital—or a casino, for that matter."

"But an aphasia patient has been calling the hospital, over and over."

"Someone capable of making numerous phone calls cannot be suffering from loss of speech. Stop making unmedical jokes."

Her mouth hanging open in astonishment, she fell silent. In my element, I gave her some instructions:

"The next time the patient calls, make an appointment for Wednesday afternoon."

There was no malice in any of this. I was merely reacting to others as I always do, with sincerity and a bit of humor.

I would like to hear the opinion of a scholar studying ill humor. But no, one can't really trust other people's research, so it would be much better to do my own, with myself as the guinea pig. Among the factors believed to give rise to ill humor are food, the weather, clothing, sleep, sexual activity, and labor. I could do comparisons to see which factors contribute to a nastier disposition: a carnivorous vs. a vegetarian diet; rainy vs. fair weather; blue-striped underwear vs. white; neckties vs. open collars; sleeping as late as one wants vs. sleep deprivation; a life of abstinence vs. erotic indulgence. Movies, music, and reading all lift the spirits, so during the experiment, I'd avoid them. Alcohol must be studied on its own. Wine is a troublesome substance that can make one feel good for a time, yet in the long run darkens the personality. During the experiment I would eliminate all drugs, from vitamin pills to marijuana.

Nothing makes me angry when I'm with Inga, neither mosquito bites nor walking into a door. Inga is undoubtedly the insecticide that kills the pest called ill temper, though how she manages this is difficult to determine. I would like to analyze her various components independently—her face, her smell, her speech, and so forth, but as simply smelling her fragrance brings her face to mind, and then her voice, I'm afraid that examining each one separately is impossible. The brain is an irrational organ that stores a mishmash of things, all mixed together. I sometimes think it would be better for a scientist not to have such an organ.

The man called Susanoo, who appeared on Wednesday afternoon, is an extremely unusual patient. He looks like an Eskimo I once saw in a movie, the title of which I can't seem to remember. He was apparently working as a chef in Arles. It was Knut Nielson who called me on the phone, wanting me to treat him.

I met Knut in a seminar on Astronomical Linguistics. At the time Knut had just entered the university, while my career as a therapist had already begun. When I happened to hear of a university seminar dealing with themes I'd thought could be found only in the fantasy/science fiction novels I'd loved as a boy, I asked for permission to attend. If Martians were to come to Earth, how would we converse with them? Is it possible that noise recorded in space is actually language? Could a metalanguage be created from elements of all the languages on Earth, and sent out to other planets? Are the rumors about the Soviet government having invested a huge amount of capital to have *Das Kapital* translated into the Martian language true? These are the sorts of topics that the professor of Astronomical Linguistics covered in his seminar.

The other students were far too immature for sustained conversation. Young people all look pretty much alike; few have distinguishing features. They are affable enough, not due to their personalities, but because they have not yet developed any special characteristics, which makes them terribly boring. Now and then I talked to Knut, but he was the only one. We invited each other to parties and such, and one time ended up spending a whole night drinking and talking in the kitchen of someone's apartment. It was neither mine nor his. One of us may have been apartment-sitting for a friend, but that part has faded from memory. As our discussion of celestial language grew heated, Knut's cheeks flushed, and his lips took on an alluring scarlet hue, burning almost. Unlike me, Knut is always cheery and upbeat; in fact, until that moment I had never seen him excited or angry. If I do decide to study "The Science of Ill Temper," perhaps I should ask him to cooperate, so that I can find out what a man who's a complete stranger to foul moods likes to eat, what sort of underwear he prefers, and so on and so forth.

While Knut stayed on at the university to continue his studies, I was employed at a research institute in Stockholm; that's all he knew; I hadn't contacted him to let him know that I'd been fired and had returned to Copenhagen, where I'd begun medical school. This was partly because the incident that had necessitated my return to Denmark wasn't something I was proud of.

That Wednesday, Knut brought along a woman called Hiruko. Although at first glance I thought she might be a member of Susanoo's family, or perhaps a more distant relative, he told me she was just a friend. Through a strange series of circumstances, Knut and Hiruko got to know Susanoo and as he seemed to be suffering from loss of speech, Knut thought he should be examined by a specialist. Many people have old friends who develop aphasia, but making friends with someone who already has it is something else again. How'd they form a relationship with this man who doesn't talk?

Susanoo comes from an area called Fukui, in a country that may no longer exist; according to Hiruko, the place name means "a well of happiness." I made a note of this, though I can't imagine its being of any use. The patient's age is unknown; after running a sushi restaurant with a friend in Husum, he worked as a sushi chef in Arles. When I pointed out that he couldn't very well be suffering from loss of speech if he'd been able to tell them so much about his past, they told me that this information came from Nanook, another friend of theirs. Furthermore, Nanook hadn't heard this from Susanoo himself, but from an employee at the restaurant where he used to work.

Knut tells me that Susanoo understands basic French, but hardly ever says anything. I couldn't help sneering when I heard that. Specialists do not regard taciturn people as aphasia patients. Isn't it merely that he can't speak French? Though he was fairly fluent in German for a number of years, he no longer speaks that language at all. But again, specialists wouldn't refer to that as loss of speech. Hasn't he simply forgotten German? He has no knowledge of Scandinavian languages whatsoever. A condition he has in common with most of humanity which, while unfortunate, is not a disease. The problem is his mother tongue. "He wants to speak it but can't," Knut declares, looking terribly earnest, "and that's a terrible psychological burden." Yet this is not something Susanoo himself ever said.

Knut has overlooked the most important point. The country where Susanoo's mother tongue was spoken may no longer exist, and even if it does, it's impossible to go there. What's the point of recovering the language of such a place?

"As a student, you were never interested in Latin or Sanskrit, so why do you want to recover a dead language now?"

I saw flames of anger in Knut's eyes and I remembered that night we'd spent drinking together, when I upset him by asserting that deciphering languages spoken on other planets would be of no use to humanity. I hadn't thought about that for years, yet now it suddenly came flooding back. Hiruko put her hand on Knut's arm to calm him down.

"our country disappeared, not one hundred percent. possibility only."

Even a Swede like me can tell that her Danish is incorrect, yet strangely enough, it's far clearer than the sort of Danish that sounds like bubbles rising from the depths of a swamp.

"i native language speaker sought. with knut. one man i found. susanoo. but he speaks not."

I heard neither dissatisfaction nor sadness in her voice. She was neither trying to control whomever she was speaking to, nor to flatter them—she seemed more to be stepping quietly from one word to the next.

"Loss of speech is your specialty, isn't it?" said Knut, thrusting his chin toward me.

"Yes, it is. And as a specialist, I'd like to suggest that you're using aphasia as a metaphor. A man doesn't talk—does that mean he suffers from loss of speech?"

I was being sarcastic, to wake him up, but he seemed to relax instead.

"If loss of speech is a metaphor, then maybe we can use the power of metaphor to cure it." He almost sang the words.

I don't believe that Susanoo is "ill," but he came here as a patient, so I decided to give him my standard test, which consists of showing objects—such as a teddy bear or a stuffed rabbit—and then asking "What is this?" My lumbago makes it too painful for me to bend over to get the box with the things I need from the bottom shelf of the locker, but fortunately Munun, the boy who washes dishes in the basement, was here to help me that day. Knowing that a careless remark to him could get me into trouble—he's a certified handicapped person with a lawyer to protect his rights—I asked him anyway. Of course, I don't mean to take advantage of him when I ask him for help, far from it—he's a pleasant lad, and I enjoy having him around. With so few other colleagues I feel close to, Munun seems like an oasis I've finally found in the Martian desert that is this hospital.

Even a simple test can tell you quite a lot about a patient. Some just give you a blank look no matter what kind of toy you show them, while others will struggle to get a word out—and when they do manage, it's often the wrong one, but these mistakes can be useful for analysis and treatment. For instance, if a patient is shown a bear and says "burr," one can hypothesize that he's substituting the "ur" sound for the "air" sound. And if he says "purr" when shown a pear, the hypothesis will be proven correct. In such cases, you must make the patient understand that if he practices saying "air" when he wants to say "ur," his condition will gradually improve. Curing a patient is never easy, but giving encouragement is part of the process.

When a patient sees a bear and says "boar," however, one can hypothesize word slippage, which means that he names the animal positioned next to the one he was thinking of. If you show him a rabbit and he says "fox," then there's a greater possibility that this hypothesis is correct, so therapy must begin by taking the patient back to scenes from his childhood, using picture books and illustrated nature encyclopedias for children. Everyone has an imaginary forest or jungle in his head. He creates it from scenes he saw over and over again in books. Rabbits and foxes run and play in that forest, but for some reason, a hunter is standing next to them with the prey he has caught. The child is loath to capture any animal; he would rather do something entirely different. Word slippage occurs when he represses these childhood feelings as an adult.

"What is this?" I asked Susanoo in French, but he merely glanced at the teddy bear and said nothing. There was tension in the air. There are many kinds of silence. Type A: Looking away while silent. Type B: The silent stare. Type C: Moving the lips without producing any sound whatsoever. Type D: Looking silently downward. Type E: Staring blankly, silently into space. Type F: Breathing irregularly, yet silently. Type G: Silently swallowing saliva. Type H: Sitting silently with clenched fists. Scientific symbols are applied to each of these patterns. *E* is the one that applies to Susanoo. And perhaps *B*. He looked down afterwards, so *D* as well. While writing down the appropriate letters, I mistakenly added an *I*. In English, this denotes the first person singular. When I looked up from my notes, I noticed the teddy bear, taunting me with those cute little button eyes of his as if to say, "You quack," which upset me, so I rapped him on the head with my fist. Hiruko then reached out and grabbed my wrist with more strength than I'd thought she possessed.

"What do you think you're doing?" I asked angrily. "Disrupting my treatment of this patient? Or is this aikido?"

A flood of words poured from Hiruko's mouth. Yet unlike that Scandinavian-type language she'd been speaking a short while before, these words were totally incomprehensible.

As I was too astonished to respond, Knut explained. Hiruko, he said, was now speaking in Susanoo's lost mother tongue. Although not born in the area called Fukui, she was from the same country. Embarrassed at having forgotten the name of Hiruko's birthplace, Knut hemmed and hawed, saying it might have been Niigata, or perhaps Hokuetsu, failing to realize that such information was of no significance whatsoever.

Hiruko's voice reverberated so strongly through the room it was hard to believe it came from that slender, delicate frame. Perhaps Susanoo's refusal to speak upset her, because she stared resentfully at him, or gazed at him with pity as she continued to talk, on and on. Like a young boy given a scolding, he turned away, trying to ignore her.

"Mightn't it be possible," I ventured to ask, "that the patient hasn't forgotten the language you're speaking, but is rejecting it?"

She then started talking again, to no one in particular: "bear equals *ku-ma*. from ku-ma, *o-ku-ma-ru*. deep, dark, invisible, hidden, private, the last room. farthest from entrance. *ku-ma*."

She said this in that strange Scandinavian language, with unfamiliar words mixed in. Hearing it, Knut leaned forward, looking excited.

"I see," he said, "so *ku-ma* isn't just bear. It's that last room, the one you hardly ever go into. The furthest one from the door. The depths of your soul."

"deep? different. deep equals vertical. *o-ku* equals horizontal."

"Got it—horizontal. So instead of digging a hole in the earth, you walk a long way, on the surface. Let's all walk together, then."

That bright, cheerful tone might have appropriate at a pop concert, but it was not suited to an examination room. I asked him a question that I hoped would curb his enthusiasm: "When you say 'let's,' who exactly is 'us'?"

Rather than having a chilling effect, this excited him all the more.

"Susanoo, me, Hiruko, and Nanook," he said, his eyes gleaming. "I told you about him before. Without him, we never would have found Susanoo, or learned about his past."

"And is this Nanook, or whatever you call him, a native of the same vanished country?"

"No, he's an Eskimo."

"Isn't the correct term Inuit?"

"He doesn't belong to the Inuit tribe."

"I see, I see, there's no need to get so worked up about it."

"Nanook is an Eskimo."

"As I've already said, I understand that—after all, this is Denmark, not Mumbai. Eskimos aren't all that unusual around here. In fact, Susanoo looks rather like one himself. Have you considered the possibility that he might also be an Eskimo?"

"That's impossible. If Susanoo were an Eskimo, that would mean Hiruko was, too."

"Why do you so strongly believe that she isn't? Because she herself says she's not? Haven't you gotten into a terrible messes before, because you never questioned anything a woman told you?"

Knut failed to respond, which I found thrilling. I relish moments when my opponent's silence tells me I've won an argument, and thoroughly enjoy observing people who don't know what to say.

"Oh well, it doesn't really matter," I assured him. "We've established that the first-person plural you used refers to the four of you."

"Sheeksu!" shouted Hiruko. Was it due to her bad pronunciation, or because I was thinking of Inga that it sounded like "sex"? Knut said it properly.

"Six. There are six of us in all."

"I thought it was four."

"There are two more. First, there's Akash."

"An Eskimo?"

"No, an Indian."

"Why should there be an Indian in your group?"

"This is Denmark. Indians aren't so unusual around here either. Akash doesn't live in Copenhagen, though. He's studying in Trier. When Hiruko and I went to Trier to look for Nanook, we just happened to meet him at a bus stop, and got friendly with him."

"Is a bus stop the proper place to make friends?"

"Some guys meet their wives at bus stops. People die of heart attacks at bus stops, and women suddenly go into labor and have babies there, too. Anything can happen at a bus stop."

"Okay, okay, enough already. Now I remember why I used to like talking to you during breaks in that seminar—you babble on about things that don't matter. Young people mustn't be too quiet. But I'm sure you haven't changed since you were in kindergarten. Anyway, is this Indian Akash coming here to see Susanoo?"

"I think so. And then there's Nora, Nanook's girlfriend."

"Nora. So, finally, the Scandinavian Ibsen makes an appearance."

"Nora's German."

"These friends of yours—there's no sense of order. It's like Moominvalley—all mixed up. Are you telling me this patient has no family?"

"We can't be sure whether Susanoo has a family or not. But we're definitely not going to abandon him."

Continuing the test, I next showed Susanoo a stuffed rabbit, but while he still said nothing, Hiruko's eyes brightened and she began to talk.

"rabbit, almost no fur, bald. crocodile the fur pulled off."

"What do you mean?"

"rabbit on an island. to the mainland wants to cross. no boat. rabbit to crocodile says. more rabbits than crocodiles there are. angry crocodile says. more crocodiles than rabbits. rabbit says. all crocodiles line up. i will count. while counting, rabbit as a bridge those crocodiles uses."

With a burst of laughter, Knut interrupted Hiruko:

"Then when the rabbit is almost all the way across, she lets the crocodiles know she's tricked them into making a bridge for her, and the last one gets mad, and, taking the rabbit in his jaws, rips off her fur. I know that story. It's an old Indian tale. I read it a long time ago for a psychology seminar in pride, arrogance, and deceit."

"You said that Hiruko couldn't possibly be an Eskimo, but couldn't she be Indian?"

Knut looked absolutely disgusted, but Hiruko smiled.

"pacific ocean equals one big picture book," she said, nodding enthusiastically. She now looked like an Eskimo and an Indian at the same time, and I was getting dizzy.

"What exactly do you want?" I asked. "To go home? But where is it—up north where the Eskimos are, or by the Pacific? Or do you just want to speak your mother tongue—is that it?"

"She definitely wants that," said Knut, breaking in, "which is why she went looking for Susanoo. She was disappointed when he didn't talk. But now she isn't just trying to help Susanoo so they can talk in their language."

"Then what is she trying to do—find out what happened to her country, why it vanished?"

"Maybe. No, probably not. Whether her country still exists or not isn't all that important. She wants to talk to lots of different people, about all sorts of things. That's why she keeps making up new words, no matter how far away she is from home."

"Oh . . . well, whatever. Work is the best way to kill time. Let's continue our examination."

When I showed the patient a rubber snake about as long as my arm, he stiffened in his chair but said nothing. Once again, Hiruko started talking instead.

"sea serpent, sea, midgard, dark night, jormungand, sky full of stars."

I thought I might have heard Midgard, from Norse mythology, somewhere in the mix.

"Do you know Midgard?" I asked, unable to contain my excitement. "And Jormungand?" But Hiruko shook her head, so hard that her hair flew out in all directions. Bringing his lips close to her ear, Knut explained.

"Midgard is a mythical place between the sky and the underworld, surrounded by water. Jormungand is a huge snake, so big the ocean can't cover him completely, with his tail in his mouth, encircling the world."

He sounded gentle, as if he were telling fairy tales to a child. But if Jormungand awakens and rises up out of the sea, humanity will drown in the flood—we'll all die. This is no time for fairy tales. That's why I can't stand Andersen and his ilk. Their stories turn the most destructive aspects of nature into Christmas decorations.

Water frightens me. Ever since I nearly drowned in the North Sea as a child, I've been terrified of floods, although I've never seen one. Even the word makes me shudder. I once read a novel in which Jormungand has an elder brother, who lives in outer space. It was about how science kept the Midgard serpent in check. Mine is the hand of science. Every doctor believes that. This hand must conquer the snake, however frightening it is. But where's my sword? A sword with magical powers is an essential element in myth. You can't find anything like that in a hospital, though—just scalpels. But not here, because this isn't an operating room. I saw a fork, gleaming brightly enough to be a hero's weapon. Brother of Jormungand, it's time to accept your fate. There! You've surrendered. Under control! Under control!

Munun had disappeared. He's the sort of person you're not really aware of when he's there, yet you miss him when he's gone. I vaguely remember shouting, "Stop making a nuisance of yourself and go back downstairs!" Not a very clear memory, but as I often scream at him, I can't say for certain that I didn't this time. No malice was intended, of course, though I regret it now.

Exhausted, I sat down in a chair and heaved a sigh. Hiruko then slipped a letter into the mailbox of my heart.

"sea serpent rivers and oceans controls. name equals orochi. lots of rice, all stomachs full. or, so much water everyone dies. full stomachs or death. orochi decides. dictatorship."

An unreasonable argument, it seemed to me, so I immediately opposed it.

"Say you invite this snake to a first-class restaurant, and soften him up by treating him to a scrumptious dinner of rabbit and fine wine. That's not democracy. It's the Asian way."

"how democracy can be achieved, with too much water?" she asked in a damp voice.

"You can't have democracy in a country with floods," I retorted, totally fed up.

"Soon Denmark will be under water," Knut replied, coolly driving in the last nail.

"As long as Sweden stays afloat, I don't care if Denmark sinks," I blurted out, then immediately regretted it. "I was only joking," I quickly added. "The country we're in is the one we care about. I'm planning to stay right here. When the seas rise, the human race will have nowhere to go."

I felt lonely when everyone had left, so I called Munun. While he was helping me straighten up the room, I chatted about trivial things, whatever came into my head. I don't remember what I said now, but talking cheered me up a bit.

I went home and had a bowl of my special mushroom soup with a drop of whiskey in it, which brightened my mood even more. I phoned Inga, who was worried that I'd called for no special reason, and said she'd come over right away. Had she asked, "Are you lonely?" when I was at my loneliest, I would have an-

grily denied it. Yet now I was excited enough to play the role of
an eager lover.

"You're coming to see me?" I asked dramatically. "I'm so relieved. I'm afraid my weather's stormy, and a bit lonely today."
A short while later I was sitting next to her on my gray VILA-
SUND sofa bed with my head on her shoulder. Pressing my
cheek into her sweater, likely hand-knitted, I felt the weight of
her breasts.

"There are so many unnecessary languages."

"What do you mean?"

"A patient came today, claiming to be suffering from aphasia.
He no longer speaks a language that has vanished."

"So, you finally have an aphasia patient. Congratulations. You
must be very happy."

"It may be too early to start celebrating. Reviving a language
no one speaks anymore makes no sense. If a patient who's had
a lump removed returns to the hospital claiming he doesn't feel
like himself without it, and wants it back, what does one do? Is
the doctor obliged to reattach it—the lump?"

"Can a person lose a lump against his will?"

"The devil might steal one, to trick someone. They say he
uses human lumps to make soup stock."

"I never thought I'd hear you use the word devil. I thought
you hated anything unscientific. Isn't that why you don't want
to go to a country where they practice voodoo?"

"The devil is just an example. This woman Hiruko is very
strange. She speaks a language she made by mixing lots of different languages together."

"You mean pidgin English?"

"No, not a language that arose naturally. She made it herself,
and there's hardly any English in it."

"Is it easy to understand?"

"Depends on the person."

"So in other words, you can understand it easily. And you find her charming."

"She has a linguistic sort of charm."

"That's the strongest kind, isn't it?"

Perhaps she was right. I wanted to spend more time talking to this woman called Hiruko.

I remembered a patient at my old hospital, a girl who looked like Hiruko. She was called Yessica, or some such name. Her mother, who was born in Nara, went to Tokyo to study law, then got a job working at the Field of Ink Ward Office. She'd had an arranged marriage, to a young man with big hands, who worked in the oddly named "Town of Big Hands" in central Tokyo, but the marriage didn't last, and she decided to make a fresh start by traveling to Canada, where she met and fell in love with a Swedish man, by whom she became pregnant with Yessica, who, because the divorce hadn't yet been finalized, was legally considered to be the child of her mother's first husband. Her country's Civil Law stipulated that a child conceived within 300 days after a divorce was legally regarded as the former husband's child. Many of her country's laws were imported from ancient China, Yessica explained, including the system of having "door documents," whereby there was one official page representing the door of each family's house, rather than identification papers for each individual person. When a woman married, her name was erased from her family's "door," and inscribed on the "door" of her husband's family. Their children's names were also recorded on that family's door. As her mother was loath to write Yessica's name on the door of her first husband's family, she didn't register her birth. This meant that Yessica was a stateless person, and couldn't leave the country. Had she gone to Sweden, she could have joined the line of refugees without passports, and might eventually have gotten citizenship, but without a passport, even this was impossible. Knowing how risky it was, her stepfather had fake identification papers made for her, and smuggled her out of the country. In Scandinavia, Yessica grew up healthy and strong. But when she was a university student, she happened to mention door documents to a second cousin who'd come to visit, and he stared at her, wide-eyed.

"You mean family registers?" he asked. "We don't have that system anymore."

As nearly all the documents stored in prefectural or city offices had either been burned or washed away in some huge natural disaster, family registers were replaced by a number, issued to each individual survivor. Though fitting, "survivor number" would have sounded awfully depressing, so it was called the Don't Worry number, a name meant to convey the message, "Don't worry if you've lost your home. Everything will be fine — cheer up!" On receiving a number, survivors were provided with a government allowance.

In the dream she had after hearing about this new system, Yessica was feeling relieved to have finally gotten her Don't Worry number. It was spring, and, clutching the document to her chest, she was sitting on a park bench, feeling out of this world. Then, a deer suddenly appeared beside her. Lovely dark eyes. Brunette fur, decorated with white stars. She had heard about these deer from her mother. They lived in a park in her mother's homeland, and since everyone fed them, they were used to human beings. This deer boldly walked up to her, stretched out its neck, and, taking the document in its mouth, started to munch. Yessica barely had time to cry out before her long awaited Don't Worry number had disappeared into the deer's stomach.

For some reason, the patient remembered this dream in detail. Had Hiruko's identification papers also been eaten by a deer? Though Scandinavian moose can be dangerous, they don't eat paper. That's what they mean by cultural difference.

Perhaps my desire to talk to Hiruko had grown stronger, for even though Inga was sleeping beside me, it was Hiruko I conversed with in my mind.

"In your homeland, people hunt deer, don't they?"

"different. vegetarian tradition. buddhist."

"So even now you don't eat meat?"

"meat we eat. yoshinoya beef bowl, kobe beef, teriyaki, pork dumplings."

"Don't you eat deer?"

"do not eat."

"Aren't there too many deer, then?"

"deer only in nara park."

"Nara ... I remember now—that's where Yessica's mother was from."

"yessica? asuka?"

"Did a deer eat your passport, too?"

"passport i have. country i have not."

"Is that so? Must have been an awfully big deer to eat a whole country. Much bigger than the moose we have in Scandinavia."

CHAPTER 3   *Nanook Speaks*

I was standing near the bottom of the ramp leading up to the entrance to the autobahn. Even looking toward Trier I didn't see any cars yet, but practiced sticking my thumb in the air anyway. Overhead was a pattern of gray patches, some closer to white and others to black—it was like I was holding them up with my thumb. What time was it? I'd forgotten my watch. The white birches behind me were all skinny, and very tall. Afraid I was too short for a driver in a car to see me, I stood on my toes, then lost my balance and almost fell flat on my face. A metallic-red Volkswagen Polo passed by. The driver must have seen me, because the car slowed down and stopped. The redhead in the driver's seat cocked her head for a better look at me. I'd once had an awful time when a guy picked me up, so I was glad it was a woman this time. She rolled down the window, and there was nothing between us.

"How far are you going?"

"To Copenhagen."

She burst out laughing and opened the door on the passenger's side.

"I can take you as far as Köblenz. It's in the same general direction, and starts with KO, like the city you're headed for."

"Copenhagen starts with a K?"

"In German it does. Well, are you getting in or not?"

I quickly slid into the passenger's seat.

"KO, so it's a knockout," she said, sounding pleased with herself.

I didn't get the connection between KO and "knockout," so I just fastened my seatbelt, pretending I hadn't heard.

"What's your name?"

"Nanook."

"I'm Bellona, with two l's in the middle."

The engine moaned and groaned as we entered the fast lane on the autobahn. I turned around and saw a black Mercedes Benz behind us, coming at top speed. After letting it pass, Bellona cautiously slid the car into the right lane. A bold talker, but a careful driver.

"Were you really expecting to find someone to drive you all the way to Copenhagen?"

"It's not that far away."

"Maybe not, compared to Colombia or the Congo, but too far to drive, don't you think? Why didn't you fly? If you hitchhike all the way you'll end up spending more than the price of a plane ticket on food." When I didn't answer she tilted her head and asked, "Are you here illegally by any chance? Not that it matters to me."

"I'm not an illegal immigrant. I'm a university student in Copenhagen."

"What are you studying?"

"Biology."

"Oh? You must be really smart."

Bellona was wearing a thin crimson sweater. Her red hair gleamed on her shoulders, and her breasts bulged like balls that would fit perfectly in my hands. The sun peaked out from between the clouds. There's a whole lot of people in the world, and among them, you meet only a few, purely by chance. Even so, sometimes guys will think they were fated to meet some woman they just happened to run into, and end up married. You could say the same about Nora, the girl I met in Trier. If some other woman had come by that time when I collapsed in the

Kaiserthermen, I would never have met Knut and his friends. Wouldn't be on my way to Copenhagen now, either. Nora would be a stranger who'd never entered my life.

Back in Greenland, people hardly ever met by chance. If you were walking along and a car passed by, the driver would be someone you knew, so when he gave you a ride, it wasn't hitch-hiking. Wasn't anything cool and ecofriendly, like car sharing, either. If you're driving and you see someone on foot you give them a ride—that's the way it's always been, ever since we first had cars. Things are a little different with immigrants coming in now, but that's pretty recent.

"Are you Korean?"

The question caught me off guard, so to buy myself some time I asked, "What made you think so?" I'm used to pretending to be from the land of sushi, but since no one's ever asked me if I was Korean, I didn't have an answer ready.

"Well, you're a foreign student majoring in biology, so you must be intelligent and hardworking. Pretty muscular, too."

Though Bellona had a sweater on, it seemed so warm to me that I'd taken my jacket off, and was now wearing only a short-sleeved shirt. The sleeves were practically up to my shoulders, too, because I'd put the shirt in the washing machine without knowing I had to adjust the temperature, and it had shrunk in the scalding hot water. Bellona must've thought Asian-looking guys only have muscles like mine from being in the army. I know a lot about sushi and kombu dashi, but if someone asked me what kind of fermented fish goes into kimchee I'd be up shit creek. I decided to tell the truth right off the bat.

"I'm an Eskimo."

Bellona was so surprised she leaned back and slammed on the brakes, then quickly checked the rearview mirror—luckily there was no one behind us.

"Sorry," she said. "But that gave me a shock."

"Why?"

"Because my husband was talking about Alaska, just this morning. He never mentions faraway places, and now suddenly he wants to go to Alaska. I'm worried. Maybe he's hinting at a divorce, in a roundabout way."

She looked like she was enjoying life, doing whatever she wanted, so "husband" didn't suit her at all. Better that than some mushy nickname like "sweetie," or "bunny," but I still felt kind of let down.

"I thought the road to Köblenz was supposed to be romantic," I said, changing the subject to a different kind of letdown, more on the surface. "I heard it had a river alongside it, and lots of old castles. All I see here is gray."

"The scenery along the Mosel River is beautiful."

"Why don't you go that way then?"

"Because I'm not a tourist. I don't care about scenery."

"What are you, then? A student?"

"Thanks, but I'm too old for university. I'm a *spionin*."

I'd heard that word before, but couldn't remember what it meant. Was it an animal, like a scorpion? Scorpion sounds like slang for someone who works in a bar. I tried to swallow my curiosity, but failed.

"What kind of work do you do, exactly?"

"I find out a rival company's technical secrets."

"What does your company make?"

"Mosel wine."

"So, you're a corporate spy."

I couldn't figure out if Bellona was really a spy, trying to steal the latest wine production technology, or if she was just teasing me, so I changed the subject.

"How long will it take to Köblenz?"

"About an hour and a half."

"What should I do after we get there? Follow the Mosel River further north?"

"You can't follow it, the Mosel River ends there."

That sounded like Köblenz was the end of the line, which gave me a jolt. Amused at how shocked I was, she watched me a while before telling me the whole story.

"The Mosel flows into the Rhine at Köblenz."

"Oh, so I can follow the Rhine toward the north."

"That's not a good idea."

"Why not?"

"You're not one of those ancient Romans, always heading north, are you? If you follow the Mosel toward Köln, you'll end up too far west, further away from Copenhagen. Extreme west. You need to go northeast. And there's no river flowing that way. You'll have to go through a deep forest, and come out on the other side. Where the sea is."

"I have to go through a forest?"

"That's right. So dense you can hardly see through the trees. Lots of swamps, too, so if you get lost, there's no way out. You won't see any church towers, or farm houses, either. The ancient Romans were terrified of that forest. My German ancestors used to hide behind the trees with spears, and attack the Romans when they passed by."

I knew she was teasing me but my hair was standing on end anyway, which seemed strange even to me.

"And there's no autobahn?"

"Sure there is. The autobahn passes through even where there're no people. There's probably one on Mars, too."

"So all I have to do is tell the driver I want to go to Copenhagen—it doesn't matter which route they take."

"No, that's no good at all. You'd get there faster on foot than if you stood on a street corner in Köblenz waiting for someone who's going all the way to Copenhagen. Tell the driver you want to go to Hamburg. Got that? Say you're going to Hamburg."

"But why Hamburg?"

"You don't really want to go anywhere, do you? You're just trying to get away from your girlfriend."

I felt like I'd just rounded a sharp curve at top speed, too shaken up to say anything.

"What's her name?"

"Nora. I met her by chance, and we haven't been together very long."

"But you haven't actually broken up with her, either."

"There's no reason for us to split up. I told her there was something I had to do up north, and left. That wasn't just an excuse. There really is something I have to do."

"Visit a sick friend?"

"How did you know?"

"It sounds like a typical reason for going north."

In the middle of this aimless conversation, we reached Köblenz. After exiting the autobahn, Bellona dropped me off on a road leading to the next entrance.

"Go straight down here and you'll come to a hotspot for hitchhikers. Take care."

"You too. Thanks for the ride."

As soon as the car disappeared, I wished I'd asked Bellona for her phone number. Maybe I would never see her again. If life is nothing more than a series of short blocks of time spent with people we only meet once, maybe the whole world will break apart and fall to pieces someday.

While I was standing there alone, a Volvo came by so I stuck out my thumb, but the driver didn't even slow down. The Mercedes Benz and Toyota that followed didn't stop, either. This was depressing. It was getting dark, so I trudged toward the lights of the town. A ride with a truck might take me a pretty good distance, but for that I'd need to come back later. I'd heard that you don't see big trucks on the autobahn until late at night.

Maybe because I was hungry, I had a picture of fried fish and white rice in my head. I wanted to eat junk food, fake Chinese.

There would definitely be edibles in town. But to put them in my mouth, I'd have to exchange them for money first. Nora had given me a credit card, but using it would seal our connection. As soon as I slid it into that strange machine, I'd be her pet poodle. For the sake of freedom, I'd have to find something I could eat for free. Though I didn't know exactly where to look, the mucous membranes in my nose get more sensitive when it's dark outside, so I can tell which smells are coming from what direction—exhaust fumes from the west, but tasty things frying in oil over to the east. My nose also detected a river. My line of vision cut off by the trees, I was treading wearily along a narrow path—more an afterthought, really—beside a street only about a lane and a half wide when I heard an engine behind me, and a Hyundai Sonata passed by, then stopped not far ahead. A middle-aged man in a navy blue knit cap stuck his head out the window and asked me where I was going. Strange, how cars never stop until I've just about given up. Maybe he thought I'd been robbed when he saw me shuffling along all alone in the dark, and felt sorry for me. But here he was, driving along an ordinary road, headed for the center of town—if I suddenly told him I wanted to go to Hamburg, he'd probably laugh at me.

"I'm planning a fishing trip, so I'm looking for a good spot."

I was amazed at how easily this lie slipped out. There was some truth to it, though. I wanted to eat fish, but didn't want to pay. So, I wanted to go fishing, but didn't have a rod. My not having one wouldn't seem so strange if I was just looking around.

"You and I have the same idea," said the driver, opening his eyes wide. "I'll show you a good place, so get in."

So, he was going fishing? That sounded too good to be true. Maybe he was plotting something, and just said that to get me in the car. But I couldn't come up with a reason to refuse, so I got in the passenger's seat. Inside, the car smelled like a hut for smoking fish.

"It reeks of cigarette smoke in here, doesn't it?" the man said as if he'd read my mind. "My name's Schuppenauer. No one ever calls me by anything except my last name. What's yours?"

"Nanook."

"Not a name one hears very often. At least not here in the Rhineland."

Judging from the way he talked, he seemed like an educated man. Which didn't mean he wasn't a criminal. I looked behind me and saw a large suitcase on the back seat, with three fishing rods leaning against it. I figured he really was a fisherman.

As the car slipped smoothly along the road we got farther from the center of town and started up a gentle slope. The scene that suddenly opened up in front of us made me catch my breath. A river like a broad, gleaming, silver belt, flowing into another one just as wide, at a slow yet unstoppable pace. Though I couldn't see it very well, there seemed to be a boiling froth of tiny bubbles just where the two rivers met.

"That's the Castrum ad Conflentes," said Schuppenauer. Turning to watch me stand there with my mouth hanging open, he added, "It's where the Mosel and Rhine rivers meet." So, this was it. That redhead had mentioned something about the Mosel flowing into the Rhine. I couldn't remember her name now. Meetings like that just don't stay in your head very long. Schuppenauer was an impressive name, but by tomorrow I'd probably forget it. He said people always call him by his last name, so maybe he was in the military.

"I'll take you to my secret fishing spot now."

Schuppenauer drove down a lonely little road and parked; then, while I carried the rods and tackle, he kneed his way through the brush down to the water's edge along a barely visible path. I followed and thought I saw him limp, ever so slightly. The leaves were rustling so loudly you'd have thought they were showing off, making sure we knew they were the ones breaking the silence. Then things opened up again, and I saw the broad river, its dark surface shining like a snakeskin.

"The fish really bite here. And the terrain hides it from the police on patrol."

"Is fishing against the law?"

"No, but sometimes patrol boats come around to check if you have a license. And a fishing license costs a lot—if you have to pay that much, you'd be better off going to a sushi bar to eat tuna. Ha, ha, ha."

"You like sushi?"

"You must be joking. Who in their right mind would eat raw fish?"

I decided not to tell him that I used to work in a sushi bar.

Where did that pale golden light reflecting off the dark surface of the river come from? Was it civilization's brightness, smoothed out into a general glow? He turned on a tiny flashlight, about the size of his index finger, and by its light took something from a wooden box to bait his hook. A short distance away I kicked the grass, trying to make enough noise so he wouldn't hear my stomach growling. Something slipped through the grass in front of me at top speed.

"That was a snake."

"Don't see them much. A ringelnatter, perhaps."

Apparently not interested in any scaly thing except a fish, Schuppenauer was busy sticking the butt end of one of the rods into the ground. He then flung the baited hook up toward the night sky, and the line whistled out over the water. He handed that rod to me, then cast another and stood beside me, holding it. I remembered when I used to fish with my grandpa, through a hole in the ice. The line was much shorter, and we didn't have rods, but we still caught fish.

"You don't live around here, do you?"

He was starting to sound like a policeman. Maybe it wasn't

just military men, but the police, too, who went by their last names only. But would a cop be fishing without a license?

"I live in Copenhagen, but I've been on a long trip and now I'm on my way home."

Depending on which bits you put on display, the truth can sound more fake than a real lie.

"Copenhagen's pretty far away. Where did you come from today?"

"From Trier."

"Do you have a girlfriend in Trier?"

Did I have a picture of Nora pasted on my forehead? I hadn't even hinted at a woman in my life, but that's what both the redhead and this guy wanted to know about.

"Yes," I answered. "She's also on her way to Copenhagen."

"Why didn't you go with her?"

"She said she wanted to fly."

"Then why didn't you fly, too?"

"Are you with the police or something?"

His Adam's apple rose and fell. Then he burst out laughing.

"Why do you ask that?"

"You're questioning me like a police detective on TV."

"I see. I used to deal with the police quite a bit, so their way of talking might have rubbed off on me. Have you ever been arrested?"

"Yes. Once in Oslo."

"For fishing without a license?"

"No. I was falsely accused of killing a whale."

"Is it illegal to kill whales in Norway?"

"I think I was actually accused of getting environmentalist groups riled up, and of plunging the city into chaos."

"You mean, you don't actually know the formal charges?"

"Right after I was found innocent I went to France, where I ran into a much bigger problem than a dead whale."

"Your girlfriend?"

"No. I ran into this lady called Inga Nielsen—she was my sponsor, and though I told her I was going on a short trip when I left, I never contacted her after that: I never let her know it had turned into an endless journey."

It's funny how when you're sitting next to someone looking out over a river you feel like you can tell them anything, even if the person's a total stranger. I didn't mean to lie, and I wasn't hiding anything, but what I'd just told Schuppenauer sounded so much like someone else's story that I wasn't sure—was it true? Does moving from place to place strip your past away, so you can't remember it anymore?

"So now you're on your way back to Copenhagen?"

"Yes, but actually, it's a little complicated."

Quiet as the night, this man didn't seem like he was going to keep on asking until he got all the details. Nora's just the opposite, wanting to know everything, breathing down my neck, hounding me until I have to blurt out a lie.

"I made us reservations on a flight to Copenhagen," she'd said this morning over coffee, sounding like she was telling me about the neighbor's dog barking the night before. "We'll leave tomorrow. I think Susanoo will be glad to see us."

I hurriedly put up a line of defense: "I can't go."

"Why?"

"I don't want to fly."

I couldn't stand the idea of taking a ticket Nora had paid for, then sitting next to her like a husband, sipping tomato juice from a plastic cup the flight attendant had poured out of a Tetra Pak as I leafed through the in-flight magazine's ads for hotels and makeup. Nora seemed shocked but kept her emotions in check.

"Are you going by train then?" she asked coolly. "I have to work, so I haven't got that much time."

"Then good, go ahead and fly."

An uncomfortable silence followed until Nora spoke again.

"I'll reserve a train ticket for you."

"I'll take care of it."

"But ..."

What would have come next was, "you don't have any money."

I said the first thing that popped into my head: "I want to hitchhike."

She didn't have a comeback for that.

I was still mulling that scene over when suddenly Schuppenauer bent his knees to steady himself, planting his feet firmly on the ground. In the distance, something was stirring up the dark surface of the slowly flowing river. Schuppenauer started reeling in his line, hard. He reeled and reeled, but no fish appeared. I held my breath, waiting, until I realized I was low on oxygen and gasped for air. Then it came dancing up out of the water, writhing, spattering gleaming droplets until finally Schuppenauer skillfully caught the line and threw the fish down on the grass. Covered in scales like a suit of armor, it landed with a thud, but in the light of that little flashlight, it was smaller than I'd expected. Its body curled so that I thought its tail fin was going to hit its head. Though it couldn't jump in the air, strangely enough, every move it made took it closer to the river. Did it know instinctively which direction to go, or could it smell the water? I pressed down on it with the palm of my hand. It wasn't as cold as I'd thought, and not slimy at all.

"It's a bream."

A river fish you wouldn't find in a sushi bar. Schuppenauer took a little hot plate out of his bag, turned on the switch and, after hitting the fish on the head with a rock, placed the limp little body on it. Sizzle, sizzle. And in response, rumble, rumble from my empty stomach.

"A cooking grill that doesn't need electricity or fire?"

I was so happy I asked him a perfectly obvious question.

"Yep, and it doesn't let off any light, either, so you can cook in the dark without anyone finding you."

As my ears picked up the low hissing of the fish cooking, my mouth filled with saliva. My fingers were trembling I was so hungry. Schuppenauer took a knife, fork, and a hunk of bread out of his bag. He gave me the fork while he sliced the fish with the knife, neatly slipping a little piece into his mouth, right off the blade. In a daze I ripped off a chunk of bread, and dug into the fish with the fork. I normally would have asked for salt at this point, but now I was too starved to even remember the word. A whiff of mud in the taste brought back a memory. When was that? An elderly chef had let me taste his carp soup, which he referred to as "koi-cook." Carp cooking. There are chefs, and cooks. So many different names for the same thing in this language that I've learned, all by myself. My life so far has been full of embarrassing moments, but this is one thing I can be proud of. A chef uses a *cleaver*; when we eat dinner, we use a *knife*; a doctor uses a *scalpel*.

Carp must be related to those monster goldfish that are so popular in Europe now. I hear that breeders who produce fish with beautiful patterns can sell one for the price of a house. Their cousins live in muddy rivers, and aren't much to look at, but—cooked properly—they don't taste bad at all.

When I'd finished eating I looked up and was surprised to find that my eyes were now so used to the dark that I could clearly see Schuppenauer's well-chiseled features.

"Shall we pack up," he asked, "and go home?"

By *go home*, did he mean he'd put me up for the night at his house? He seemed kinder than he had all evening when he said it.

"We met tonight by the will of God," he went on. "I may not look like it, but I'm a man of faith. And well off financially, too.

I'll buy you a ticket to Copenhagen. Let me have your full name, as it's written on your ID"

A sternness in his voice told me I couldn't refuse, so I gave him my name. I felt a nagging regret about that while I was helping him load the fishing equipment back into the car. Once someone knows your real name, he's got you where he wants you. I sat in the passenger's seat, waiting, but Schuppenauer was taking his time. I was so worried I got out of the car again, and saw him a short distance away, with his back turned, bending over his phone. He was talking an awfully long time, which made me even more nervous.

Taking a different road from the one we'd come on, the car suddenly pulled up in front of the station. After he'd parked behind the taxi stand, Schuppenauer started giving me instructions, like a teacher in school:

"I'm going to buy you a ticket to Hamburg. It's a night train, due to arrive tomorrow morning. When you reach Hamburg, don't get off at the central station, but at the one called Dammtor. Go out the exit where there's a tall building, and you'll see a botanical garden. A man will come to meet you outside the exit. There's something I want you to give him, a bag, in exchange for the plane ticket to Copenhagen."

I don't want to get mixed up in criminal activity, I wanted to say, but I'd lost my voice: in a mystery novel, the guy who's wise to the secret but refuses to go along with the plan always gets rubbed out.

I'd keep playing the part of a much younger friend while we were together, and decide whether to take the bag to the police after I'd figured out what was inside. Schuppenauer had said he sounded like a cop because he'd spent so much time talking to them. Was he called only by his last name because he'd been behind bars for a long time? While busy making up my own story about him, I smiled and nodded to hide my anxiety.

"You won't have much time at Hamburg, so hurry. Your ticket will take you directly to the airport."

When he'd got out of the car, Schuppenauer opened the trunk and, lifting out a black leather bag, put the strap carefully over his shoulder before heading into the station. I hurried after him. To my surprise, the ticket he handed me when we were inside was for first class.

"You'll have to transfer at Köln. Got that?"

"But Köln's too far west," I said, parroting what the redhead had told me like a little kid. "You're asking me to take the long way around to Copenhagen. Why should I go to Köln—I'm not an ancient Roman, you know." This didn't seem to surprise Schuppenauer, or to irritate him, either. In fact, he sounded a little lonely.

"On trains, the long way around often gets you there faster. Because the tracks don't run straight through the forest. Köln is a hub, so from there you can go just about anywhere. This is where we part. Good luck. The train leaves in two minutes. Hurry or you'll miss it. I doubt we'll see each other again, but I'm depending on you."

I took the black bag from him, slung it over my shoulder, mumbled a goodbye to the old fisherman, and then, turning my back on him, raced up the stairs to the platform, taking them two at a time, and stepped into the car clearly marked 1. It was practically empty—the only other passenger was sitting at the opposite end, a man in an expensive-looking suit, busy working. I carefully placed the black shoulder bag in the seat by the window. The leather was too thick to tell by feeling the outside whether what was inside was hard, like a gun, or something softer, like plastic bags full of drugs. I was just about to open the bag when I heard a loud voice from behind bark, "Ticket, please," so I quickly shut the door on that darkness, took my ticket out of my hip pocket and, turning around in my seat, stuck it out. The conductor, a tall man, stared at my ticket for a long time but didn't punch it. Immigration officials will sometimes take so long over your passport, their faces a total blank, that it creeps you out. This guy looked like he was decoding a secret sign that showed this ticket had been bought by a suspicious character, or maybe he was deciding what to do about it. But even if a murderer had bought it, if he'd paid good money, it wouldn't be against the law for me to use it.

Though the conductor finally punched my ticket and walked away in silence, as long as he was in the car, I was afraid he'd come back, and couldn't relax. Fortunately, he had only one more ticket to check. But in fact, as it turned out, there wasn't one to check. That businessman in the classy suit at the other end of the car didn't have a ticket. What's more, he refused to accept that when you buy a ticket on the train, you have to pay extra, and launched into a lecture on methods they should use to inform passengers ahead of time that their tickets will cost more than the standard price. The man used lots of big words, making sure we knew how articulate and well educated he was. But the conductor wasn't about to give in. Refusing to pay is a crime, he said. So, I guess the criminal wasn't me, but this man in expensive clothes.

I couldn't resist looking inside that shoulder bag, lying on the window seat like a baby, so I picked it up and, very carefully, so there wouldn't be a loud click, opened the clasp. There were two bundles inside, each wrapped in a blue towel. I unwrapped one, and found it was a darkish brown teddy bear. A vintage Steiff, with its fur worn off in spots. Staring into its black button eyes I felt a chuckle coming on, like a tickle inside my nose: I wanted to laugh out loud, to blast all my worries away. Maybe Schuppenauer had had this bear for a long time, and wanted to pass it on to a grandchild. What if the mailmen voted to strike, but tomorrow was the kid's birthday? If that's how it was, I'd really gotten a good deal. I wrapped the bear up again, put it back in the bag, and picked up the other bundle. It was about the same size but much heavier, and cold to the touch. I unwrapped it, and discovered it was a robot. It had the katakana letters ミコ トクン on its side. The first one, pronounced like "me," means "three," and the next two together make the word *koto*, or thing. The last two are *kun*, an honorific for a cute little boy. Being able to read katakana made me feel like I had something on all the rest of the people on this train.

The robot's eyes were like the teddy bear's—black, round, and kind of cute. It was about a foot long. Not only did its arms move from the shoulders, and legs from the hips, but the other joints bent, too—elbows, knees, even fingers. A silvery color, tinged with blue, the robot looked like it was about to stand up and start walking. I didn't see anything like a switch, though. How were you supposed to turn it on? Maybe it moved by remote control. I felt around the bottom of the bag, but didn't find any extra parts, or instructions, either. Figuring the robot must be another present for his grandchild, I wrapped it back up in the towel, laid it next to the teddy bear, and closed the clasp.

With the toys shut up in darkness again, there was nothing to see, and I got bored. The glass window was a pitch-black mirror, showing only my own reflection. I stared at it. What sort of guy was that, anyway? What if I didn't know myself, and that face belonged to someone I just happened to be sitting across from? I'd notice his black shoulder bag, lying on the seat next to him instead of up on the luggage rack. Why? I'd wonder. Probably because he was carrying drugs, or maybe a bomb. The powder wouldn't be sprinkled in the bottom, but wrapped in neat little plastic bags, hidden inside that teddy bear, I'd think. If a sniffer dog came by, it would howl like crazy, but we weren't in an airport, and no sharp-nosed mammals were on duty here. That robot looked like a child's toy, but there was a bomb inside, I'd tell myself, and as soon as someone far away flipped a switch, it would start walking toward its destination, where it would blow everything up, including itself. I'd read somewhere that there weren't so many suicide bombers these days—we had robots instead. But was that guy, sitting across from me, really capable of such horrific crimes? Wasn't there also some goodness in his face? I could see him doing environmental research in the Arctic, kneeling down to pat a husky on the head, then breaking the ice to take a water sample in a test tube, which he'd carefully take home to his laboratory.

I decided to take the bag to the police. There'd probably be a police station at Hamburg's Central Station, so I'd go straight there. But then again, they'd probably ask me lots of questions. They'd find out that after wheedling scholarship money out of my sponsor, I'd quit the university without telling her and gone traveling; that I'd passed myself off as a native of the land of sushi, and nearly led a dashi workshop under false pretenses; that I'd deceived Nora, too—when all those threads were pulled, my story would unravel. Knowing just how irresponsible I'd been, they probably wouldn't let me off so easily.

I'd better just do as I was told, and not worry about what might happen. If there was an explosion in Hamburg, and the bomb was found, it was Schuppenauer who'd given it to me—I was simply the courier. Like when explosives are sent through the mail, they don't arrest the mailman. I'd thought the things in the bag were children's toys, so I couldn't be found guilty.

I might still be interrogated, though. If Schuppenauer, or the guy I'm supposed to meet, had left a record when they'd reserved my plane ticket, the cops might get my name from it.

Even with all these worries on my mind, I fell into a deep sleep. Now that I think of it, I've been sleeping my worries away ever since I was a kid. When you're asleep, you don't have to think, so it's a pretty convenient habit. The train shook, and when I opened my eyes it was already light outside; we were on the railway bridge, crossing the Elbe River. There were rain clouds in the sky, but it was still morning, and the brightness cheered me up.

I followed Schuppenauer's instructions, and got off at Dammtor, rather than the central station. A cold wind hit my cheeks, and I thought I smelled the Arctic. I was happy to be heading north. Why had I gone to Trier in the first place? Or Arles, with its southern culture I didn't understand, which kept people's hearts chained to the past. Sure, the Mediterranean had food so good it melted on your tongue, and clothes that made you want to have sex as soon as you put them on. But I hated the idea of rubbing oil into my skin, having women lick me all over, and in the end, being eaten by a lion. I was meant to be wrapped in fur, playing with huskies on the ice.

The platform was raised like a little hill, and looking down from it I saw a street lined with stately old buildings on one side, and on the other, a thick grove of trees—a botanical garden, maybe.

I slowly went down the stairs, holding the black bag to my chest so passersby wouldn't bump into it. I smelled coffee, but then remembered I didn't have any money. Using Nora's credit card would leave evidence that I'd been here early this morning.

Walking along the fence around the botanical garden, I soon came to a large entrance gate. There was no sign saying "Botanical Garden," though, and no booth where you could buy a ticket. The gate was wide open, and through it I saw boulders piled up near the front and a small grove of trees reaching straight for the sky in one corner, and lots of plants spreading out behind.

Placing the shoulder bag gently on the ground, I stood there with my arms folded across my chest and my feet planted firmly on the ground, hoping to attract attention. I remembered Schuppenauer saying I wouldn't have much time in Hamburg, but what time was my flight, anyway? Among the people coming out of the station I saw several who might be the guy I was supposed meet: a young man with a hoody pulled down over his eyes, hands stuck in his pockets; a man in a business suit, glancing around as he walked; another in sunglasses, even though it was a cloudy day, but they all passed me by.

Off to the side, a skinny, dark-skinned guy was sitting on the ground, strumming a guitar. He was awfully good for an amateur. The music he was playing reminded me of a Sinti Roma guitarist I heard once, a favorite of Nora's. No one stopped, or threw coins into his flat cap. The varnish had worn off his guitar: it matched the greasy-looking sheen of his old jacket and trousers, limp from many washings. Where would he sleep tonight, and where would he be tomorrow? Switching to slow, easy chords, he started singing a sad song. The words sounded like Italian, though the rhythm was Slavic. What language was he singing in, anyway? It sounded familiar. His song finished, he slowly got up and started walking toward me. I wanted to give him five euros, to thank him for the music, but didn't have any money. Instead of putting out his hand, he took a small, folded paper out of his pocket and stuck it under my nose. I unfolded it, and discovered that it was a ticket for Copenhagen with my name on it. Expressionless, the man took the shoulder bag from me, went back to where he had been sitting, and picked up his guitar. I wanted to talk to him, but when I looked at the ticket, I saw that I had only an hour until takeoff.

With the weight of that bag off my shoulder, I felt much lighter. I went straight to the airport, and by the time I checked in I was perfectly calm. I was terribly thirsty though, when I got to the gate, and since I didn't have any money and there was no drinking fountain, I searched quietly through the trash until I found an Evian bottle with a little water left in it. I was about to pick it up when a hand reached out and snatched the plastic bottle. A typical scrounger, lugging a big cloth bag with handles. If he returned an empty bottle to the shop, the deposit would probably be enough to buy some stale bread left over from the day before. Five would get him a sausage at a stall.

"Wait," I said. "Just let me drink the water."

The skinny guy eyed me suspiciously from under his cap.

"I promise I'll give you the bottle afterwards."

With a trembling hand he gave me back the bottle. I unscrewed the cap, and gulped down the water.

"Thanks."

A mundane thought about how words of thanks show gratitude ran through my head as I watched a line form at the gate, even though boarding hadn't been announced yet. People here must like to line up for things. Even if you're the last one they let you on the plane, which seems like a miracle. A baby started wailing as if all the loneliness in the world had collected in its little heart. After boarding was announced, that kid was the first to disappear. Slowly, the line began to move. The seat next to mine was empty, and I had the uneasy feeling that Nora might come sit down there.

On the flight, they passed out sandwiches with wilted lettuce and ham the texture of rubber when you bit into it. When I'd finished mine, I swallowed my pride and asked for another. Smiling down at me, the flight attendant opened the bottom drawer on her cart and handed me a sandwich. Before, I'd have been too embarrassed to ask—I should have tried that sooner. Now I had something for dinner.

We reached Copenhagen in no time, still early in the afternoon. Nora had said she'd be coming on an evening flight, so I'd beaten her here. And I hadn't used her credit card even once. Nora was probably expecting me to arrive sometime next week, looking exhausted. I got a kick out of that.

Five people were lined up at the taxi stand. Which of them

would give me a ride? Rather than ask them one by one, I said in a voice loud enough for everyone to hear, "I have a sick friend, so I need to go to the Royal Hospital. Could anyone here give me a ride?"

A fiftyish woman in an old-fashioned lady's hat looked me up and down as if she'd like to get her hooks into me. "Come with me," she purred. "I live near the hospital." I thanked her, trying not to look her in the eye.

"You speak Danish so well," she said. "Are you from Greenland?"

"Yes. I came here to study. I was traveling around Germany, but came back when I heard my friend was sick."

"Is your friend from Greenland, too?"

"No, he's Asian."

"Is he very ill?"

"He's been robbed of something fundamentally human. I hear he's really suffering."

When the taxi pulled up, she got into the front seat, so fortunately our conversation stopped there. The taxi sped along without braking once, as if there were no traffic lights here. Sometimes in my dreams I'm like an omnipotent god, and all the traffic lights turn green just as I get to them: I'm always driving a dogsled. I've never told anyone about those dreams, though— I'm sure they'd laugh at me.

"What are you studying at the university?" she asked, turning around in the front seat.

"Biology."

"That's wonderful. What are you planning to do after you graduate?"

"I want to research species diversity in the Arctic."

I wasn't exactly lying, but it felt like some different person was saying all this—someone studious and well brought up, someone I didn't know very well. His life might start up again back at the university, but I'd have to retreat somewhere behind the scenes.

When the taxi pulled up in front of the hospital, the woman handed me her card. As I was getting out, I heard her quietly tell the driver to go back, toward the airport. So she'd lied about living near the hospital.

When I went into the hospital, I heard an announcement in Danish over the loudspeaker—that made me feel one step closer to home. Since the whole idea of "homeland" is relative, you can have more than one. I wasn't born and raised in Reykjavik, but it seems more like home to me than Copenhagen, which in turn feels homier than Oslo. But Oslo is closer to home than Hamburg. There are holes in the earth, but everything's still connected. And it's the sea that brings places together. Places I've never been, like Alaska and Siberia, are linked to the land where I was born by icy seawater. And when water freezes, it's just like solid earth, firm enough to drive a dogsled over. Susanoo and Hiruko, who come from far away, look like me because of all these connections.

When I asked about Susanoo at the front desk, the receptionist told me he was probably on the third floor, but possibly on the fourth—she didn't seem sure. I got into the elevator and pressed 3, but felt the floor under my feet going down. People sometimes press the DOWN button and then, changing their minds, get out. This elevator, unable to shake off that useless command, was now taking me downward. The door opened and I saw a boy in white work clothes. "Hellooo," he said, stretching out the last syllable. Feeling like a kid myself, I got out.

"You didn't want to come down here," he said, "but you came anyway, right? My name is Munun."

"A friend of mine, named Susanoo, is here in the hospital," I replied.

"He's on the fourth floor. Or maybe the third. He might be talking to a bear or a rabbit."

"A bear or a rabbit? Why?"

"Doctor Velmer thinks Susanoo can't speak, so he's treating him."

"He *thinks* he can't talk? You mean he really can?"

"Yes, he can."

"Did he say something to you?"

"He said *Tsukuyomi.*"

"What does that mean?"

"It could be my name. I'm called Munun, not Tsukuyomi, but then again, maybe my name's Tsukuyomi. What's yours?"

"Nanook. Is this elevator broken?"

"Ghosts live in it, and they take it wherever they want."

"Ghosts in the elevator? What is this, a horror movie?"

"Yes," Munun said, pointing at the room behind him. "It's a horror movie." Looking in that direction, I saw a girl who could have been his sister, watching TV. The woman patient on the screen was on the elevator, watching a loose, wobbly board in the ceiling, listening to the voice of a ghost, coming from behind it. I laughed out loud to show I wasn't afraid, but it was such a creepy scene that I felt myself shrivel up below the waist.

"I'll use the stairs."

"You can't use the stairs."

"What do you do if a fire breaks out?"

"Fires are very dangerous."

"Would you mind riding in the elevator with me, up to the third floor?"

Though I'd never begged anyone to come with me because I was too scared to be alone, I thought it would be okay to ask Munun. He nodded, rode up with me, and when we got there, knocked on a certain door, which Dr. Velmer opened. The doctor stared at us menacingly, but Munun was unfazed.

"This is Nanook," he said. "He's come to see Susanoo."

"Since when are you a tour guide?" the doctor barked. "Oh, well, I guess it's okay. Go on back to your post now."

He certainly didn't seem very kind, scolding the boy when a thank-you would have been in order, and yet both the doctor and Munun were grinning all the while. I was wondering whether I should sit down on the square stool in the room when, instead of, "Have a seat," Velmer came out with, "This is NILS." I gawked around the room, looking for this Nils he had just introduced me to, but there was no one here besides us.

"You don't know NILS?" he laughed. "That's the stool's name." I was bracing myself for a conversation with an alien from outer space when Velmer, as if objectively aware of his own strangeness, explained, "It's what Ikea calls this line of products. They're like family to me. Don't let it bother you." I was relieved, and not only that—even if this guy was definitely weird, I was starting to feel like I could trust him somehow.

While Susanoo might not actually be ill, Velmer told me, he was a fascinating subject for research, so he'd asked him to stay on for a while. His own work consisted mainly of comforting wealthy hypochondriacs, but he explained that he saw in this new patient a chance for clinical trials that would gain this mediocre hospital recognition from the medical research community, adding that since Susanoo wasn't sick, he was living in the guest house next door, and that I should go see him there. He was paying for Susanoo's living expenses out of his own research funds.

"I envy him," I blurted out. "Couldn't you do some research on me, too?" Hearing my cheeky request, Velmer's eyes took on a sheen like a fish's belly.

"You're Nanook, aren't you? You're the one who heard about Susanoo while you were working at a sushi bar, and then told Knut about him, am I right?"

"You're well informed."

"Knut and I have been friends a long time. He mentions so many people I have a hard time keeping their names straight, but yours has a primitive ring that stuck in my mind."

Most people in wealthy European countries won't use a word like "primitive" for fear of being accused of racism. This doctor was an unusual man.

"Are you a student?" he asked.

"That's right. My major's biology. I was planning to study medicine at first, but that was mostly to please my parents."

"Do you blame everything on your parents? I'll bet you don't have any hopes and dreams of your own."

"Yes, I do. I'm interested in creatures that live in the sea, and in the health of people who eat them, but I'd never be able to cut human flesh with a scalpel."

"Are you trying to say that it takes cruelty to be a surgeon, and you're much too sensitive?"

"No. But when I don't like taking medicine myself, I can't see myself ordering patients to take theirs. Besides, I don't like being indoors all the time, and I'm not sure university life suits me. That's why I started traveling."

"And what happened after that?"

"I was studying dashi while working at a sushi place. But I didn't tell the person who sponsored me as a foreign student that my trip had gotten much longer than I'd originally planned— endless, in fact—so now I feel like I really should."

"Then why don't you?"

"It would be awfully hard to explain ..."

"Why is that?"

"She'll probably be angry with me."

"She's not going to kill you, is she?"

"No, but she'll be very disappointed in me, and terribly sad."

"If she's sad, that's her problem. You don't have to worry about that."

"Well, actually I also have a girlfriend in Trier. I lived with her for over a month, and now I'll have to tell her that I'm going to stay in Copenhagen. It's going to be hard to break the news."

"Why?"

"I'm afraid she'll be hurt—wounded."

"Listen, *wound* is a word that should only be used by doctors—amateurs have no business using it as a metaphor. And there are no wounds of the heart. There is only heart disease. But why are you so worried about how other people feel, anyway?"

"I'm not sure."

"There's no sense always thinking about other people. They're not you, so you can never really understand them. You're just imagining their emotional reactions. She'll be disappointed, or she'll be sad. What meaning is there in that? Other people don't matter. Who cares what they think? All you have to do is say honestly what you believe to be true."

"I really envy you."

"How about switching personalities with me, for about a month? I have a feeling that things will go much better for you that way."

"Can we really just switch personalities?"

"With modern medicine, nothing is impossible."

"You mean a brain transplant?"

"The only time psychologists cut into flesh is at the dinner table. There's no need for an operation."

"That's a relief."

"It'll be an experiment. We'll keep it secret until the results start to show. I can't pay for your living expenses, but I can give you some remuneration. All you have to do is come here two or three times a week while you continue your studies."

As Velmer, I'll have no qualms about looking Mrs. Nielsen in the eye and telling her what I've been doing, and what I'm planning to do. And when Nora arrives in Copenhagen, I'll come right out and tell her that I won't be going back to Trier with her. I'm Velmer, I have nothing to fear, I thought, thumping myself on the chest with my fist.

CHAPTER 4   *Nora Speaks*

I was staring off into space, thinking about travel. Not trips I've taken, but one that was about to begin, and that didn't have arms or legs yet. Or, more accurately, it had arms and hands, but no legs. Arms reaching out, searching for Nanook, who'd already left; hands that grasped only air. Fingers anxiously scrolling through my phone for a number, a palm pressed to my forehead because I didn't know what to do. So, plenty in the arm-and-hand department, but no lower limbs. I needed to start moving, yet I couldn't find my feet.

After I reserved two plane tickets, Nanook announced he was going to hitchhike, and set out on his own. I'll probably end up flying to Copenhagen alone, and waiting for him there. I hate waiting around for people, and not knowing when they're going to show up is really the pits. I fantasize about turning into a huge wave that will come crashing down on the car he's in, zipping along the seashore, pulling him under, and then—even though I'm disgusted with myself for having imagined a scene straight out of an anime—I scour the map in my head for the nearest sea shore. None close by. In fact, both the North Sea and the Baltic feel as far away as the moon. Perhaps I should turn into the moon, then. But "moon" is a masculine noun in German, so that's out. What about a gust of wind, strong enough to flip the car over? No, "wind" is masculine, too. Thinking about how many nouns are off-limits keeps me awake, slowing the hours down as I toss and turn in bed until dawn breaks, but even on the saddest morning the sun doesn't stop being a feminine noun, or lose any of the energy she had the day before. Since the sun burns constantly, you'd think she'd gradually grow smaller as her fuel gets used up, but that never happens. She must run on renewables.

I recently found a handy site to consult when planning a trip, where you can check how much energy will be used, and how much damage it'll do to the atmosphere. As Trier doesn't have an airport, I usually use the nearest one, in Luxembourg. According to this site, an Airbus A320 flying from Luxembourg to Copenhagen uses 462 kilowatts of unrenewable energy per passenger, which is equal to eleven gallons of gasoline. It takes ten gallons to drive that far, not so different from going by plane. But you can fly that distance in one hour and forty-five minutes, whereas it takes ten hours to drive. Framing the demerits of going by car cheered me up a little: Nanook shouldn't have hitchhiked. It's good I didn't go with him. Or at least I'd like to think so. I checked the carbon dioxide emission for each mode of transportation. By plane, 265 pounds per person, by train 1.75 pounds, by car 230 pounds. Which means cars are terrible—much slower than planes, and they still dirty the air almost as much. I was right about Nanook being wrong. Or so I'd like to believe.

About to suffocate, I opened a window. That was when I noticed the one thing I'd overlooked. If I had hitchhiked with Nanook, the cars that picked us up would have been carrying at least three people including the driver, which means the total amount of gasoline divided by three would come to just a bit more than three gallons per person, so less than my going by plane. I started to waver. Maybe I should have gone with Nanook after all. Then the word "train" reappeared out of nowhere, and like Superman, swooped down, picked me up, and gently set me down in a first-class compartment on an Intercity Express. I could go by train. Rail is truly the King of Transportation. Though it takes nearly fifteen hours to Copenhagen, and might cost more than a plane ticket, a train only uses 70 kilowatts, much less than either a car or a plane. And there was something else I'd forgotten—considering the volume of emissions, trains really are the most efficient. When judging how important something is, volume is a better measure than weight—this applies to lots of things besides emissions. Love, for instance. In my own experience, it can be small but heavy, like the diamond in an engagement ring, while sometimes it's very light but takes up more and more room in your heart until it's awfully hard to handle. Where is Nanook on this scale? Anyway, if you compare the volume of emissions, for a car it's 14,000 gallons, not much different than a plane, which emits 15,850, while for a train it's only 90 gallons—an amazingly small amount. I'll definitely go by train. You'll probably say that while women who travel by train might be morally superior, they have no sex appeal, but men like you—insisting on hitchhiking—are just deluding yourselves, thinking you're keeping yourselves pure by not spending any money, despite the fact that hitchhiking wouldn't even be possible without cars, and the automobile industry is one of the pillars of this money-grubbing society, I say to myself, silently arguing with Nanook. But he's never actually condemned capitalism—I'm just superimposing the views of an old lover of mine onto him.

It's just occurred to me that Nanook may really like cars. Once when we were walking together, he stopped to look at a parked car, his eyes narrowing over this bright, shiny object.

"The latest Toyota model," he murmured, breaking into a smile.

"Is Toyota the name of the man who started the company?" I asked.

"No," he said, looking as shocked as a kid taking an oral exam when the teacher throws him a really strange question. "It's a place name. A really nice town."

Not knowing he was an Eskimo at the time, and wanting to find out more about him, I asked, "Did you live near the town where this car was made?"

"Huh? This car? No, it was manufactured in Kentucky." Why there, I wanted to know, but seeing the frown on his face I decided not to ask.

Why do I take his decision to hitchhike as unspoken rejection? What should I say if he arrives a week after me and stands there, showing off his filthy, crumpled clothes and greasy hair? *You're not the least bit cool—if you'd really made up your mind to trade a life of decadent luxury for honest poverty you would have walked, because bumming rides with strangers is like refusing to get a job while sponging off your parents.* But pounding on his chest with words wouldn't melt his icy silence. It's best to counter action with action. My walking all the way to Copenhagen, for instance, against his hitchhiking. He'd be really surprised if I showed up several weeks after him, my sunken eyes gleaming in my gaunt face, and casually mentioned that I'd walked from Trier. Then he wouldn't be able to dismiss me as an older woman using money and logic to foist conventional morality on him anymore. For I would have just completed a trip that was harder, more dangerous, and at least as outrageous as anything he's ever done. Pulling that off would really feel good.

After daydreaming a while with my eyes closed, I opened them again and noticed that "on foot" was one of the modes of travel you could choose on this site. Next to the airplane, train, and car icons were some I'd overlooked: a bicycle, a motorcycle, and a human figure with a rucksack. When I clicked on it, the figure started walking awkwardly from left to right until it stopped, right in front of a sign that said Copenhagen. The amount of time required came to "twenty days, one hour and seven minutes." The fine print above this data noted that "twelve hours of rest per day" were included. That would mean you'd have to start at 8:00 a.m. and keep on walking until 8:00 p.m. without a break. Much too grueling a schedule for someone like me—I'm ready to stop at a coffee shop after even a short walk. And because the amount of energy a person expends while walking apparently can't be converted into gallons of gasoline, the entire trip would take "58 pizzas." Since I'd only be able to walk about six hours a day, it would take me forty days to get there, and I'd consume 116 pizzas on the way. Or would I only eat half that many, because I'd be using up half the amount of energy?

I pictured myself waking up to my alarm clock, gulping down a cup of instant coffee, gobbling a pizza the size of an old-fashioned LP record, and then rushing out of whatever inn where I'd spent the night. Why am I walking? I mustn't think— it's a waste of calories. I have a nauseatingly long stretch of time ahead of me until noon. Why did I choose to travel this way? Why Nanook? My doubts have wide open mouths, like baby birds clamoring for food, *Pi-chiku, pa-chiku*. I'm not imagining these sounds. Real birds are chirping. Their voices travel up and down a scale full of gaps. Or shoot out a single note, sharp as an arrow. I see a red-tailed warbler. Another has a yellow throat. I'm in the middle of a forest. Then I woke up. I had not started out on foot. Or on any other kind of journey, for that matter. I was still collecting data.

I suddenly wanted to eat pizza with a thin, crisp crust. I got one I'd bought several weeks earlier out of the freezer and spread olive oil and tomato paste over it. The red tomato reminded me of the phrase "covered in blood." To me those words were more frightening than blood you see in the movies. Probably hardly any hitchhikers are actually murdered and left by the roadside "covered in blood," though. There's a much greater possibility of being killed in a terrorist attack at an airport. Nanook is probably dozing in a car right now, next to a driver he doesn't know. I took a small onion, so white it seemed cold, and sliced it as thinly as I could. When the pungent smell hit my nasal membrane, my eyes blurred with tears. I looked for the big, sweet kind, last week, but these smaller, sharper ones were all they had in the shop that day. Perhaps there were tears in Nanook's eyes now, too. Maybe because the driver was telling him a sad tale about how he'd lost his love. Nanook never seemed to turn his own sadness into tears, so this would be his first chance in quite a while to have a good cry and clean out his tear ducts. I was weeping with the aid of this onion. Against all odds, the two of us might, at the very same time, both be in tears.

I added thin strips of green pepper, then green olives, thinly sliced mushrooms, and finally, as if covering a wound with bandages, carefully placed oblongs of cheese across the top. Standing by the window after I'd put the pizza in the oven, I heaved a deep sigh. Sighs, too, emit carbon dioxide. By breathing deeply, letting out sigh after sigh, a person in love might cause more pollution than someone breathing normally, so did that mean that long-distance hikers would damage the environment more than people doing office work? I thought about that until my curiosity got the better of me, and I found myself back in front of the computer screen. Walking from Trier to Copenhagen, a person would exhale a third of a pound of carbon dioxide, the data said. That was approximately one-fifth as much as a car—a surprisingly large amount.

I had a dream. Everything was floating in white. I had no idea where Earth ended and the sky began. Something grayish appeared. A sled. I approached, and saw that polar bears and snowshoe hares were pulling it. The driver was dressed in a white arctic outfit with a hood that covered his face. That must be Nanook, I thought, my heart beating faster. But when the sled stopped, and the young man roughly pulled the hood back, I realized that although they looked a little alike, it wasn't Nanook.

And yet that slender youth with the sunburned face looked familiar. The wrinkles on his forehead and around his eyes made him look old and young at the same time. Could this be Nanook in the future?

"I'm looking for Nanook."

He didn't answer.

"Do you speak German?"

"Nicht ich du versteht spreche Deutsch."

Though I understood certain elements, they were put together in the wrong way, so I couldn't grasp the meaning.

"Do you speak English?"

He opened his mouth wide and pronounced one word very slowly and carefully, but I couldn't understand it. Maybe we only seemed to be here, together in the same space, but he was already dead. Or was it me who was dead, I thought, feeling a piercing pain as if gills were sprouting open on my cheeks—and then I woke up.

Who was that? Not Nanook. Once I was outside the dream, I couldn't even remember his face very clearly. I ran my hand along the cool wall next to my bed, then got up and gazed at the square of gray sky framed by the window. Nanook felt very far away. The ancient Romans called the area around Copenhagen Hafnia. Though they traded wine there for animal hides, Hafnia to the Romans was remote beyond their imagination, a complete backwater. Eskimos couldn't possibly have come to Trier in those days. But though the Romans took a jaundiced view of places like Hafnia, the Eskimos probably wouldn't have found their imperial cities particularly attractive. Not because they were ignorant—they wouldn't have envied city dwellers even if they'd known how they lived. Nanook might never come back to Trier. If that were the case, I'd have to leave for the far north. Could I make such a bold leap?

I was staring into space again, holding my coffee cup at mouth level without actually drinking any when the phone rang. It was Akash.

"How've you been? Knut and Hiruko have gone to the hospital to see Susanoo. I envy them, being so close by. Copenhagen's pretty far away, but if you and Nanook are going, I'd like to join you."

"Nanook left by himself. I had two airplane tickets reserved for us, but then he refused to go with me."

"Why?"

"His mind got swept away by the romantic notion of hitch-hiking, alone."

"That sounds dangerous."

"Not any more than going by plane. Bombs go off in airports, there are hijackings, and planes sometimes crash. I'm not particularly worried about him hitchhiking, but it makes planning hard."

"Because you don't know when he'll get there?"

"That's right. And I'm not used to leaving everything up to fate. In fact, the word 'fate' has almost disappeared from German, except as a metaphor."

"But wasn't it fate that brought you and Nanook together? Not that I want to be like an Indian guru, giving you words of wisdom."

"You're an Indian realist, aren't you—not a guru."

"Yes, so, asking as a realist, what'll you do?"

A great idea that a moment before wouldn't have occurred came falling out of the sky.

"Why don't you come with me, as my traveling companion? You needn't worry about a ticket."

"I can't go for free. I'll pay for the ticket."

"Just treat me to a cup of coffee in Copenhagen."

"That's much too cheap."

"These days there's coffee that costs more than a plane ticket.

A cup of Russian coffee might be more expensive than the fare to Moscow."

"Don't you mean Irish coffee, or maybe Russian hot chocolate?"

"You know a lot about coffee."

"It would be nice if cafeteriology were a field of study."

"Can you skip your seminars?"

"Friends are more important than academia. I can hardly wait to see Copenhagen, and Knut."

"I wonder if we'll be of any help to Susanoo."

"I'm sure that if we put our heads together, we'll find some way to help him. You'll be taking the bus to Luxembourg, am I right? So, let's meet at the central bus station."

After I hung up the phone, I imagined myself walking next to Akash, who'd be dressed as a woman. He has a firm, slender build, and his skin is golden brown. Mine is almost white as snow, which makes me seem kind of flabby even though I'm not fat. My hair's so blond it spreads out like flames when the sun catches it. I rather like that, but I don't want to look too voluminous next to Akash. Maybe I should tie my hair back. Though wearing black would give me a firmer appearance, it doesn't really suit me. And the red jacket I have is a different shade from Akash's sari. Side by side the reds would be "clashing," a term that used to be synonymous with bad taste. But wasn't my colleague talking about designers who deliberately use clashing shades of red? The topic came up because the gift shop in the museum where we work has now started selling a magenta, crimson, and scarlet T-shirt.

She was the one who answered when I called the museum.

"This is the Karl Marx Haus," she said in the official voice she used with customers.

"It's Nora."

"Oh, hello Nora, how are you enjoying your vacation?"

"Actually, I have to go to Copenhagen to visit a sick friend, so I can't come back to work just yet. Can I take another week off?"

"That'll be fine. We don't have many visitors these days, and we've finished working on the garden. So I'll give you exactly another week. In return, I'll be counting on you when my son's summer vacation starts."

"Got it. Thanks a lot."

Even from a distance, it was easy to pick Akash out of the crowd. Dressed in a bright red sari, he had a navy-blue sports bag—the kind high school kids carry—slung over his shoulder, and white sneakers on his feet. Does he think this mismatched ensemble looks cool, or does practicality dictate his choices? While everyone else was bent over their phones, staring at screens as their fingers moved over them, Akash gawked around until he saw me, then smiled and lifted his thin arm straight up.

In the bus, things seemed strange somehow. Everybody besides us had only an attaché case or a handbag. Were we the only ones going on a trip? I was going ask Akash what he thought, but he suddenly veered off on a completely different topic.

"I'm wondering about Susanoo's condition. The inability to speak is certainly an illness. But then again, there are diseases you recover from by not talking."

"That must be why silent retreats are so popular now. A colleague of mine who recently went to one told me all about it. She took a whole week off work, and stayed in a retreat center without saying a word. Everybody had all their meals alone in their rooms, and though they'd gather in a large hall for meditation, conversation was forbidden."

"So, they paid a fee for not talking. How much, I wonder?"

"About a thousand Euros for the week, she said."

"Including room and board, I assume. But the silence itself— I wonder how much that costs."

"I don't know," I said. "Room and board should go in a separate column on the tax return, so maybe tax officials know how much is left over—the cost of silence."

"Can silence be a commercial product? How are prices determined anyway?"

Seeing how serious Akash looked, I burst out laughing.

"Are you asking me because I work at the Karl Marx Haus?"

"No, I was thinking of Susanoo. What he's producing is silence."

"Who's he selling it to?"

"By not speaking, he's generating all sorts of economic activity—people are paid to give him medical treatment and see to his daily needs, his friends travel to see him, and maybe even buy him flowers."

"So, if we all refused to visit him, it would be like going on strike—a friendship strike." Though I was only joking, it was already too late when I realized how ominous that sounded. "Hijack" and "terrorist attack" are things you always avoid mentioning on the way to the airport, but "strike" can be disastrous, too.

When we got off the bus and went into the airport, there was hardly anyone around. Seeing a woman in a poison-green uniform turn away from the checkout counter, I hurriedly called out to her.

"Is there a strike or something?"

"It's not our airline that's striking," she said coldly. "It's the entire airport." In other words, everyone who worked there. The people who load the baggage; the ones who put "Maintenance" signs on the restroom doors and mop the floors; the women at the information counters, who crisply answer all your questions without changing expression or moving their lips. All those people were definitely not around today.

"So, all flights have been canceled?" asked Akash, voicing the very question I'd had in mind.

Giving him an *Of course, you idiot* look, the woman in green silently walked away. We wandered aimlessly around the airport until we found a travel agent's sign. Several people were lined up at the window, all looking very anxious. Akash was cheerful as usual, like a kid on a school field trip. When our turn came, we asked the fastest way to get to Copenhagen, and were told it would be smartest to fly from the Köln Bonn Airport, but discovered there were no tickets available.

"There are no direct flights. But maybe you could take the train to Frankfurt or Paris, and then fly from there." Like an enthusiastic volunteer assisting migrants, he tried to find us tickets.

"The only flight I can find has an eight-hour layover in Paris, and costs two thousand Euros. It would be cheaper to go to New York and catch a plane to Copenhagen from there."

Akash let out a shimmery sort of laughter, like a triangle being tapped, but I had serious objections.

"No matter how much time or money it saved," I countered, "a flight to New York would use tons of unrenewable energy— think of the air pollution that would cause."

Apparently unperturbed by my earnest environmentalism, the agent nodded gently while his fingers continued the search for another route.

"I know what you mean," he said. "Why not try taking the train to Rostock, and the ferry to Copenhagen from there? The train trip takes a long time, but the ferry's only a couple of hours, and the whole trip costs about a hundred Euros. With this strike on, it might be faster than flying."

Akash was slowly moving his head from side to side as he stared into space. Watching him, the travel agent looked puzzled.

"In India," I blurted out, "shaking your head means yes."

That brought Akash to his senses. "How did you know?" he asked, looking surprised. "An old habit must have resurfaced while I was daydreaming."

A boat trip had never occurred to me. I rarely travel over water. Though I have taken tour groups on ferries down the Mosel or the Rhine, I've never crossed the ocean on a real ship. Mist hung over the map in my head, but through it, I saw a port to the north, and began thinking, oh, that must be the Baltic, the way out of Germany, and there'd be lots of boats moored there, each with a sign indicating its destination. Sweden, Finland, the Baltics, the Russian city of Kaliningrad, Poland. I started to worry. I'd have to find the boat for Denmark.

"You were daydreaming too?" asked Akash, peering into my face. Startled, I whisked the dream away with my hand as if brushing off a fly.

"What kind of dream was it?"

"I saw a port with lots of boats, but couldn't find the one for Denmark."

"Mine was much more dramatic. The Balkans and southern Europe had turned into an uninhabitable desert, so billions of people were heading north. But is something wrong? You look pale. Here comes the train. We'll be boarding as soon as everybody gets off. Let's get as far toward the back as we can."

Akash darted forward, slipping nimbly through the crowd, but came back for me when he noticed I'd fallen behind and took my hand, pulling me along. We didn't see a single empty seat until we got to the middle of the train, where there was a table for four with the two aisle seats free. Sitting across from Akash, I realized why no one had taken them. The two men next to us, by the window, had faces covered with tattoos. They looked as if the tattooist had started to imitate a Maori pattern, then decided it was too much trouble and got sloppy. The men's foreheads and cheeks were red and swollen, as if the skin was inflamed. Akash gave them a look, but didn't seem the least bit upset.

"It's not nearly as crowded as I'd thought it would be," he said with a smile.

I laughed, thinking he must be joking, but then realized he might not be. Perhaps this really wasn't crowded compared to trains in Asia. That's a whole world I've never been to. The closest I've come is a walk I once took through the "Asian side" of Istanbul. I imagine a mindboggling display of colors, smells, and sounds, starting in India, crossing China, stretching all the way to that country Hiruko and Susanoo are from, and I vaguely label it all "Asia." Akash took a thermos out of that navy blue sports bag of his, along with two paper cups, and poured us some chai. Next, he produced two boxes—the kind kids pack their school lunch in—and like a mother, briskly handed me one. It had some kind of fried buns inside.

"Piroshkis?" I asked.

"Do I look Russian? They're supposed to be samosas."

The tattooed duo next to us let out high-pitched notes of laughter that sounded like flutes. Rather than starting a conversation, though, they soon retreated behind their tattoos.

As the sun peeked out from between the clouds, everything I saw from the window brightened up. Crumbling castle walls, farm houses, tree-lined streets, and hills all rushed by and disappeared behind us, which felt like a terrible loss. As long as the train was speeding forward, this was inevitable, perhaps, but I felt as if going forward meant pushing the scenery away, and nothing more. And yet I wondered if there wasn't something odd about me, finding this so disappointing.

A smile spread across Akash's cheeks.

"You look happy," I said.

"Yes, for several reasons," he replied, "First, I'll be able to see Knut soon. Second, I'm not having to travel alone. And the third is—"

He was about to tell me when we heard a loud grinding underneath, and the scenery that had been zipping past outside stopped as if it had suddenly run into a wall. The car froze in silence for a few seconds until someone calmly said, "I'm going to get some coffee from the dining car." There was no announcement over the loudspeaker. "Don't worry, we'll start up again. This sort of thing happens all the time," said another passenger, trying to comfort his traveling companion. "If the conductor comes, we can ask him what's going on," said a woman. "He'll never come," a man fired back. Hearing that voice gave me a jolt. He sounded just like an old boyfriend of mine. When we were stuck in situations like this he'd sit there, waiting for me to speak, and when I did, he'd snap at me, telling me I was wrong no matter what I'd said. How would Nanook have reacted? He'd probably be eyeing me with an *I told you it was better to hitchhike* look on his face.

"I wonder why we've stopped. Maybe a herd of cows is crossing the tracks. But we're not in India, are we?" Akash joked as he poured me another cup of chai. Just then we heard some thorny static, as if someone was rubbing the mic with a cactus, and then a voice that announced, "A herd of cows is now crossing the track, so we cannot move. Please wait a little while longer." We heard smothered giggles here and there.

"Dairy farmers always come first," one passenger said. "Maybe we'd get there faster riding one of the cows," laughed another. Amid the humor, a loud, angry woman's voice protested, "Activists have sabotaged the train. They're driving cattle across the tracks on purpose!"

Whether her voice carried naturally, or she was shouting to make sure everyone heard, she succeeded in silencing the entire car.

"Activists do this sort of thing?" I whispered to Akash.

"There's a movement to protect the routes animals use," he said. "I've heard about a road through the woods with a special crossing for deer. Drivers have to get out of their cars and raise the barrier. And I've seen a Rabbits Use This Road sign, too. So it's possible that someone intentionally drove the cows over the track."

"I wonder if the railroad company isn't behind it. They're getting a lot of bad press because so many trains have to stop for repairs—maybe they asked a group of activists to send a herd across the tracks."

The static on the mic started up again.

"The train will now start," a voice said. "Due to a problem with our dining car system, service will be suspended."

"They probably gave all the dining car food to the cows to make them move," said Akash. More flutelike whistling from the tattooed pair beside us. But with those wrinkly laugh lines completely hidden beneath their tattoos, they looked just as grim as before. Though we talk about laughing eyes, or kind eyes, the eyeball itself is always cold. It's the wrinkles around them that make eyes look warm, or gentle, or clever, I was thinking to myself when the loudspeaker came on again.

"We will be moving slowly to Koblenz Station, where the train will undergo repairs and a maintenance check. We are not certain how long this will take. Passengers who wish to do so may transfer to the incoming train bound for Amsterdam. However, this train is expected to be extremely crowded. All seats are taken, including in first class."

We exchanged looks. Rather than having to stand all the way, I thought it would be better to stay in our seats and wait. Even if they weren't sure how long the repairs would take, they hadn't ordered everyone off the train, so it couldn't be more than a couple of hours. But Akash wanted to take the train for Amsterdam as far as Hamburg, then go from there to Köln. Never hesitating, he moved freely across the globe, while I lost all sense of direction as soon as I left my own neighborhood. The name Amsterdam was so unsettling I wanted to cling to this train, even if it rusted away on the tracks and wouldn't move for another ten years rather than risk being dragged off in an unknown direction. Akash, on the other hand, would have boarded a train bound for Siberia as long as it was headed in the right direction, certain that he could transfer to another one at some fork in the road.

Joining the stream of people who got off at Koblenz, flowing like water down the platform steps into a dimly lit passage, Akash and I melted in, me holding on tightly to a thin finger as we climbed the staircase to the opposite platform, jostled like salmon swimming upstream to spawn until before I knew it, we were on a crowded train for Amsterdam. The space between the outside doors and the restroom was so full of people that we couldn't get into any of the compartments.

"It's only an hour to Köln," Akash whispered. "Try a little packed-train yoga and we'll be there in no time."

"Packed-train yoga? What's that?"

"A sort of exercise, a way to kill time when you can't get a seat on a train. First, put your feet together and, keeping your balance, slowly raise your heels until you're standing on tiptoe."

I pitched forward and grabbed onto his shoulder.

"Next, slowly bend your knees a little. Pull your hips forward, and push your spine back—just a tiny bit."

I was bending my knees when the car lurched, sending my nose straight into a big white bowl that turned out to be one of the headphones the person diagonally across from me was wearing.

"Since this is packed-train yoga, remember to restrain all movements that can be seen from outside. Expand and retract your body from within. If your spine grows even 0.1 millimeter, that's quite a revolution."

Hearing the word revolution, a nearby passenger looked nervously over his shoulder at us. He was probably hoping there were no terrorists around. Akash took so little notice he seemed to be encased in an invisible eggshell.

"Next, expand your chest. Outward restraint is still important. But inside, your lungs are so full of oxygen that your chest is puffed out, and you can feel both shoulder blades being pressed out and down."

"Did you used to teach yoga?"

"Actually, I know nothing about it. But because I'm Indian, I've been asked to lead classes so many times that I eventually figured some things out."

"That's a little like Nanook almost giving a workshop on umami."

When the train slid to a stop beside a platform covered by a domed roof, it was announced that we'd arrived at Köln Station, but there was none of the usual information about incoming trains or layover times for transfers. Fortunately, as we had very little luggage and were near the door, we had no trouble getting off. Standing on tiptoe, Akash stretched his neck up like a crane and gawked around the station.

"There's something strange going on."

"You think so? It does seem awfully crowded."

"That's not all. It isn't Christopher Street Day or Carnival, either, but everybody's up in the air somehow. Not worried, exactly—more like they're ready for a festival. I wonder if something's happened."

Afraid we'd be separated in the pushing, jostling crowd, I took his hand again.

"For the time being let's just go with the flow until we get to the sign board, and look for a train to Hamburg. It'd be great if we found one that went straight to Rostock, but let's thank the gods if we can get to Hamburg."

Rows of train numbers, starting times, destinations. Almost all had been struck through in red: "canceled." The few that hadn't were apparently all bound for Brussels.

"I'll usually try any train, even if it's not headed where I want to go," Akash sighed, "but Brussels is in the opposite direction."

"Brussels is on the verge of collapse," someone behind me said, and I felt as if a hand had reached in and grabbed my heart. What if our only possible destination had been destroyed? From fragments of the following conversation, though, I realized that "Brussels" meant the EU.

The volume must have been out of control, because the next announcement sounded like voices lifted in prayer reverberating through a cathedral:

"Our valued customers, due to a malfunction in our computer system, the electric sign boards are not working properly. The information you are now seeing may not be accurate."

As the crowd around the sign boards dissolved, I turned around and saw that there was already a long line in front of the information booth. We would have to wait for our turn, and when it came, it didn't seem likely that we'd get much help.

"Let's go out," Akash said. "I can't find anything on the internet. At times like these, real people are often the best source of information. I know someone who works at a broadcasting station near here, so let's go see him."

He sounded casual, as if he were deciding where to have a cup of coffee. I can never choose a course of action when something unexpected happens, because my head fills up with useless thoughts. If a dictator suddenly took over the country where I was living, and I wanted to escape, I'd have to pick a destination right away. In desperate times, wishy-washy people need friends like Akash. I'd feel even more relieved with Knut and the others by my side too. Akash now turned to me with a comforting look.

"Don't worry. If you go straight ahead, there's always something blocking your way. That's why you should instead try moving a little to the right, then a little to the left."

"Like a snake."

"Not just snakes. Rivers flow in a winding path, too. Only

shooting stars fall in a straight line. But since we're not falling, we shouldn't hesitate to meander."

The Köln Cathedral, all lit up, looked like a giant crystal. Slipping nimbly through the tourists taking selfies in front of it, Akash went down a narrow road off to the side. Through a glass window I saw a café where people were drinking coffee; the building next door was probably the station. Akash headed straight for an entrance that looked like the back door to a theater, and once inside, loudly greeted the man at the reception desk.

"Akash?" he replied. "I sure wasn't expecting to see you here."

The man's brown eyes shone in his tanned, manly-looking face, as his red lips, surrounded by a black beard, twisted into a grin.

"There was a strike at the airport and then all the trains are canceled, so we're in a bit of a bind. We need to get to Rostock—any ideas?"

"Rostock? To people living here, that's like a foreign country. I've never even been there."

"How about Hamburg, then? That would be far enough."

His eyes half closed, the man riffled through his brain, looking for useful information.

"Stay with me tonight. You miss sleeping on a hard mattress, don't you? I'm having a little party, so drop by sometime after 8:00. I'll come up with something by then. There may be someone who can take you to Hamburg tomorrow. Or at least as far as Hannover—that much I can guarantee."

"Hannover..."

"Don't ask for the moon. If you get to Hannover, you're practically there."

"But after that we have to go to Rostock, and then catch a boat from there. Actually, our final destination is Copenhagen."

The man opened his mouth wide and laughed out loud: "So

what? Remember that time we went to the Hijra Festival? How many days it took to get there?"

Judging from Akash's smile, this immediately put him at ease, but it made me nervous. Hijra—that word seemed like it would carry me off to the far side of the globe.

As soon as I'd sat down with the cappuccino I bought at the café next door, I asked him: "Exactly what is this Hijra Festival he mentioned?"

"It's a gathering for transgender people from all over India, to celebrate a god who travels back and forth across the gender boundary. That's where I got to know Chris. I was really happy to discover we're both living in Germany."

"You have this web of friends stretching all over Europe."

"It's not a spider's web, though—nothing to fear!"

"He's called Chris?"

"It's not his real name. He told me he uses it because it sounds universal and is easy to remember. His real name might be Krishna, or maybe even Christopher Columbus."

"Was he born female?"

"Biologically speaking, he's always been a man. Since he looks like a man, too, sometimes his friends ask him which border he's crossing. But as far as he's concerned, he's a woman in the guise of a man, who loves women."

The word *party* takes me back to when I was about fourteen and we'd get together at a friend's house to listen to techno-rock, loud enough to shatter the windows, switch to Ecstasy when we got tired of beer and cheap wine, and dance until morning. With that sort of party in mind, my first thought was that I'd have to watch whoever we'd be riding with the next day, to make sure they didn't get too drunk or take drugs. But when we got to Chris's place there was no music or dancing, just five students— boys and girls—sitting primly on the sofa sipping chai. After listening to their conversation for a while, I realized they were discussing whether strikes are an effective means of changing society, but they might as well have been talking about rheumatism, the way they hung their heads, speaking in hushed tones. Only Chris seemed happy, humming to himself as he fried samosas in the kitchen.

"I've found someone who's driving to Hamburg tonight," he said, turning to me, looking pleased with himself.

I was about to propose a toast, but when he started pouring milk into a pan, offering to make more chai, I couldn't very well tell him that I wanted wine instead. Patting him on the shoulder, Akash thanked him.

"I'm so grateful. I hope you didn't have to call up a hundred friends."

"Not that many. Five, maybe. I know some guys who're always talking about Hamburg, so I started with them."

When the spices bubbled up in the white milk, Chris took the pan off the stove.

"I'll let the flavor seep in for a while," he said, then, hearing the doorbell, went to see who it was. A woman in glasses, dressed in a suit, carrying a bouquet of roses. She had a completely different atmosphere from the students, and seemed over forty. What sort of acquaintance was she? Thinking I could relax if she were the one who'd be driving us to Hamburg, I introduced myself.

"How do you do? I'm Nora, a friend of Akash's. We're going to see a sick friend in Copenhagen."

"I'm Marianne. The one standing over there—is that Akash?"

"That's right."

"Well, you're going to have a hard time getting to Copenhagen with the transportation strikes."

Marianne apparently wasn't the one who'd be driving us.

"Are Akash and Chris classmates, or maybe cousins?" she asked.

"No, they met at a Hijra Festival," I replied, pleased to be able to pass on this bit of information. "Where did you meet Chris?"

Looking somewhat embarrassed, Marianne smiled for the first time.

"I had some business at the station last month, and we just happened to be in the same elevator. He works at the reception desk, but he'd been called to the personnel office, which is on a higher floor."

"So, you got friendly in the elevator?"

"Well, actually we got stuck between floors, and it took an awfully long time before help came."

"It was only about half an hour," said Chris, who'd brought Marianne a cup of chai.

"It felt a lot longer—I thought I was going to faint. Then Chris started telling me about some myth—I don't remember exactly, but there was a snake with lots of heads, and as I listened, I was surprised when my own memories of India came flooding back. I'd heard from my mother about a trip to India when I was small, but was certain I didn't remember it. She'd just gotten divorced, and suddenly decided to travel. I was about four at the time. I was shocked when that door to my childhood, the one I'd believed was closed for good, suddenly swung open. Holding my mother's hand, I was walking in the courtyard of a Hindu temple ..."

Not that I didn't want to hear Marianne's story about a snake, but I was having trouble concentrating on what she was saying, because I was much more interested in finding out which of these students would be giving us a ride. Chris came by with a huge platter heaped with samosas.

At about 9:30, the doorbell rang again and an elderly, white-haired couple came in, saying they'd just been to a concert. They apparently lived next door, and had stopped in for a cup of chai. As they were pensioners who said their hobby was traveling, I wondered if they might be the ones, but a little while later they left, saying they'd been up since 5:00 and were now getting sleepy. No sooner were they out the door when the bell rang again, and two long-haired young men with makeup on, dressed in leather from head to toe, came in. Each carried two helmets. With a knot in my stomach, I raced to the kitchen where I found Akash and Chris standing together, laughing and talking.

"You don't mean to tell me we'll be riding to Hamburg with those bikers?" Though I'd meant to restrain myself, my voice came out very shrill, like an accusation.

"They're the ones. Seems they're going to a big gathering at a church in Hamburg. They don't have any money so you'll have to pay for fuel. For the motorcycles and for the people, too. There won't be much traffic on the autobahn late at night, so you can really get up some speed."

His eyes bright, Akash seemed to be looking forward to this motorcycle ride, but I was furious—playing at Easy Rider would be even dumber than hitchhiking, what with the cold, the noise, the bone-shattering vibrations, and of course the danger.

Though the bikers, named Thole and Kurt, seemed eager to get started, for the time being they sat on the sofa, side by side, quietly sipping chai. There had definitely been a motorcycle icon on that internet site where I'd researched different types of energy and their impact on the environment, but I'd been so certain I'd never ride on one that I hadn't even bothered to check it.

"Let's see how it fits," said Thole, carefully placing the metal sphere on my head and fastening the chin strap.

Knowing that all the little bones from my ears to my cheeks would be protected felt kind of good, yet I couldn't help snapping, "It's awfully heavy." Letting my head droop to one side, I added, "I'm sure my neck's going to get tired."

Thole burst out laughing. "You have to sit with your back and neck perfectly straight," he said. "Bend your neck like that and it might stay that way."

Akash was all smiles when Kurt put his helmet on. Though Thole's was curly and Kurt's straight, their hair was the same shade of chestnut brown and the same length, down to their shoulders; they both wore the same makeup, too—white faces with a hint of rouge on the cheeks, eyes rimmed in black for a Goth look. I wondered why they made their faces up, but if someone were to ask why I did mine, I wouldn't know how to answer. Because I'm a woman? Why *do* women use makeup? And why shouldn't men?

My original plan had been to sit side by side with Nanook like a middle-aged couple, ordering a glass of wine and flying straight to Copenhagen, and now here I was straddling a black machine as if it were a horse, feeling the rumbling of the engine all through my body. Exposed to wind and darkness, a metallic roar in my ears, clinging desperately to the torso of a man I didn't know to keep from falling off, I would travel north. I squeezed my eyes shut when we started, and by the time I cautiously opened them again, we were already leaving behind the lights of the city.

CHAPTER 5

Akash Speaks

The roar of the engine made the night air tremble as we drove straight through the darkness. I clung to the body in front of me, afraid I'd be flung off into the abyss if we didn't become one. I knew nothing of this biker other than his name—Thole. Did he have a family, what sort of work did he do, where was he born and raised, what was his personality like? The torso I was hugging from behind like a lover belonged to a complete stranger. What's more, I was bent over, my back curved forward so that my nether regions pressed somewhat indecently against him. This was because of the seat—long and raised in the back. I wouldn't have had to sit this way on a bicycle, where the saddle and luggage rack are separate. The leather under my palms was smooth, with a soft, downy layer beneath it; further down, a firm layer of flesh covered the ribs and muscles to protect the internal organs. If only this were Knut . . . Just the two of us, heading north through the European night, it would have been the sweetest of dreams, yet still, something was missing. Perhaps what I was looking for was not a world just for two after all. If romantic love was nothing more than lingering warmth left by older generations, totally unrelated to the new frontiers we're speeding toward, we'd have to find new ways to connect with other human beings. I thought of Hiruko. Maybe she understands better than anyone that we are people of the future. She and Knut are a couple, yet they've never become lovers. She manages to glide lightly through life with neither lover nor family.

Though I'd always wanted to ride on a big motorcycle, now that I was on one, there was something disagreeable about it. I love to talk and it's hard for me to keep still. Not that I was dying to have a serious discussion about, say, the possibility of a country's actually vanishing, or of several languages blending into one, but it would have been nice to be able to casually say, "The wind's not as cold as I was expecting," or "Maybe I should have changed into denim," or "The autobahn's practically empty tonight." On the bike, I was overwhelmed by all the engine noise before I even opened my mouth. If I talked naturally, I wouldn't be heard, and if I shouted, I would no longer be me. The thought of not speaking all the way to Hamburg was depressing. Poor Susanoo, who can't talk, even if he wants to. Perhaps he, too, hears a roaring in his ears that breaks his will. He puts his hands over his ears, or shakes his head from side to side, but nothing can get rid of that metallic groan, loud enough to shake the earth, and what's more, he's the only one who hears it. How unbearable that would be! The mere thought was so frightening to me that I squeezed Thole's body all the more tightly. Which took me back to my childhood, when I'd ride on the back of my brothers' scooter. Even after they got jobs, and had plenty enough money to buy a car, they held on to the scooter they'd had since adolescence, treating it like a pet, even giving it a nickname, "Mo-mo-pet." They hardly talked at all, so sitting around chatting over a cup of chai as the women did was out of the question. Joint ownership of this scooter, repairing it together, may have been the only "social life" they had. I remember a time when old-fashioned vehicles were all the rage in our town. People sold their Porsches and got rickshaws instead, paying artists huge sums of money to paint gaudy pictures on them in striking shades of pink and blue. Rich men paid through the nose to proudly show off doorless, three-wheeled autorickshaws. Long before that fad took hold, my brothers had pledged eternal devotion to Mo-mo-pet.

Maybe Thole bought this motorcycle because he's rather like them, wanting companionship, yet not very good at talking to people. He'd like to travel with a friend, but finds the banter on the way a pain, perhaps. On a bike, you don't need to make conversation. Even if for some reason you're forced to give a chatterbox like me a ride, the roar of the engine makes a long, nuanced talk impossible. In a quiet coffee shop, where you can hear the most delicate shading in a voice, simple remarks like, "It's not as cold as I expected" could mean all sorts of things. The listener might hear something like, "I was nervous at first because I'd never been on a bike, but the wind wasn't very cold so I enjoyed the ride, and am hoping we can do it again sometime." If, on the other hand, it sounded more like, "Because I'm always buffeted by society's cold winds, I like that strong back of yours, protecting me now from real headwinds," accompanied by an appropriately alluring facial expression, it might be the opening line of a confession of love. Yet when I imagine yelling, "It's not as cold as I expected," in a voice loud enough to compete with the noise, I realize that any delicate emotion I was trying to express would be lost, leaving only a statement of fact. And while the listener could take a line like "The wind is cold" at face value, and assume that the speaker was wishing he'd worn a jacket, the words "It's not as cold as I expected" would sound like nonsense, as he would have no idea what the speaker was really trying to say.

I suddenly longed to see Nora, whom I'd spent the day with. She was on Kurt's bike now, so she must be somewhere back there. Turning my head wouldn't give me a clear view of what was directly behind us. I was too afraid of falling off to let one hand go and twist all the way around, so I leaned forward and peered over Thole's shoulder, trying to catch a glimpse of them in the rearview mirror, but though the mirror was pitch black, lights from the street lamps lining the highway leapt into that dark space, one after another, aiming straight into my eyes. They looked like falling stars. We couldn't avoid them, yet because they always veered off to the side at the very last moment, they never hit us. Having come only to give us light, they meant us no harm. The troubles we run into in life are like that—we don't actually collide with them and hurt ourselves. People who cry out in pain, mistaking their problems for real smashups, are just pitying themselves, I thought, turning what I'd just seen into a philosophy of life—a habit I've had since childhood, which led my brothers to call me "the little guru." Back then I used to say whatever popped into my head, and—once I got talking—lost control and couldn't stop, until finally they'd shout, "Shut up!" That didn't stop me, though—I'd babble on, my voice getting higher and higher. Sometimes they'd get so fed up they'd whack me on the head, and I'd have a real temper tantrum. "You're always telling me to be quiet," I'd scream, "but when the river was overflowing, would you refuse to warn the neighbors? Would you accept any awful thing the government does without a word of protest? If you saw Mama crying, wouldn't you say something to comfort her? Does keeping your mouths shut make you worthy of my respect?" When faced with something they couldn't handle, my brothers wrapped themselves in the armor of silence. Like on that night. The memory is wrapped in darkness and rather vague, but for the first time, our father didn't come home. My brothers were silent as stones, leaving only my mother to patiently answer all my questions. The next morning my sister, who was married and lived in another town, came over, looking troubled, and after talking to my mother for a while, answered more questions. At times like that, the women could stay in that stream of words, but my brothers always clammed up. I remember thinking that if men went on this way, they'd go extinct. Brash beyond my years, perhaps, but that's how it seemed to me at the time.

I saw a pictogram up ahead—a knife and fork—coming closer. A sign for a rest stop. Thole raised his hand, signaling to Kurt, then changed lanes to exit the autobahn. As our speed dropped, my pulse slowed down. The parking lot was practically empty, with only the white lines shining coldly in the dark. I heard Thole's boots roughly scuff the pavement, then the motor stopped, and a heavy silence fell on my shoulders. Feeling fatigue in every muscle, I looked up to see an expanse of forest behind the plain one-story rest stop. The trees blotted out the light from the parking lot, keeping it from reaching the night sky. Though I couldn't see any stars, I sensed waves in the cosmos, rising and falling. The joints that held my bones together had been loosened by all that shaking. Hoping my body wouldn't fall apart, I very carefully got off the bike. I was slightly dizzy. My brain was so packed with the words I hadn't said during my ride that I was afraid they'd all come spilling out when I took my helmet off. Then I saw Nora. She was shaking her head to loosen her hair as she talked and laughed with Kurt. Watching her blond hair dancing wildly in the breeze gave me the courage to remove my helmet, and when I did, my head felt light and airy. The dizziness came back, though, and my stomach wasn't quite right.

"How was it—part one of our night journey? Are you tired? Let's take a break here before going on to part two. This is my favorite rest stop in the whole of Germany." I had Thole down as a man who didn't talk much, so it was odd to hear him sounding so open and friendly. But his favorite rest stop in the whole of Germany—wasn't that a little over the top? Did he also have a favorite gas station, a favorite autobody shop? Then again, maybe he thinks libraries are all merely buildings filled with books, and would find it just as strange if I were to tell him that a specific one was my favorite. We were strangers, separated by a yawning gap. And that was okay. The same black leather jacket I'd been clinging to a moment before was right there, in front of me, yet now even touching it was forbidden.

"How was it?" I gently asked Nora.

"I feel great!" she shouted, her eyes opening wide. "Like when

I've been dancing—that same kind of rush. But you look a little pale, Akash. Are you all right?"

I'd been hoping she'd say that she still hated motorcycles even though it hadn't been as bad as she'd thought, so I felt let down.

"My stomach's still churning, as if it's a cocktail shaker. And listening to all that noise has put my sense of balance out of whack, so I'm woozy, like on a boat. But I'm getting better by the second, and should be back to normal soon."

After explaining all this, it occurred to me that being silent for so long might have been the real problem. Talking has always been my way of staying healthy. As I exhale, I send out words that flow through my body, waking up all my cells, destroying all the nasty outside germs that have taken hold. If I had to listen without speaking to the cacophony of this world, I'd surely grow sicker with each passing moment.

Thole looked happy as he handed each of us a cream-colored plastic tray.

"These fried potatoes are really good with mountains of ketchup and mayonnaise," he told us.

Looking as if she'd never eat fried potatoes, Nora laughed uneasily. "I'm Secretary of the Treasury for tonight," she then announced, suddenly sounding like everyone's big sister, "so don't be shy—have whatever you want." Chris had told us we'd have to pay for meals, since Thole and Kurt didn't have any money. Nora hadn't forgotten that. Yet my memories of what had happened before our ride lay scattered in fragments on the autobahn. The sausages lined up in a steaming case looked like washed-out penises. A basket held sliced bread, dry as white skin. The potato salad was in a bucket, the kind usually used for paint. A short distance away was the dessert corner, with a surprising variety of yogurt and cakes.

Sitting down for the first time at a table for four with the food we'd chosen, we were embarrassed to realize that this format seemed perfect for self-introductions. After silently eyeing one another's trays for a while, somebody finally laughed, and the others joined in. Nora and I had exactly the same things, arranged in the same way. On the right, a small cup of coffee and a glass of water, on the left, apple cake without whipped cream. This wasn't like me at all, as I normally drink only chai or English tea, and don't really care for apples, but if asked what, at this rest stop, was "like me," I couldn't have answered. Nothing "like me" was served here, so I'd just have to show what I was "like" by choosing things that weren't, casting off the image I'd formed of myself. That's what it means to travel. But saying that out loud might disappoint Thole, who'd brought us to his favorite rest stop, and certainly wouldn't show my appreciation to Nora, who'd paid for all this. I ended up silently picking at the apple slice on top of the cake with my fork. Did Susanoo, too, worry so much about hurting people's feelings? And that's why eventually he stopped talking altogether? Words always cause someone pain. Using only euphemistic, roundabout expressions so as not to offend anyone can give you a clearer grasp of the sorts of words and phrases you avoid saying. Just as when after a figure has been cut out of paper, you can see its outline in the sheet that's left.

I've heard that in the country where Susanoo spent his childhood, they had very advanced writing tools, including a special pen you could use to write letters in the air. It was used by people who were so afraid their words might hurt someone that they couldn't say anything at all. Sometimes there were so many words scrawled in the air that the inhabitants had trouble breathing. From an early age, children were expected to read this air writing at a glance, and then walk by, pretending they hadn't noticed. Those who couldn't perfect this skill choose to be outcasts, apparently, and stay shut up in their houses or go on to successful careers as politicians.

The mountains of fried potatoes on Kurt and Thole's trays were covered in an avalanche of ketchup and mayonnaise. The sausages let out little sighs of steam as they were being cut in half.

"Have you guys ever been to MOGO?" Thole suddenly asked. Kurt could tell from the looks on our faces that we didn't know what he was talking about.

"It's a worship service for bikers," he explained. "MO is for motorbike, and GO is for *gottesdienst*—service."

"Chris said you were going to Hamburg for some gathering, but didn't tell us what kind."

That reminded me of a saxophonist I once met at a neighborhood bar. It was drizzling outside. I'd heard from the girl I was supposed to meet that, even after her three-day bout of flu, the healing goddess had yet to appear, so I was all alone on a Saturday night. My sneakers were waiting in the hall, urging me to put them on. I washed off my makeup, took off my sari, and put on a T-shirt and jeans, like a male student. My friend said she liked me in women's clothes, but if the people in that run-down bar saw me in a sari they'd freak out, and no one would talk to me.

I sat at the counter and ordered a Virgin Mary. I felt a little guilty, as if I were in disguise, trying to trick people. Since biologically I am a man, it's not a lie to dress like one. Yet I can't help feeling that that's not actually what I am. The bar was empty, except for some rough-looking guys at a table near the back. After a while the door wearily opened, and a man shuffled in. A worn-out yellow windbreaker hanging on his thin frame, he leaned against the bar and ordered a Virgin Mary.

"I envy guys like you who can handle a Bloody Mary," he said, glancing at my glass. "I'm sick, so I have to stick to nonalcoholic ones." When I told him my drink was also a Virgin, he sat down and asked, "Don't they drink alcohol in India?" He'd decided I must be from India. While he wasn't wrong, he might have been, and ignoring that possibility seemed arrogant to me. Feeling indifferent, turning away from his pale, greenish face, I rattled off an explanation.

"Drinking alcohol and eating meat used to be against the law for religious reasons. While the law didn't apply to heathens, they had difficulty finding work, so most people refrained from drinking or eating meat. Now that times have changed, anyone is free to eat veal or drink whiskey, yet because many assert that vegetarianism and prohibition made our current economic boom possible, and vegetarians and teetotalers tend to succeed in life, people who drink wine and eat steak are seen as losers."

"So, Indians who live abroad don't drink either?"

"Some do. I don't, though, because drinking makes me feel lonely."

It seemed odd to be sounding so sentimental after my transformation into a male student, when I avoid saying things that make me seem weak while dressed as a woman.

I was prepared to hear something like, "Prohibition goes against the Western spirit of freedom," but what he actually said was just the opposite.

"Germany should have prohibition, too," he declared, carefully wiping his mouth—which wasn't very dirty in the first place—with the back of his hand. When I asked him why, he stared over at me and, little by little, told me about how alcohol had ruined his life, how if he hadn't started drinking he'd now be making music with his friends.

"What instrument did you play?" I asked.

"Alto."

"Alt? Isn't that a kind of beer?"

For the first time he laughed out loud.

"I've never liked the word saxophone. Sax sounds too much like sack. And phone is short for telephone—something I really hate. Love the instrument, can't stand the name. A real tragedy. But in musical terms, I'm neither alto nor bass now—more a rest, or a caesura, maybe. You see, I need a liver transplant, and I'm waiting for a donor. That's my only occupation now—waiting."

His name was Jork; his parents had already relocated to the

other side, and he had neither siblings nor children in this world. Not that having relatives meant they'd be ready to give you an organ or two any old time, but waiting first for someone to die tragically, and then to see if your body would accept that person's innards, was as lonely as waiting for a loan shark to fall out of the sky, he said. Even though his drink was nonalcoholic, Jork was soon slurring his words, his head swaying from side to side.

Several months later, I met him again. Just like the first time it was drizzling, only it was a Tuesday, and though my eyes were blurry after reading in the library all day, I was too excited to sleep, so I decided to stop off at that bar. Jork, sitting at the counter, raised his hand and waved as if he'd been waiting for me,

"How've you been?" he asked. "I finally got it!"

Remembering his liver transplant, I congratulated him. His face was much brighter than last time. When he stuck out one arm, motioning for me to sit down, it kept going until his hand hit the counter. He seemed to have more energy than he could control. I ordered a glass of tonic water.

"Wow, you're in great shape."

"I feel great. I got a young guy's liver—fantastic. It's like I've got my youth back, all over. I mean, the transplant shouldn't have anything to do with my plumbing, but my pee comes gushing out now and I can get it up any time."

I couldn't believe this was the same man I'd had that dreary, sentimental conversation with. His eyes were sharp enough to see right through you, and his lips, now a healthy pink, twisted into a smile. What sort of young man had the donor been? Jork couldn't have gotten his personality along with the liver, could he?

"I love walking down the street, feeling everybody's eyes on me. The women look like they want to get me in bed, and the men wish they were me. That feels really good."

I quickly changed the subject before he could start tallying up his recent sexual conquests.

116

"Did they tell you who the donor was?"

"Not his name—only that he was a biker, around twenty, who died in an accident. Too bad—he was so young. But bikers are beacons of hope for sick, old guys like me. Young people have the best organs, but they don't often die. Maybe they do in countries where all the kids have guns to shoot each other with, but we don't even have gangs in Trier. Most bikers are young men, though, and accidents are usually fatal."

He must have realized that he was talking as if those young lives meant nothing to him, for he suddenly laughed out loud, "HA, HA, HA!"

"I really do feel sorry for him," he went on, "and I'm very grateful. I wouldn't mind praying for him, so his soul can go to heaven."

"So, while his soul is in heaven, a part of him lives on in another."

"Not bad, when you think of it. A sort of recycling."

"If I were to die suddenly in an accident, I think it would be better if someone could use my organs."

"Mine are chock full of poison, so I wouldn't recommend them to anyone. When I die, I want to be cremated, so that nothing remains of my bones or genes. But anyway, have you ever seen a large group of bikers gathered outside a church?"

"No."

"I did once, a long time ago. They'd come to pay their respects to a friend of theirs who'd died. Looked like a convention of black angels. I'd forgotten all about that until just recently, when I had a dream about them."

"Perhaps the young donor's memories were collected in his liver, and entered your body that way."

It was just something I'd thought of—nothing serious—but Jork pulled away as if I'd hit him, and got very angry.

"What are you talking about?" he shouted. "Are you trying

to say I have no personality of my own? Do you have any idea what you're saying?"

Pulling my head in like a turtle, I ran out without paying my bill. Fortunately, Jork didn't come after me.

I've upset people by blurting out whatever came into my head any number of times. Still, I had the good sense not to bring up the topic of organ transplants with these two bikers. Nora, who'd run into an airport strike after letting the word "strike" slip out, would surely think it insensitive of me to start talking about motorcycle accidents.

"Don't you get tired, riding for so many hours?" I asked, unable to keep quiet any longer. "You can't let yourself doze off, and you have to keep your eyes on the road." This seemed a harmless enough subject.

"When you're in danger," Thole replied, a french fry sticking out of his mouth like a cigarette, "your body produces a chemical substance that makes you want to stay alive. It gives you a high that's better than alcohol, or any drug. It lasts, too, so you can drive for hours without getting bored."

"So that's how you do it," Nora said. "I may take up biking."

Hearing that made me choke and spill my coffee. Sometimes, meeting a stranger can awaken a person's hidden desires. Still, the idea of Nora turning into a biker was too extreme. Seeing how flustered I was, she laughed.

"Relax. I'm not going to buy a motorcycle in Copenhagen and insist on riding it back to Trier."

I was about to say we'd probably be coming back separately anyway, but that felt so lonely that I thought better of it. Nora would meet her lover Nanook in Copenhagen, and they'd return to Trier together. Leaving me on my own. What I really wanted to do was stay in Copenhagen, where Knut lives. Susanoo was in the hospital there, and Hiruko was working in Denmark too, in Odense, so maybe we could all settle down in Copenhagen, like a family. Wouldn't that be fun?

"What's the longest trip you've ever taken on your bike?" Nora asked Kurt. She was really getting into motorcycles.

"To the south, Sicily. To the north, maybe Sylt Island."

"So, you crossed the sea on your bike?"

"Well," Kurt replied, looking far off into the distance, "I went by ferry, of course." Those eyes are seeing the ocean, I thought.

"And did you survive on sausages all the way?" I asked pointedly, so that Nora wouldn't get too rosy a picture of the biker's life.

"No. Bikers have their own networks, so we often eat dinner at a friend's house." Kurt was speaking directly to Nora: "We have salad, and stir-fried vegetables, too. If you like that sort of food, you'd be fine." He was trying to please her. This irritated me so much that I ended up asking a question I'd been meaning to avoid.

"I hear bikers have a lot of accidents—do you know the statistics?"

Apparently not at all upset, he nodded quietly.

"Twice as many as cars, and the death rate is five times higher."

Thole, who'd been busy eating, now looked up.

"I used to keep my donor's card in my pocket when I was on the road, but last week I tore it up and threw it away."

Hearing him bring up what I was determined not to mention, I opened my mouth to change the subject, but Nora didn't give me the chance.

"Donor's card? Not long ago, I saw a scary film, and now I wonder if it was based on a true story. It was a horror movie, where a biker whose organs are being removing is actually still alive, feeling the pain."

"That may not happen for real. But as long as there's even a slight possibility, I won't be a donor. I told my parents, too."

"Can you feel pain when you're dead?"

"Seems the organs aren't much use if the person's completely dead. So, they take them from a patient who's brain dead. Sometimes muscle spasms jerk the body around, so they tie him down before they operate. Some people say that a brain-dead person can still feel pain—they just can't tell you about it. That might not be true. But the idea's still out there, which bothers me."

The more Thole talked, the deeper his voice got.

"I've heard that the term brain death is used only in the context of organ transplants," Kurt added. "That the transplanters need a concept like that, because it's illegal to take organs from a living person."

"Yeah," said Thole, shaking his head, "but if that's wrong, the survival rate of people waiting for donors goes way down— would you want to be responsible for their deaths?"

"What if there's even a one percent chance of your organs being removed when you're near death but can still feel pain?"

Thole nodded deeply before answering. "I've heard awful stories from people who've lost a family member in an accident. There's a pulse, and the body's still warm when they operate. Sometimes they see him move, even though he's tied down."

"Makes you sentimental, looking at it from the family's point of view."

"But defiling a corpse has always been a grave sin, ever since ancient times," Nora broke in. "In all history, there's never been a time when people didn't care how the dead were treated. A young woman in a Greek tragedy gave up her own life so that she could bury her older brother. That's how important dead bodies are."

She's wary of anything that seems superstitious, but when a discussion like this starts, she'll jump in with arguments of her own, escalating things further.

"What about people with old, worn-out brains whose livers are still healthy? Mightn't someone think of classifying them as semibrain-dead, so they can be killed for their livers? Thinking it's okay to sacrifice people who can't work anymore for the sake of those who can is just plain wrong. Everyone's life is equally valuable."

The word "semibrain-dead" made me feel sick, so I went to get another glass of water. It was all my fault that the conversation was turning out this way.

I had no idea where I'd sleep the following night, but there was one dream I definitely didn't want to have. Of being thrown off the motorcycle, and losing consciousness when my head hit the asphalt. Then waking up lying on a bed, looking at stars on the ceiling. But wait—those aren't stars, but rows of fluorescent lights. I can't move my arms. My thighs are also pinned down. Five men wearing blue masks, blue hats, and thin blue plastic gowns are looking down at me. Fortunately, though their masks keep them from talking, my mouth is still free. I'm not dead, so if you cut me open with your scalpels, you'll be committing murder, I tell them. Troubled, they exchange looks. Only words can save me now. I keep on talking. You want to believe I'm brain dead, don't you? But can a person whose brain is dead use language? The fact that I'm talking shows that I'm alive. No one has the right to cut into a speaking subject. Suddenly, the fire alarm sounds. The men in the blue masks cast their scalpels and scissors aside and hurry out of the room. I struggle, but my arms and legs are securely fastened. In time it begins to seem as if the fire started in order to save me ...

"Do you feel sick?"

Nora seemed worried after watching me gulp down a large glass of water.

"The stimulation from my own imagination is sometimes so strong I nearly pass out."

Kurt and Thole burst out laughing. Judging from the ripples of good will I felt flowing toward me, no scorn was intended.

"It's not good to OD on illusion," said Thole. "How about

coming back to reality, and part two of our trip? On our bikes, I mean, not drugs."

Back on the autobahn, though speed once again threatened to carry me away, oddly enough my heart felt so calm that I was no longer afraid of falling off if I loosened my grip on Thole. I gasped only once, when I saw a rabbit tearing across the highway in front of us. The headlight caught its grayish-brown leg leaping into the air.

The edge of the world gradually grew whiter, and while my foggy brain was trying to figure out why, the whiteness turned first to blue, then red. So that was it—the sunrise. A phenomenon I'd never thought had much to do with me, yet now that it was wrapping all around me, I felt it sinking in.

After Kurt and Thole dropped us off at Hamburg Central Station, Nora and I caught the train for Rostock. As soon as she was settled into her seat, Nora nestled her head against the jacket she'd hung on the hook next to the window and dozed off. Watching her, noticing how mature she looked when she was asleep, my own eyelids began to droop, though I tried to stay awake to avoid frightening dreams.

By the time we boarded the boat in Rostock Nora was young again, babbling away like a girl. She was finally nearing Denmark. The sea let her know that.

"When you're traveling, you're not responsible for anything!" she said, looking down at the dark green waves. "I didn't pick those colors in the water, so they keep surprising me. When I was going to repaint my apartment, I spent hours poring over catalogues, so I felt invested in the color I chose, as if it must reflect my whole personality, but what I see from the boat has nothing to do with me. It's odd how refreshing that feels."

The wind was cold but we stayed on deck anyway. A teary-eyed sort of feeling passed by from time to time, carried on that salty wind.

"I wonder what Susanoo is doing now," I said. "I hope it's a good hospital. He doesn't really need constant care, but they're apparently letting him stay there for free in return for participating in some sort of project."

"His doctor is a friend of Knut's, isn't he?"

"Not a close friend—just an acquaintance, I think."

"How do you know that?"

"It's just a feeling I have. When we get to Copenhagen, I'll go straight to the apartment of the guy I'm staying with. He's a taxi driver, so he may not be home, but I asked him to leave the key with his next-door neighbor."

"I booked two rooms in a hotel, because I thought Nanook and I'd be staying together. I'll check in there, then take a taxi to the hospital."

"Okay, let's meet there in an hour."

As my friend the taxi driver was out, I got the key from his neighbor, put my stuff down, wrote him a note saying I'd be back that evening, and went to the hospital by bus, changing several times on the way.

Nora was waiting for me in front of the reception desk with a face like a tangled knot.

"What's wrong? Can't we see Susanoo today?"

"Nanook's already here."

"Really? He got here awfully fast considering he hitchhiked."

"He said he's in the middle of something, though, and that in about forty-five minutes or so I should go to Room 719."

"Did he seem okay?"

"I haven't actually seen him yet. I just talked to him on the phone."

"It sounds like there's some kind of work he has to do at the hospital—or maybe … ?"

"That's what I think. He might be hurt, and getting some kind of treatment. Maybe someone beat him up. I was about to ask when he hung up."

"It's best not to worry too much. You'll be seeing him soon, and he can tell us about it then. Besides, if he's using the phone, he can't be too badly hurt. After coming all this way to see Susanoo, it seems we'll be visiting Nanook instead."

We sat down side by side on a sofa. The smell of disinfectant in the air made me all the more nervous. That odor reminds me of illness. I thought talking might calm me down, but when I looked over at Nora, I realized it would be best not to intrude. Her head was surely like an echo chamber, full of conversations she'd had with Nanook, and about things she felt she should say to him now. I'd thought Nanook was pretty self-centered at first. Hiruko, Knut, Nora, and I were on this endless journey because he'd lied about his country of origin. He was immature, running away from something—even he didn't seem to know what—dragging in complete strangers along the way, yet you couldn't stay mad at him for very long. I was mulling over these thoughts when Nora suddenly looked at her watch, stood up, and, as if drawn down that long corridor, started walking, mumbling as she went, "Room 719." I hurried after her.

I was startled to see Nanook. This was not the man I'd been expecting. Not wanting him to see how rattled I was, I hid behind Nora. The Nanook I remembered was like a puppy from a loving home who got lost in the wild and had survived on his own long enough to realize that there were wolves among his ancestors. When you held out a hand to him, he'd keep his distance at first, but then soon come running, wagging his tail, wanting to play. The man who opened the door of Room 719 was more like a petty bureaucrat than a doctor, looking down his nose at us, his chest puffed out under his white coat.

"Sorry to keep you waiting," he said. "Did you have a pleasant trip?"

You're much too young to be using words like "pleasant"—
wait another thirty years or so, I thought. Before he could go on
in that vein, Nora cut Nanook off.

"Why are you in the hospital? Are you hurt?" The fear bottled
up inside her came pouring out.

Smiling slightly, Nanook lifted his chin an inch or so and said,
"Now, now, calm down. Do I look as though I've been injured?
I'm not *in* the hospital, I'm just staying here so that I can work
on a certain project."

"Staying?"

"I'm living in a hospital facility. I also have this laboratory at
my disposal. Susanoo will be here soon. Then we can start today's experiments."

Nora now seemed too depressed to speak, so I stepped in.

"What sort of project are you working on?"

"It's difficult to explain, but I was told I could decide its actual
contents. Which means, of course, that the doctor has placed far
more trust in me than in his research assistants. He said I was
to do whatever I like. Though of course I had to find a theme
that was related to Susanoo. I finally chose Multilingual Silence.
What is the difference between silence in a single language, and
silence in several different ones? I got a number of hints about
this from all of you—especially Knut—for which I'm very grateful. Though of course, when I wrote the proposal, I mentioned
Hiruko's name far more often than Knut's. Placing women at the
forefront brings success, while insulting them can get you fired."

"What's going on with you, Nanook?" asked Nora, furrowing
her brow.

"Nothing in particular."

"Has something happened?"

Just then there were three knocks on the door in an odd
rhythm, and Susanoo came into the room. I was much happier
to see him than I could ever have imagined.

"Susanoo, how are you? Nora and I just got here. We wanted to come sooner, but it's a long way from Trier to Copenhagen. There were strikes, and some other stuff, so it was quite a journey, but I am glad to see you."

When his eyes met mine, the muscles in his face relaxed ever so slightly, but that was enough for me. Susanoo, who didn't speak, seemed much closer to me than Nanook, whose personality had changed so drastically. Perhaps Susanoo simply wasn't very talkative, and didn't actually need medical treatment at all.

"So, you two are participating in the same project," I said.

"I am the researcher entrusted with this project," Nanook replied sharply, glowering at me. "Susanoo is the patient, the object of my research."

"So?"

"Doctor and patient mustn't be seen as playmates."

"What has happened to you?" asked Nora angrily. "You act as if you're way above the rest of us."

Sensing a storm brewing, I quickly stepped between them.

"Why don't we all get a cup of coffee later, and exchange stories about how we managed to get here?"

"Leave nostalgic travel tales to the old folks," Nanook said, snorting with laughter. "I've got work to do. Susanoo, sit here."

When Susanoo duly sat down in the chair, Nanook put a helmet covered with nubs, a cord coming out of each one, on his head. I thought of those labels you see on shampoo or face cream that say "Cruelty-Free/Not Tested on Animals."

"Nanook," I said, "have you got Susano's consent for this?"

"There was no need to, because I'm not officially a doctor, and he and I are friends."

"But didn't you just say that the doctor entrusted you with this project, and that doctors and patients are not friends?"

Nora said: "That's right, Nanook, and you're wrong."

"Let's stop arguing about this," he said, casually pointing upward with his chin. Looking in that direction, I saw a camera in the ceiling. "I'm not going to hurt Susanoo," he added, suddenly switching back to his old self. "I'm just measuring the nature of his silence."

CHAPTER 6   *Mrs. Nielsen Speaks*

The sperm and egg that met soon after I got married slowly grew in the temple of my womb until a bundle of screams heralded the birth of a human being. Perhaps he was howling because inhaling air hurt, but the chemicals coursing through my brain must have undergone some change, because I listened to those cries in ecstasy, from somewhere far away.

I awoke to see faces—my husband, my mother-in-law, my sister-in-law, and close friends—floating above me like clouds. Each had a mouth that opened and closed, competing to be the first to say, "Congratulations!" But why all the fuss? You'd have thought I'd done something right for the first time in my life. Though there *is* something wonderful about producing a new human being, I detected a whiff of tyranny in this undiluted praise. There was definitely something wrong here, but I didn't know quite what, which was irritating, as if I were suddenly appearing on one of those "What's wrong with this picture?" quiz shows, and couldn't find the solution no matter how hard I looked. Finally, I gave up and closed my eyes.

The next time I opened them I was all alone in a white box, my own body below the waist drifting off like some distant island, my arms stiff as parts borrowed from a robot, my neck too rigid to turn, the inside of my nose dry and scratchy—the only thing that still felt even a little like me was the liquid flowing through my brain. That was when the painful days started. Or, to put it more accurately, looking back, "painful" is how I want to describe them. At the time, I'd forgotten the word even existed. My husband would lean over to touch me, gently whispering, "How do you feel, Inga?" and without the slightest feeling of shame, I would say, "Overjoyed!" A word I'd never ever used in my life. I was swaddled in orange air tinged with pink, warm and sweet with a hint of sour, air you could call "joy" without sounding the least bit sarcastic. But then again perhaps the word "joy" refers only to the air, and has nothing to do with the person it surrounds. If so, a miserable person could be wrapped in a blanket of "joy." Which would be like a dolphin wearing a knitted sweater—a mismatch, unacceptable. You'd want to strip it off the poor creature immediately. I myself was that out-of-place feeling.

Now I am taking the past into my own hands, to squeeze it, knead it, flatten it out, roll it into a ball, flatten it again, cut it into squares, color it, and add some scent, trying different techniques to make it into a story. The listener I have in mind is not Velmer, my current lover. Our relationship began after our children struck out on their own, so I'm sure hearing about birth and child-rearing would disgust him. My imaginary listener is my son, Knut. As he hates old stories as much as wool socks, and puts flaps over his ears whenever I say more than ten words in a row, he only listens in my imagination. Ear flaps are an invisible yet convenient body part, found on more than half the male population. But Knut keeps jutting his chin up, passing judgment on me, so even if he doesn't actually hear it, I simply have to tell him my side of the story. To lay out my defense, before he hands down a life sentence. He might even order my execution if we lived in a country with the death penalty. It's frightening. And yet so childish it makes me laugh. I'd love to turn my trial into an anime, in which my son, the judge, appears as a polar bear in a black robe, and I, the defendant in the witness box, as a pathetic rabbit with hardly any fur left on her back. "Why did you give birth to me?" the judge asks. "You weren't really thinking, were you? You didn't want a kid—your birth control didn't work, is that it? Or were you hoping society would pat you on the back for being a mother? Did you take care of the baby after it was born? Why did you stand by the window swinging your boobs like a pair of bells instead of breastfeeding your infant? And why did you sit there giggling and jiggling your thighs instead of comforting your screaming child? Why did you need other men—wasn't your child's father enough?" And then comes the ultimate question: "Why did you kill my father?"

When a sweet, milky baby-smell filled the air, and I knew he was the source, he was too close to be so critical. Then, after I'd gotten used to holding him, doubt appeared, like a crack between us: Perhaps this child isn't mine. I was seized by the fear that he might be a completely different organism, who as time passed would mature into a creature I couldn't understand, until one day he left for some faraway place. Had I been his father, this notion of radical difference wouldn't have occurred to me—I would simply have wondered, "Could this child's father be some other man?" But being a mother, I had difficulty imagining a stranger's egg entering my body, and being fertilized of its own volition there. Was I actually a surrogate mother, who only believed the child was mine because my memory had been erased?

A nurse hovered around, asking if I had chills, or was nauseous. Rocked by waves of uncertainty that came and went, I felt seasick. Since I myself had worked as a nurse, I had a pretty good idea of how she was interpreting my condition. Afraid that if I didn't say something, her anxiety level would go shooting up, setting off a siren in her inner ear, I blurted out something I wasn't actually worried about.

"I'm not sure I'll be able to raise this child."

Relieved, she settled down and gave me a pep talk. "Everyone feels that way at first. But just think a minute. The city streets are full of people. That means that anyone—whether they're lazy, or sickly, or much too busy, or habitual shoplifters, or terrible egotists, or were poor students at school—can raise children. If a fine woman like you couldn't care for a baby, the human race would have gone extinct thousands of years ago." Even now, that nurse's words come back to me when I'm sitting in a coffee shop, staring out at the passersby. I sigh in amazement, thinking about how all those people were brought up by adults, which shows how many have managed to rear children. Some as biological parents, others by adopting, still others by caring for little ones in orphanages, yet they all did it. Despite the problems each of them had—perhaps they were bullied after falling behind at school, or smoked too much marijuana and couldn't hold down a job, or had crushing debts after playing the stock market, or ruined their health through some diet scam, or could never quite keep the rules about trash disposal and recyclables straight— children grew up under their care. It's truly astonishing.

After I left the hospital and no longer had the nurse to talk to, I spent my days in silence. Loath to let anyone other than my husband into the house, I refused my mother-in-law's offers to come help with the baby and stopped friends who wanted to drop by for a visit with a few brief words over the phone. Until evening, when my husband came home from work, my son and I were alone in the house, the scene outside the window as still as a watercolor.

Sometimes he would stare gravely up at me, his fingers and toes wriggling like amoebas in the air. His eyes, covered with a watery film about to overflow, gleamed in the dim, indoor light. Struck by their frightening beauty, I would throw myself down on the sofa and lie there, motionless, hugging my whale-shaped cushion. When the wall deep in my brain suddenly turned white, standing up seemed such an arduous task that I'd prod myself, picturing the act as a scene in a movie, yet all the while I'd still be on the couch. A nonexistent glass wall separated me from the plates I saw on the table. The self I watched putting those dirty plates into the dishwasher was not me.

Every morning my husband got up just before the yellow alarm clock went off, then reset it for a later time before tiptoeing out of our bedroom. As if he'd been waiting for his father to rise, my son would start crying, and I'd hear my husband changing his diaper and giving him his bottle. Then he'd turn on the shower, which sounded like a persistent workman filing down metal. After that, the coffee machine started making a commotion in the kitchen. Each new model seemed to sound more vulgar than the last—even now I can't stand coffee machines. Mornings were a dreadful din. In the crackle of eggs frying in the pan I felt pain and frustration. The door sounded angry when my husband closed it. As he was a gentle man, I'm sure he shut it quietly. I decided it must be the door that was angry, rather than him. In fact, the whole house was in a rage. Because my husband was the sort of man who couldn't feel anger, the house had taken on that role in his stead. Enclosed in that ill-tempered house, I stayed in bed. Around noon I would finally get up, and go straight to my second bed, the sofa in the living room.

If I were to make a movie of my life, I would include a closeup of my husband's glass with a trace of black currant juice in the bottom. And his plate, shiny with the last drops of grease from his omelet. I'm sure I could capture these images quite nicely. But I wouldn't want to film myself, eating cereal alone. It would look as if I were chewing on sand, and besides, you can't capture flavors with a camera. I'll probably never make that movie anyway.

When my son started howling, the woman who flew to his crib, unable to bear it, was my alter ego. The real me was lying on the sofa. Without a body, my alter ego wasn't able to deal with diapers or baby bottles. She would run back to the real me, take hold of my hand, and pull. "I can't do anything without you," she'd beg, "so please, come with me!" Finally, the real me would heave herself up. At first, she walked as if she'd twisted her ankle. Yet once she'd started moving, she quickly went over to the baby and easily did what needed to be done. Like a machine that's been switched on, she suddenly sprang into action, turning on the washing machine, giving her baby a bath, powdering his little bum, doing one mundane chore after another without a break. But then, when she was least expecting it to, the battery would run down, and the real me would flop down on the sofa, unable to lift a finger, even if there was still work left to do. I used to wish I were a robot. They always move when they're turned on, whether they feel like it or not.

On days when my switch stayed off, rays of evening sun would slide slowly down the sides of the coffee cups and plates left on the table. When my husband came home from work, he would gently ask, "Did you have a good day, Inga?" never mentioning the dirty dishes. He sometimes sounded like a psychiatrist. Though his kindness should have warmed my heart, it didn't make me the least bit happy. It merely showed me that he was a model human being, while I was hopelessly flawed.

I would occasionally turn on the TV, but turn it right off again if a talk show or family drama was on. Only science fiction movies held my interest. There's one film I particularly remember from that time. On Mars, all the women were professionals who worked from morning until night at jobs they found truly fulfilling, creating a shortage of daycare centers, which led the government to adopt a policy of sending Martian babies away to be brought up by Earthlings. To achieve this, Martians sneaked into homes with a newborn in the middle of the night, switched the baby with one of their own, and brainwashed the sleeping parents into believing that the little Martian was their own child. The hapless Earthlings then poured themselves into raising the changeling. Meanwhile, the Earthling babies were sent to Saturn. Since children were no longer born on that planet, the adults there were happy to adopt any child, no matter where it was from. This might make you wonder why the Martians didn't just send their own children to Saturn, but in fact they were determined not to, and with good reason. Saturnians loved their children so much they ended up causing them pain. They often said things like, "You're lazy and not very bright, so you'll have a hard time finding a job when you grow up. And even if you do, you'll probably be fired. But don't worry, you can stay here with us forever." This was a Saturnian expression of love. Unable to bear the sorrow of parting with their child, they tried every means possible to keep it from becoming independent. The Earthlings in the film fail to notice that their children have been raised on Saturn. Except for one woman who studies cosmology to prepare herself for a journey in search of her child and finally succeeds in sneaking aboard a space ship.

What if my son were sent from another planet? Might inhabitants of some other world with frighteningly well-developed technology have brainwashed me, induced maternal love by injecting me with some special hormone, then foisted their child on me, leaving him for me to raise? Considering this possibility helped me to stop blaming myself for my uneasy feelings about my son, which made everything simpler.

After several months, my husband took the baby for his regular checkup and returned looking very pleased. Knut was in excellent health, his height and weight exactly average for a Danish child. I took this as evidence of alien developmental control. That "exact average for a Danish child" simply wasn't natural. I'd have been relieved to hear that he was much smaller or much bigger than other children his age.

I decided I must be one of the few Earthlings who was unaffected by the hormones the aliens had injected into all of us. Other women diligently raised a new generation from another planet until about the age of thirteen, when the child they'd loved and cared for was taken from them and the one they'd given birth to returned, yet due to the brainwashing they failed to realize this and were left wondering why a boy who used to be so bright kept failing his university entrance exams, or why a girl who was so sweet when she was little was now suddenly threatening them with a knife. They were sure they'd done something wrong, but couldn't figure out what it was.

One day, the difficult relationship I had with my son suddenly improved. He started speaking *munya-munya*, a strange, new language. Although beyond the understanding of adults, one could sense the complicated structure at its base. It included a wide range of vowels and consonants I could never hope to imitate. Perhaps it was spoken on the planet he came from. If so, I wouldn't have minded. Knowing that my son possessed an excellent linguistic system all his own eased my burden. I needn't worry about his not maturing properly due to his mother's inferior parenting skills; knowing he had this extraordinary ability, I could just sit back and watch, savoring any bits of knowledge that happened to trickle down to me.

Until then, he had expressed hunger, the discomfort of a messy diaper, or sleepiness with loud, metallic cries that appealed directly to my nervous system. Rather than expressing any particular desire, however, *munya-munya* was a purely artistic medium—talking for talking's sake.

"Let's hope he gets over this *munya-munya* soon, and starts saying real words," my husband said. That upset me as much as if he'd said about my favorite clothes, "I wish you'd stop playing dress-up like a little girl." From the start he called him Knut, the name on his birth certificate, whereas I preferred Mumu, my nickname for him. To my ears, Knut sounded more appropriate for an old man with the experiences of a lifetime than for a baby.

Mumu seemed genuinely startled by the discovery that he

could produce the sound "ma" by humming deep in his throat with his mouth closed, then suddenly opening it. That first "ma" must have been accidental; apparently not yet able to say "ma" whenever he wished, he sat with his mouth open, making a sound closer to, "Nyaa, nyaa." Even as an adult, he'll sometimes say, "Nyaa, nyaa" in the middle of an argument, to defy me while at the same time putting a stop to the stream of words flowing in his direction. Whenever I hear that, I'm reminded of those strange sounds he used to make as a baby.

I believe that repeating the combination of the "m" and "a" sounds delighted Knut more than having me there with him. Or was it my fault that he loved the word "Mama" more than his Mama? I'm quite sure that he preferred his Papa to me. I know this because whereas he cried only to express his basic bodily needs while we were alone in the house, when my husband came home, he cried all the time, begging to be held and rocked. Yet linguistically, Mama was his favorite. He repeated it over and over again, hardly ever saying, "Papa." With Knut in his arms, my husband pretended not to mind. "*M* is much easier to pronounce than *p*," he'd sigh. "That's why he calls for you all the time, not me."

Had I recorded his speech in a Pronunciation Diary, my son might be grateful now, but at the time, writing was simply too much trouble. Although I can't be certain without a record, it seems to me that "ah-oo" followed "ma." Thrilled to find that when he pursed his lips while saying "ah" the sound turned into "ah-oo," he made this new sound over and over again. As his breaths came in quick little gasps when he was happy, he'd sometimes look up at me and emit a sound closer to "Haa, haa" than "Mama." The sound "ah" was a toy he never tired of. He even tried sophisticated experiments, such as shaking his head back and forth to make his "ah" quaver.

I couldn't understand why my son kept imitating cat voices.

We didn't have any pets, and I don't believe he heard cats meowing outside, either. Nevertheless, his sticky cat mewls and growls never stopped.

"Why do you suppose he mews like a cat?" I asked. At that moment, my husband had a red ring around his mouth, from eating watermelon.

"I'm not sure," he replied, "but it might be just the opposite. I mean, cats might be imitating humans. Maybe they could only make scary-sounding growls at first, like tigers, but then started crying like human babies to get attention."

As I'd hardly ever heard him explain a personal theory of his in such a humorous way, I've never forgotten that. He could have amused me with lots of funny stories had his natural talents not been crushed by his work, causing his interests to narrow, so that I often had trouble finding topics of conversation that would draw him out. I couldn't understand the world of finance where he worked, and had no interest in it anyway. The rising level of the North Sea, which had begun to attract his attention, didn't seem real to me. He said that if the Arctic ice floes continued to melt at the current pace, the ocean would rise until Denmark was drowning in seawater. A certain corporation was apparently developing a huge ice machine that would be placed in the Arctic to prevent that from happening. When completed, it would use solar energy to produce blocks of ice the size of a compact car, which would then be emitted into the sea. As expenditures for research were skyrocketing, and there was no telling when the project would be completed, several banks had already frozen their loans. The last remaining bank, where my husband worked, was now exploring ways to use the partially completed ice machine.

"I may be going to Greenland soon," I remember him saying, "for observation." It wasn't as if he was going to the moon, so I didn't think much about it at the time.

When a couple has nothing to talk about besides their child, the marriage is over. My husband would sometimes bring me a bouquet of roses. I smelled soap the moment I took it from him, and always pricked a finger on a thorn while I was putting them in water. Roses are a symbol of love filled with malice. Perhaps he'd just given a bouquet to another women, and was motivated by guilt to buy one for me as well, or had belatedly realized that chivalry was dead, and hit on the idea of roses to hide this discovery. Avoiding his eyes, I put them in a vase, which I placed near Knut's crib, whereupon he crinkled up his little nose and sneezed. Flowers think only of emitting the dustlike pollen that enables them to reproduce, and children are the first to sniff out their egotism.

"Knut just sneezed," I complained to my husband.

"You shouldn't put flowers right by his crib," he coolly replied. "We don't want him to develop an allergy, so why not put them somewhere farther away?"

This made me positively spiteful.

"Roses smell like soap, don't they?" I asked.

"You've got it backwards," he said with a wry smile. "It's that soap you use, scented with rose perfume, that smells like the flowers."

Knut's pronunciation-training period continued for a while after that. I'd always thought that parents taught words to their children, but perhaps there's an instruction manual that parents know nothing about embedded in the genes, which children study on their own. Or have I been seeing too many science fiction movies? Knut listened carefully to whatever I said, but rather than imitating me, he stubbornly insisted on practicing a language all his own.

When he started speaking *munya-munya*, I regained the will to live. By "will to live" I don't mean anything grandiose—it's simply that I now wanted coffee as soon as I woke up in the morning, felt refreshed after having eaten my cereal and done the dishes, then was able to prepare his baby food and change his diaper as I listened to his *munya-munya,* after which I went downstairs and took out the garbage. That was when I realized something perfectly obvious—that the garbage wasn't overflowing because my husband had been taking it out. And that the refrigerator wasn't empty because he'd done the shopping on his way home.

When my son had a specific desire, such as wanting to be fed or have his diaper changed, he still produced that metallic wail so characteristic of babies. When he simply wanted to talk for the sake of talking, he spoke that *munya-munya* language of his that was so pleasant to the ear. Though I feigned disinterest, looking out the window, I could have listened to it forever.

Munya-munya was an incredibly rich language. It had magical explosives I had never heard before, an exotic melody, an acrobatic dance of the tongue, and abundant sprays of saliva and sweet breath. Listening to it, I had visions of places I had only seen on TV—the savanna, tropical forests, the bottom of the sea, views from the peak of Mt. Everest. Perhaps this son of mine who couldn't yet walk was tasting all the languages of the world, wondering which to choose. Cheeks soft enough to melt, a tongue that wriggled and raced freely around his mouth, bright red lips, always moist. Love for this child hit me like dynamite.

My husband sometimes picked Knut up while he was speaking *munya-munya,* looked into his eyes, and asked in a jocular tone, "Are you Hamlet? Your soliloquy's kind of long. Too long, in fact. Besides, I can't understand it at all. Why not try saying 'Papa' for a change?" Pleased that his father was talking to him, Knut cackled with laughter, then continued his speech in that incomprehensible *munya-munya.* Not to be outdone, my husband gave it his own interpretation, determined to pull the child into his own world.

"What's that you say?" he asked. "Papa's a great man? You bet he is. Just one look at me and the Arctic Sea freezes over with fear. That's how great I am. But you're going to be even greater."

In time Knut began to speak Danish, just as we had once, and by the time he started primary school, he seemed to have forgotten that he'd been fluent in a completely different language. To me, that baby who had belonged to the *munya-munya* linguistic tribe and this lively, articulate boy were two different people. Could this one be a changeling, raised on another planet? I missed that baby, for this child, who seemed like a miniature version of my husband, wasn't nearly as interesting. Now that I was performing household tasks, my husband went back to doing only his share, which was exactly half, and I returned to the hospital, going in several times a week.

My memory from this period is a little foggy. This is an important time, though, so if I don't explain it properly, my son won't find this account convincing. Even if I intend to be honest, were I to fill in the gaps in my memory with what I merely imagine to have happened, my story will turn into fiction. My husband definitely left me. I can't remember exactly what he said when he left, though. "I'll be going to Germany for a meeting." That was the dragon's body. With the addition of "Depending on what happens there, I may head on to Greenland," a tail sprouted from the beast's rear end, and when my husband called me on the phone several days later to say, "I'm so tired I'm thinking of spending a few days by the Mediterranean," wings unfurled, after which I received a letter. "I've met some people involved in truly meaningful work, and now that I've found my mission in life I want to quit my job at the bank," he wrote, causing horns to grow on the creature's head. I hid that letter, way in the back of a dresser drawer. For two months I heard nothing until, on the very day I'd decided to take the letter to the police, he called to say, "I've been duped into taking part in a crime, and have changed my name and my entire lifestyle, so don't contact the police—I'll be in touch before long." The voice, which I recognized immediately, didn't tremble with fear; in fact, he sounded groggy, as if he'd taken a sleeping pill. My husband is not the sort of person who gets involved in criminal activity. It seemed far more likely that he'd fallen in love with another woman but was too timid to tell me. Yet if that were so, it was odd for him not to have contacted Knut, on whom he'd lavished so much affection. Perhaps he'd been brainwashed. I made up a story about his having been tricked by a terrorist organization posing as environmentalists, then brainwashed into embezzling money from the bank where he'd worked. Otherwise, I would have spent my days thinking of jumping off the windy roof of some skyscraper. And then a man suddenly appeared beside me on that precarious roof, put his arms around me, and gently led me back down to a quiet room on the ground floor. He was known by his nickname, Klaudie, and I'd met him in a bar late one night. I was sitting at the counter, gulping down vodka, when he asked me, "Are you interested in volunteer work, to help immigrants?"

Only a swindler or an oddball would ask a drunken woman who'd left her child at home such a question.

"Do I look like the sort of woman who'd be of any use to society?" I asked provocatively. Soberly, Klaudie nodded. Looking embarrassed, as if he were sure he'd done something wrong, he clumsily maneuvered himself—he was large, both vertically and horizontally—onto the stool beside me. When I saw his hand resting on the bar, my heart beat faster. His middle finger was much longer than the others. There was no going back now. I let him take me to the office of his volunteer organization, where we looked at pamphlets side by side until before we knew it, we had our arms around each other. I started doing volunteer work. Although Klaudie told me his regular job was in aerospace development, there wasn't a trace of either the 'E' of elite or the

'K' of kroner in his face. The feminine curves of his body put me
at ease, but though he seemed gentle he was strongly attached
to sex, enclosing my body like a deep cave while we were together, never letting me out. I sensed that masculinity in him the
moment I saw those extremely long middle fingers of his. For a
time, I was able to forget that my husband had disappeared. And
that wasn't all—a new sensuality opened up in my own body. "If
you have enough money saved, you'd best quit your job and concentrate on our volunteer work until you're used to it," Klaudie
said, yet even after I stopped working as a nurse, I was a prisoner
of those long middle fingers of his, and never had enough time.
Finally, he asked a student named Maria, the daughter of a friend
of his, to babysit Knut; she took him to school and met him afterwards, fixed his dinner, played with him, and sometimes put
him to bed. Meanwhile, Klaudie neither irritated me nor show-
ered me with flattery. When he talked, he'd say things like, "A
says he's more afraid of going to City Hall than the dentist, but
I find the dentist much scarier," or, "B was complaining there's
nothing he wants to eat at the local supermarket, so I took him
to a shop that specializes in Middle Eastern food some distance
away. He bought some hummus there, and liked it so much that
now he's always asking to go back." Though he didn't look or
sound particularly sticky, those extra-long middle fingers would
run through my hair, then start down my neck to my breasts,
stopping to caress them before edging their way down to my
thighs, extracting all my free time.

"Your son Knut gives me the creeps," he suddenly said one
day. Startled, I asked him why, and he told me that Maria had
been watching him play with some paper dolls he had cut out.
He had staged a little drama, in which the Klaudie doll was killing his father. And in a very gruesome way: the Klaudie doll
was forcing a strip of paper, long and thin like a snake, covered
with overlapping scalelike rows of indecipherable letters, into

the mouth, nose, and ears of the doll representing Knut's father. Shocked, Maria made him stop, and demanded an explanation. "This is Klaudie," he said, "killing my father." I laughed, refusing to take it seriously. How could Klaudie kill Knut's father when he had never even met him? But in the following days, Klaudie and I began arguing about trivial things, and after walking by a coffee shop one day and seeing Klaudie and Maria inside, holding hands, I decided to break it off. I never asked my son if the girl's story about that scene with the paper dolls had actually happened. Much later, I discovered that the "aerospace development" work Klaudie was involved in was actually a project to turn food consumed by astronauts in space into children's sweets. It was apparently successful, because one day when Knut brought home a box of cookies a friend had given him, with "You can be an astronaut, too!" on the front, I recognized the name of the company on the back, and remembered that that was where Klaudie had worked.

At age thirteen, my son started growing very quickly, and stopped eating pork, beef, and chicken. He announced that moose steak was the only kind of meat he'd eat. That wouldn't have been so bad if he hadn't also started accusing me of being responsible for my husband's disappearance. Even when I'd told him all I remembered, it wasn't enough. He said I must be hiding something, that perhaps his father hadn't simply disappeared but had been rubbed out, and even threatened to go to the police if I didn't tell him everything. In the old days, parents would assume this sort of behavior was due to the difficulties of adolescence and would eventually pass, but recently children apparently either skip puberty altogether, or enter it in their early teens, and are stuck there until their parents die. Though he acted like an adult with everyone else, Knut either attacked me or stayed away.

In his midteens, he began bringing girls home. A different one each time, though, which suggested that he didn't have a steady girlfriend. Afraid he was flirting with lots of girls, and might be hurting some of them, I asked him about it.

"We're out of honey and toilet paper," he replied with a contemptuoius look, "so why don't you quit worrying about things you know nothing about and go to the store?"

Once he spent so long alone in his room with a girl that, wondering what was going on, I put my ear to the door, only to hear him sounding witty and charming, apparently delighting her. Yet when she eagerly started telling him about a bicycle trip she'd taken with her boyfriend while he laughed now and then like a good listener, I realized that she had no romantic interest in him whatsoever, which must mean that my son was gay, but then why on earth would a boy hide that sort of thing from his mother in this day and age—a century ago, perhaps, but surely not now. During the next few weeks, I tried to discover who his real partner was, but found no possible candidates. Another science fiction movie I once saw depicted a world in which young people no longer have any interest in sex. Aware that a steady increase in the human population will cause them to go extinct, cedar and white birch trees emit clouds of pollen that smother people's desire to reproduce. Only one weak, sickly boy, who always has to wear an oxygen mask due to his faulty immune system, avoids breathing in the pollen, and falls in love.

Knut majored in linguistics at the university, then went on to graduate school. He hated it when I talked about the university; if I so much as mentioned the word "linguistics," he would retort, "I'm not sure that's the exact term for what I'm studying," but never explain what he meant. After he started grad school, I let the word "scholarship" slip out, only to be immediately corrected. "It's a research grant," he snapped, but when I used that term the next time I saw him, he corrected me again, saying, "It's not money I was given for a specific research project."

One day, when I was exhausted from dealing with my son, I happened to see an article on volunteer work in a magazine, detailing a program that allows individuals to support students from Greenland. I phoned to ask for details, and was told that there were various ways of lending assistance. You could provide a room in your house for a token fee, take a student out for a talk over dinner now and then, or become a sponsor, paying for their transportation to Denmark and living expenses. I started by taking students out to a restaurant, to hear what they had to say. A young person starting life in a foreign country needs someone like an aunt or an uncle. Not exactly a surrogate parent, but someone to talk to, who will treat them to a good meal once in a while. Giving young people from Greenland a helping hand seemed to me like a natural thing for Danes to do. But when I told my son about it, he responded coldly, saying, "That's just an extension of colonialism." Though his criticism upset me, I knew how lonely I'd be if we got into an argument and I didn't see him again for months on end, so I didn't protest. Nor did I tell him when I invited a girl who had just arrived from Greenland to have dinner with me at a restaurant in the Danish Royal Library. She told me she wanted to study fertilizers in the future, and had just started studying Danish at a language school. Her English was very good, and listening to her made me want to fly to Greenland right away, to help her plant potatoes. Due to global warming, she said, they were now growing cabbages as well. But they needed cash to buy foreign imports. Her parents worked for a call center, answering customers' questions on the telephone all day, never taking their headsets off, and because her English was better than theirs, and she needed money to buy clothes and things, she got a job there, too. But one day when she happened to look outside while she was on the phone, she saw a hare hop over to the window and stand up on its hind legs, looking at her. As she returned the animal's gaze, the customer's voice, speaking

English from somewhere abroad, suddenly grew faint, and she tore off her headphones and ran outside to chase after it. That was when she started thinking about studying in Copenhagen.

The next student I took to dinner was a large yet shy young man, with a habit of fidgeting around on his chair as if searching for something to say. This gave him an oddly sexy air. Though he didn't seem very articulate at first, what he finally said was so sophisticated, the words chosen from such an overly rich vocabulary, that I realized the field of his thoughts must be too finely cultivated for him to speak fluently in any language. Just imagining what he might do in the future warmed my heart.

And then one day I received the news that an aunt who as a young woman had moved to Washington, on the west coast of the United States, had died of diabetes. She had no children or male cousins, so I, her only niece, had inherited her entire estate. Though I considered using this windfall to travel through Central and South America, I knew how depressing it would be to travel alone. After buying an antique chest of drawers I'd had my eye on for some time, there was still a large sum of money left. I thought of spending it to fully sponsor a student from Greenland. My spirits were immediately lifted, and the decision was made. When I told Knut about my plan, at first there was no reaction, but as time went on, he began to make caustic, sarcastic comments. He'd say things like, "Can't you just make friends like a normal person?" or, "Do you have to give money to some kid and see how grateful he is to feel good about yourself?" or, "Isn't it awfully arrogant for people from a country that destroyed the Arctic to start giving aid at this late date, acting like some kind of savior?"

This word "postcolonialism" that immature, self-centered young people are so fond of using these days makes me angry. If, as Knut claims, Europe's wealth came from exploiting marginal territories, shouldn't youngsters like him, who grew up without having to worry about money, be all the more eager to share their ill-gotten gains with people on the margins, wherever that may be? After all, that wealth makes it possible for him to conduct useless research with no fear of going hungry. It's the height of arrogance and ignorance, sitting there basking in privilege, ignoring his contemporaries who can't go to university no matter how badly they want to. Of course, I never spoke this harshly to my son—I simply couldn't. I might have let my feelings slip out once or twice, but if he was hurt, it never showed. Besides, I didn't want to argue with him. As any sort of contact with me put Knut in a bad mood, I decided to stop worrying about him, and concentrate on Nanook, the young man from Greenland I was going to sponsor. Though of course, I couldn't entirely squelch my determination not to let any chance I had to spend time with my son slip away.

The first time I saw Nanook, I felt he was going to be my new son. He had such a talent for languages that during our first meal together, he was speaking better Danish while we were finishing dessert than he had when the appetizer had been served. Smiling, he looked as cute as a seal, yet staring off into the distance, his face took on such dignity. Time and again I imagined him in a white coat, gently smiling down at me, his patient, whispering, "You'll be fine." After years of working as a nurse, I neither idolized nor idealized doctors. I had seen the petty jealousy and childish egotism that could lead them to hurt those weaker than themselves. Yet when I pictured Nanook's future as a doctor, he looked like an angel in his white coat.

After he finished language school, just as he was about to start at the university, Nanook went on a trip and never came back. Remembering my husband's disappearance, I felt as though a barn door had slammed shut in my face. Suddenly I couldn't drink coffee, my hair became dry and unmanageable, I had sharp pains in my elbow.

When I finally met Nanook again by chance some months later, I couldn't help feeling betrayed, but I was reluctant to harbor a grudge, or browbeat him into going to school, so I decided to forget everything related to the word "son" and make nursing the center my life. Before I quit to give birth and raise my child, my heart had been calm. It would seem that what's often said about women becoming sadder after they stop working outside the home is true. At the hospital, patients would tell me how grateful they were, my superiors praised me now and then, and because bad things happened as well, I had my ups and downs, but never did I feel as if I were tumbling down a steep slope. Until then I had worked only part-time, sometimes several times a week, usually to fill in after several nurses had all quit at once, but now, for the first time, I was returning to nursing full-time. You might say it was as if I'd been sent back to grid one in Snakes and Ladders.

Yet somewhere in the sky, a careless angel must have tossed the dice that determined my fate. At the hospital, something outrageous happened. I fell in love. And not with a white-haired knight on a white horse, but with a doctor named Velmer, whom the entire hospital staff agreed was "an awful man." I am finally old enough to understand what's good about "awful." The embrace of a "good man" is never annoying, yet as time goes by, one tends to think of him less and less, while with an "awful man," there's always something to push back against. While brushing him off, shooing him away as if he were a fly, I sometimes feel laughter bubbling up, or a desire to scream. The more passive I am the more irritating he gets, giving me the incentive to irritate him in equal measure. I build him up, argue him down, caress him, jab at him, hurt him by intentionally telling him all the nasty things people say about him, then make him believe that I'm the only one who sees the good in him, striking at his weakest point, all the while enjoying his various reactions. Though

I'm occasionally wounded when he mounts a counterattack, I know the pain won't last very long and I wait a while until it's safe to go back to pinching, prodding, kneading his heart. Tormenting each other with words makes sex all the richer. Like an exotic dish, simmering with herbs and spices that give it its peculiar taste. If the young are truly no longer interested in sex, I can't imagine what they're living for.

"Old age is worth the wait," I whispered one day to Hanne, my best friend at work, over a cup of black coffee, which tasted good to me again. "When I was young, I couldn't have imagined how happy I'd be now."

"You certainly seem to having a good time," she said with a grin. "But can you trust a man like that?" I detected a note of doubt in her voice.

"Why, of course I can. In fact, he's a lot more trustworthy than most men. He doesn't flatter me, or promise me anything, so how could he possibly be trying to trick me? He says the most dreadful things, but that's how he shows his love."

"I remember an insult about your hips."

"Like a cabinet."

"That's awful."

"Well, there are various types of cabinets, you know. He got flustered when I asked if he meant a MALM or a HEMNES. But his seeing me as a piece of furniture made in his home country may well mean that he's recognized me as a compatriot."

In fact, that's what first made me aware of this doctor named Velmer—someone told me he'd compared my hips to a cabinet. In my twenties I would have been angry or hurt, but now, knowing he was interested made me want to tease him a bit. I decided to catch him off guard when I had the chance, by asking, "Did you mean a MALM, or a HEMNES?" I was looking forward to that.

When we were finally alone, our bodies almost touching, I knew he would be mine. As is usual with talkative, confident men, he didn't seem to realize how strongly he was attracted to me, yet when we touched, suddenly it all became clear, and despite his inner turmoil, he gave himself to me. I'm afraid I lost out as a young woman. I was so busy avoiding awful men that I completely overlooked the ones like Velmer, and ended up marrying a rather boring fellow instead. Klaudie, who appeared next in my life, always came on so strong that he left me no room to play. But now I've reached the right age for love. One day, hoping to get a rise out of Velmer, I said, "I'm interested in voodoo, and would like to go to Haiti sometime. Do you want to come along?"

Though I didn't realize it until I'd said it aloud, I had long dreamt of going to Haiti. Velmer frowned.

"Women and savages," he said, "pretend to be attracted to the irrational, believing there's some special sort of culture to be found there."

"I guess this means I'll have to give up my dream of spending my vacation with you," I replied, dramatically lowering my head and biting my lip.

He clumsily repeated what I'd just said. "Hang on a minute. Does this mean you want to go to Haiti with me?"

"If not with you, who else?"

"Nobody, I guess, but if being with me is the point, why go so far away? Wouldn't it be more natural for us to spend our first vacation together in Rome?"

"Why Rome?"

"Because that's where I want to go."

"Voodoo's popular in Rome, too. No, wait—that's Roman Catholicism. But Catholic priests seem to have far more legal problems than their Voodoo counterparts."

"Let's discuss our vacation later, and for now, take an inter-body trip."

The fleshy hand that had been caressing the back of my neck slipped under my arm, pushing me down and across until I bumped into a pile of little packages, sending them scattering across the floor. I could tell from his impatience that not only did he not want to go to Haiti, but that he'd try to put off our vacation for as long as possible. I'd have to take my time finding out why.

I recently caught the flu, and took two weeks off work. Wanting to surprise Velmer, I didn't phone ahead of time to tell him when I'd be coming back. Having asked at the reception desk, I knew exactly where he'd be examining a patient, and freshened up my lipstick as I waited for him in the corridor outside. Like a schoolgirl, you might say, but my plan was vulnerability followed by nastiness. If I showed him my weakness, he was sure to make some horrible comment. The door opened, and he came out. Preparing myself mentally, I looked up with a soft, melting smile and murmured, "I was longing to see you." I waited for the insult he would surely hurl at me. Yet he simply smiled back and said brightly, "My feelings exactly. Why didn't you call me?" This made me all the more wary, for I was sure he meant to catch me off guard, then come in for the kill.

"My telephone's out of order," I said, knowing how stupid that would sound. He normally would have countered with something along the lines of "It's more like your excuse-making-machine is on the blink." But today he nodded and said, "I'm done for the afternoon. I'm going to take you to a café on the waterfront where we'll drink champagne to celebrate your recovery. Then, I'm going to buy you flowers, so many you won't be able to carry them all. Not roses, because I've noticed you're not very fond of roses."

Taking my hand, he started to run. What movie was he parodying? It couldn't be *Melody*, could it? I was about to ask when he looked back, and I gasped in astonishment. There wasn't even a hint of a sarcasm in his face.

"What's wrong?" I asked. "Are you sick?"

"I'm just excited to see you," he replied, "after being apart for so long."

Still holding my hand, he ran down the long hospital corridor toward the front entrance.

CHAPTER 7

Knut Speaks

I was rummaging through a trash container as I listened to the rain pour down on the pavement outside. Luckily, there was a roof—otherwise, all this paper people had thrown away would have gotten soaked. There's something sad about paper wet enough to see through, that dissolves in your hands. When I pulled up the heavy lid, the container was halfway full of the stuff, with those free newspapers they hand out on the street on top. The first thing that caught my eye was a drawing of a wolf, straight out of *Little Red Riding Hood*. Probably from an article about Wolf X, an animal recently sighted here in Denmark. A sketch is odd in a newspaper—usually there'd be a photograph. I could tell the contents without reading it. A lone wolf who'd managed to escape the hunters has been showing up at bus stops or soccer fields at night, throwing the city into confusion. Wolf X hasn't attacked anyone yet, but people are afraid to walk around at night the way they used to. A certain political party has started saying things like, "Only in backward countries with Morality Police do people stay indoors every night. Why must citizens of an advanced, democratic nation feel they have to do the same? To prevent more wolves from entering the country, we should close our borders at once, and exit the European Union as soon as possible." These politicians claim that wolves started coming in because we extended the border as far as Romania and Bulgaria. Which is utter nonsense, of course, although it is true that wolves—supposedly extinct—started being sighted in northwestern Europe just around the time when southeastern European immigrants were granted free entrance into Denmark. Political parties that spout anti-immigrant rhetoric scare me a lot more than wolves, but I'm not going to waste my time reading about that now. I'm looking for an article I threw away, one that Hiruko asked me to find. Actually, I'm in a real fix, because people I don't know keep sending me loads of copied-out articles in the mail, and they take up a lot of room. These days everyone's afraid that if they send data by email, some hacker might alter it and sell it on the internet, so they're careful to send only handwritten documents through the post. I miss the old days, when we believed our data would be protected if we used a special format like PDF. The safest data of all is in handwriting too sloppy for a character reader but a scrawl that can still be deciphered by the human eye.

Paper takes up an awful lot of space. Stack it and the pile gets so high it falls over, start putting it in boxes and you end up with a whole lot of cartons, and they're awfully heavy to haul out to the trash. I feel bad for the people who spent their time writing this stuff, but there's nothing to do but throw it away. At first, I was planning to read each one, noting down the content before I threw it away, but that takes too much time. Now I just leaf through them before they go into the trash.

I got into this mess because of a stupid rumor about my editing a collection of scholarly papers that's sure to be a bestseller. The editor of a famous magazine is supposed to have interviewed me about this plan, but I don't remember it, and besides, no well-known magazine would approach me in the first place. In fact, no magazine, famous or not, has ever contacted me. What's really strange is that even though lots of people claim to have read it, the interview itself is nowhere to be found. Are there sites that roam the internet like ghost ships, occasionally appearing out of the mist, only to fade away again?

There's usually a letter attached that says, "This paper deals with an important theme essential to the collection you are editing." When not even I, the supposed editor, knows what that theme is. Some of the titles are: "Characteristics of the Language Used by Dog Owners When Talking to Their Dogs"; "An International Comparison of the Phonetic Systems of Intoxicated Speakers"; "Parts of Speech Most Likely to Slip Your Mind." Most are casual essays aimed at the general reader, rather than scholarly papers. Easy-to-forget parts of speech is a topic that interests me, so I read about a third of that one. Considering how often you hear people say something like, "I know her, but the name escapes me," it's not surprising that proper nouns would top the list. Common nouns come next, like when you're fixing a shelf with tools you haven't used in a while. "Could you hand me the . . ." you ask, but then can't remember the word for what you're looking for—claw hammer? screwdriver? According to this paper, people rarely draw a blank when it comes to adjectives. That's definitely true. Probably because there are fewer adjectives than nouns, and you can make do with just a few basic ones. I feel sorry for all the people who die without realizing what a tiny portion of the total adjective supply they've used. They order a *large* beer, drive a *fast* car, eat a *delicious* steak, see a *beautiful* singer on TV. Satisfied with these few, they never give a thought to all the adjectives that are lacking in their lives. When it comes to expressing frustration with their jobs, or their bosses, they can usually think of a lot more, though. There's a limited number of adjectives in this category too, but I've never seen someone scream, "You . . . what's the word I'm looking for? . . . grimy, no, that's not it . . . grouchy . . . nah, not that either . . . wait, I've got it—you greedy bastard!" If "greedy" doesn't come to mind, "grabby," "grubby," or even "greasy" might do. Even if the meaning's a little off, the listener will get the general idea. That doesn't work with nouns, though. When you need a "screwdriver," it's no use asking for a "hammer." And the pain of seeing that screwdriver in your mind but not knowing what to call it can leave you gasping for breath. But it only hurts because you know exactly which word you want and can't find it—if not for that, you'd never notice you'd forgotten the name. What if my memory of that interview was buried somewhere where I couldn't get to it? There could be lots of other things as well, like having injured a friend by mistake when I was a teenager, or being sexually abused as a toddler—but if that were the case, I'd be living with a separate self I knew nothing about.

The letters people send along with their papers give me hints as to what I'm supposed to have said in that interview. "You have a book you want to get out, so you're starting your own publishing company. I'm truly impressed," one said, so I'm apparently not just into editing, but publishing as well. Another one, from abroad, said: "I hear that young Scandinavians often dream of becoming editors. Here in my country, almost no one does, so it makes me jealous. I'm sincerely hoping that you, who might be called the frontrunner of this new editorial movement, will read my paper." This nonexistent interview seems to have made me into the pillar of a new Scandinavia with a bright future, full of people who love books and young people who dream of editing them. Still another letter, written in Icelandic, said: "You asserted in the interview that academic papers should be written in the minor languages. Otherwise, these languages' range of expression will narrow, until they are dull and flat, with only the capacity for everyday discourse, causing scholarship to grow even farther away from people's actual lives, becoming empty theory, suitable only for the ivory tower. When I read that, I was so happy I cried. For that is exactly what I've been thinking for about fifty years now, although hardly anyone agrees with me." I began to see my ersatz alter ego more clearly. Unlike the real me, he seems to be an active young man, skilled at spreading new ideas, with a charm that draws people to him.

What if I were to pretend that the interview really happened, edit the book, and start a publishing company? Take on the role of my alter ego. When I actually started reading the papers, I realized that would be impossible. Though this is partly because I'm naturally lazy and tire easily, it's also the fault of the papers themselves. All these writers are studying linguistics, yet most of them have no feel for the rhythm of language. You can't read them at a steady pace, as if you were walking. I think it's because they're too busy filling up the tiniest holes in their argument, making sure no one can object. When actually it's best to leave open spaces, to let some air in. I can't even make it through the dry, technical prefaces, and the autobiographies—self-portraits that go on and on—are depressing. Why should I have to read about some guy who was in despair because nobody would read his poetry until he met his current lover, who helped him to discover linguistics, a field of study that's become his life's work, when I'm not a friend of his, or even an acquaintance?

When I do find an essay I want to read, it's almost always written in several different languages, which makes for heavy lifting. A translation machine can usually turn correspondence into Danish no matter what language the letters were written in, but with these papers the handwriting's too bad for a character-recognition device to decipher, so I can't even use the machine.

Lately I've been having trouble sleeping. I always prided myself on my ability to fall asleep anytime, anywhere, but recently a fluorescent light keeps flicking on in my brain late at night and I can't find the switch to turn it off. Then the doorbell rings and I stand there half-asleep while the postman dumps a huge pile of mail at my feet. All I can do is open the envelopes one by one, take out each bundle, covered with strange handwriting, and look it over. After that, I blot out the name, address, and title with a magic marker. By noon I stop using the letter opener and just rip them apart. In the evening, I load my knapsack with papers, along with the envelopes they came in, and take them out to the trash. Since there're too many to take all at once, I have to make several trips. I must look suspicious, pulling stacks of paper out of my knapsack in the semidarkness, tossing them into the bin, because passersby sometimes stop to watch. Back at home, I'll get the sneaky feeling that I've pitched my own research along with the other stuff, and open the file on my computer to see if it's still there. Though I should feel relieved to find it, I still can't get to sleep. Once I awoke with a start in the middle of the night, certain I'd thrown my passport away. I rummaged through my desk drawer, where I always keep it, and there it was.

Hiruko called me on the phone.

"I'm having trouble sleeping," I told her.

"cause?"

"People keep sending me all these papers ..." I explained the situation to her.

"tomorrow's tomorrow on you i call."

"Oh, you don't have to do that. I'm just surprised, because I've never had this problem before. But they say about a third of the population has insomnia, so it's probably a natural phenomenon, like aging. Nothing to worry about."

"worry equals roof of friendship."

"Rooves are definitely important. Especially in places where it rains a lot."

"about susanoo i worry, so to copenhagen i go."

"I see. Let's go see him together then. Akash, Nora, and Nanook are at the hospital almost every day, but I've only been once even though I live here."

"tomorrow's tomorrow in copenhagen. thirteen o'clock all right to your house reach?"

"Sounds great. I'll make you a hotdog. After we eat, we can go to the hospital. Why not stay at my place tomorrow night? My sofa turns into a bed."

"night metamorphosis."

That gave me the jitters. Those words made me think of characters that morph into wolves or vampires when the moon comes out. I can't believe the kids who play those computer games actually want to be like that. No matter how dark or creepy the night gets, I'd never want to turn into a werewolf or a vampire. Or a Roman warrior, or a square-shaped, black-belted guy, for that matter.

"Anyway, I'm really glad you're coming. Oh, I just remembered something. One of the people who sent me a paper had a name something like Hiruta. It was about patients with brain injuries after a traffic accident. Some of them remembered ideograms even though they forgot phonetic letters. It looked kind of interesting, but as I said before, I've decided to throw them all out, so I pitched that one, too."

"away threw?"

A sharp blade hidden in her voice made my heart skip several beats. I should have held onto that one. Hiruta was probably the surname, but it sounds like Hiruko. And considering that the paper dealt with ideograms and phonetic letters, this Hiruta might well be from her home country. Why hadn't I taken that in at first glance? All this time Hiruko's been looking for someone who speaks her native language. She's determined to follow every lead, no matter how tenuous, and keep searching until she finds someone. After deciding to join her on this journey, how could I have tossed out such an important clue, not even keeping the envelope with the address on it? There must be a hole in my brain—a hole of forgetfulness.

"Actually, I threw it into the bin right near my house. They don't collect the trash very often, so I'm sure it's still there. I'll go out now and get it back."

"to away throw equals play," she said. "to retrieve equals work." I generally get what Hiruko says, but that hits me like a flash of light—asked whether I'd fully grasped her meaning, though, I couldn't really say.

"Okay, I'll go out and retrieve that paper. I'm looking forward to seeing you the day after tomorrow—be sure to bring me some Andersen's Fairy Tale Cookies."

I quickly hung up, making that last little joke so she couldn't tell how rattled I was. She works at the Märchen Center in Odense, but they probably don't have a gift shop, and I don't even know if there's a bakery that makes that kind of cookies. Though I'm not interested in fairy tales, I do find myself thinking about fairies now and then. There's something fairylike about Hiruko, something that keeps her one step removed from the everyday. If she were to say, "The train was crowded so I rode here on the back of a swan," I'd probably believe her.

I put on my leather jacket to go out, but it was raining so I came back and changed into something waterproof. Then, for the first and I hope last time in my life, I started rummaging through the trash.

The recycling bins are lined up in a lonely little alley off the main street: one for paper, another for bottles, still another for clothing. I lifted the lid—not of Pandora's box, but of a trash container. Using a tree branch lying on the ground nearby to prop it open, I bent over double and somehow managed to haul out some newspapers on top of the pile, but couldn't get to that thick layer underneath. So I brought something to stand on from my apartment, but still couldn't reach the bottom. I'd have to actually get inside the container. I started to swing my leg over the edge, then stopped. If I got in, the thing might slam shut like a coffin lid, and I'd be trapped inside. After all, only a single branch held it open...

Then it came to me—why not ask Akash? I was sure he'd be happy to help. As he's "moving between genders," I'm never quite sure which pronoun to use, whether *he*'d be happy or *she*'d be happy.

Only third-person pronouns are gendered. I can't understand why, though. One theory is that it's a matter of visibility: because I (the first person) and you (the second person) are looking at each other, we can tell each other's gender at a glance, but because the third person—the one we're talking about—isn't here, we need the pronoun to show whether or it's a man or a woman.

I can't accept that. It's awfully old-fashioned to assume you can tell someone's gender just by looking, and besides, isn't there something grotesque about a third person who isn't there, but whose gender alone is somehow perfectly clear?

Akash came over about two hours after I called him. He was staying with an Indian guy he knows in Copenhagen.

"You have Indian friends wherever you go," I said.

"To me, the whole world is a hotel," he replied. I don't speak German nearly as well as he does, so we always speak in English. (I had several years of German at school, so I'd probably get better at it if I tried, but speaking it now takes so much more energy than English that I get awfully hungry, so to keep myself from eating too much and putting on weight, I avoid speaking German.)

"I hear you came with Nora."

"That's right. It was a pretty rough trip—fun, though. Nanook wanted to hitchhike, so he left Nora and took off first. There's something not okay about Nanook these days."

"What do you mean?"

"He's acting like someone other than himself."

"What for?"

"I'm not sure. Maybe his personality's suddenly changed. But is that possible? Why don't you ask him when you see him? I have a feeling he'll be honest with you."

Akash, who's very slender, was wearing his usual red sari, carrying a blue umbrella. Though I hated to spoil his elegant appearance, for the work we were about to do I had to ask him to wear a raincoat over his sari so he could use both hands, and put on a pair of sweat pants underneath. Forcing someone to dress in clothes they don't like is really a form of violence, so I was hemming and hawing, but then he casually asked what sort of job I wanted him to help me with.

"Actually," I said, taking a deep breath, "we'll be fishing through a trash bin."

"Oh, like raccoons," he said, laughing out loud. "When they can't find food in the mountains they come to town and search through the garbage."

"I'll be the raccoon, and climb inside the container to look through the stuff, but could you stand outside, take the papers as I hand them to you, and put them on the ground? Don't worry—it's not garbage. It's a recycling bin for paper."

"And you're going to climb inside?"

"You mean I'm more like a big brown bear than a raccoon?"

"No, that's not what I wanted to say. It's just that I think I'd be the one to get into the bin. I'm smaller than you, and thanks to yoga, I'm pretty flexible, too."

"Do you practice yoga?"

"No, I never have, actually, but with so many Europeans asking me to teach them, I keep having to demonstrate, and now my imitation is starting to look like the real thing."

"So maybe if I played the role of a young Scandinavian about to set up a publishing company, it would come to me naturally."

"Are people hoping you'll do that?"

"Their hopes are based on a misunderstanding, but maybe

most hopes are. Anyway, let's go out to the bin. But before that, there's something I have to ask. Would you mind changing into work clothes? Otherwise, your sari might get torn or dirty."

Akash readily agreed, which was a relief, so I got out a pair of sweat pants, a T-shirt, and a parka I had stashed in a drawer.

"Everything's gray," he said. "Is that your favorite color?"

I saw laughter in his face. He definitely had a point. While I'm not especially fond of gray, reds remind me of fire, so too hot to wear; blues are embarrassingly young, like I'm trying to be Little Boy Blue; in black I'd be trying to pass myself off as an artist; and I'm not pure enough for white.

In trainers and a T-shirt, Akash looked like a different person. When we got back to the container, it was gleaming silver in the sunlight streaming through a break in the clouds.

"It looks like a spaceship," Akash joked as he lifted the lid and peered inside.

"Let's tie up the lid first." I'd brought tools in my bag. I pulled the lid up and tied it to the fence behind. As if he were weightless, Akash darted up the stepladder, lightly lifted one leg over the edge of the container, and dropped down into a squat on top of the paper carpet inside.

"I'm not sinking down at all. The papers are packed solid. The top layer is all newspaper."

Akash started by stacking the newspapers into neat piles, which he carefully handed over to me one by one with his long, delicate fingers. Beneath them was a layer of the essays I had thrown out. I had a reason for not shredding them. I once read an article about a criminal organization that collects shredded documents, which it reconstructs and then puts to ill use. Apparently, with a computer and a special machine, you can easily put back together even the tiniest pieces. But this gang assumes that intact papers won't contain any information they can use for criminal purposes, so they don't bother with them. That's why I never shredded the essays that came in the mail, although

I did black out all the names, addresses, and titles with a magic marker. I regretted that now. It would have been much easier to look for a name like "Hiruta." But I had to leaf through the papers Akash handed me, page by page, looking for some trace of Hiruta's essay. If I found nothing, I'd set them over to one side. There were now several snowy white mounds around the container, which of course I intended to return to the spaceship when we were finished. Fortunately, the ground below the roof was paved with concrete, keeping the rain that had soaked the ground outside from seeping in.

"Hey, what are you guys looking for?" Hearing a man's voice from behind, I turned around and saw two policemen. This was a quiet residential neighborhood where you never saw the police, especially in this back alley. Maybe someone had spotted us and called them.

"I threw away an important scholarly paper by mistake," I answered slowly, looking as dopey as possible. "It's on linguistics." I was thinking how I'd made them believe my lie by playing the role of a graduate student with his head in the clouds, when I realized it wasn't a lie at all. I'd told the truth.

"Oh, I see," said one of the policemen. "Just make sure you put everything back when you're done." After they'd left, we looked at each other, shrugged our shoulders, and went back to work.

Paper is awfully thin. You could only fit about fifteen chairs into one container, but each sheet of paper is less than one-tenth of a millimeter thick, which meant there were tens of thousands of sheets inside, all covered with a frightening number of letters. I got weak in the knees just thinking about it, but Akash's oddly soothing voice helped me regain my balance.

"Do you remember the content of the paper we're looking for?"

"Sure—it's about patients with brain injuries who remember ideograms but forget phonetic symbols."

"Hiruko would naturally be interested in something like that."

"The guy who wrote it might be a countryman of hers."

"Yes, definitely, but more than that, she'd want to see if there was some hidden clue that might help Susanoo regain his speech."

I hadn't thought of that, but he was right. I must have a potato for a brain to have tossed that paper out with the others. We'd been quietly working for a while when Akash suddenly asked, "Why do you think Susanoo lost his ability to speak?"

"I'm not sure. But he seems to avoid talking to Hiruko. Maybe he doesn't want to share his memories with her. He has his own story about their homeland, and keeping silent is a way of protecting it."

It was nerve-racking to look at a page with no title, not knowing whether it was from the beginning or end, trying to tell at a glance if it was what I was looking for. If Akash hadn't been there, I would have given up long ago. I was sorry I'd told Hiruko about Hiruta's paper over the phone. But because I had, there was still a possibility that I'd find it again. If I'd forgotten all about it, the sort of clue you only come across once in a decade or so would be lost forever, turned into recycled paper. The pile in the container seemed just as high as before.

"It's packed in a lot more firmly than I thought at first," Akash sighed. "I can feel it pressing up against the bottom of my shoes. Shall we ask Nora to help, too? Since she doesn't have anything to do besides visit Susanoo at the hospital, she said she'd try acting like a tourist, but she might be getting bored with that."

"I'll take a pass. Nora's so competent, she'd be disgusted to know what a mess I've made of this. She wouldn't bawl me out or anything, but she'd probably give me one of those *How could you be so stupid* looks, and that would really hurt. Can't we ask Nanook?"

"I'm afraid not."

"Why?"

"He'd just stand there, laughing at us."

"He's changed that much?"

"I'm afraid so."

My hand stopped. My eyes were drawn to one sentence on the page, then down to the next, and the one after that, as if I was being sucked into a pit. "An infant's babbling can have a great psychological impact on its parents. The father and mother often read different meanings into their child's babytalk, which can give rise to arguments. The writer will deal with an extreme case, in which a father who thought his son was delivering him a message from outer space left his family and disappeared." A brief summary of the total content, so I figured this must be a part of a preface. I wanted to read the whole thing. Unfortunately, the papers above and below were by a different writer. I could tell that at once, by the handwriting.

"Here's something interesting, Akash. It's not the one I'm looking for, but I'd really like to read it. Can you hold on a minute?"

I looked through the papers scattered on the ground, the ones I'd already checked, and found several others written in the same hand. After I'd put them into my knapsack, I asked Akash to keep on with his work. I was ready to take a break, but since we couldn't leave things this way and go out for a coffee, I decided we'd better keep going a little longer.

The rain returned as a lazy drizzle, then stopped altogether before starting up again, repeating the pattern about three more times until, damp with a mixture of sweat and the moisture in the air, we finally hit bottom. The last thing I found was a sheaf from that paper on babytalk I'd wanted to read, but no sign of Hiruta's paper.

"That's strange. I'm sure I would have noticed it."

I had Akash take pictures of both the inside of the empty container, and the mountains of paper piled up outside it. Tomorrow

I'd tell Hiruko about how we'd gone through the whole bin, all the way to the bottom, but I was afraid she wouldn't believe me. Not because she didn't trust me, or was generally suspicious, but because even to me it seemed incredible that there were actually people who'd spend hours and hours doing this sort of thing. To show my gratitude to Akash for helping me with this nonacademic task, I decided to treat him to dinner.

"There's an Indian restaurant I think's the best one around," I laughed. "Want to try it?"

"Sounds interesting," he said, his head cocked to one side.

It was an old place, not much to look at from the outside, a bar as much as a restaurant where the same people had been coming since it opened. I had stumbled on it by chance about a year earlier when I sprained my ankle one Sunday, and discovered the only things in my apartment you could call food were ketchup and mustard. I knew that if I called my mother she'd come running with a basket full of everything from appetizer to dessert, but I wasn't going to get caught in that trap. I normally would have walked down to a hotdog stand by the station, but that was too far to hobble on my sprained ankle. And taking a taxi to a hotdog stand would have been kind of weird. That's when I remembered there was a place nearby I'd never tried. Even if it was a bar, they'd probably serve some kind of food as well. When I got there, dragging my aching foot, I was surprised to find it was an Indian restaurant. There was no sign outside, but when I opened the door, I was hit by a wave of spices. I was the only customer; the dour-looking, bearded man behind the counter brought me a menu. Still wary, I let my hunger decide for me—I ordered a lamb curry, and was astonished when it came. The meat, so tender it melted in my mouth, turned into wild-animal energy as it started to burn inside my stomach. It was a little expensive, so I hadn't been back there since, but a hotdog wouldn't be enough to show Akash how grateful I was, and besides, he might be a vegetarian, so I figured an Indian place would be the safest bet.

I went in first and, seeing that the place was practically empty, turned to Akash, who looked a little nervous. He normally would have smiled at the man with the moustache who came out from the back to show us to a table, but not this time.

"What's wrong?" I whispered, leaning across the table.

"This place is Pakistani, not Indian."

"Oh? Sorry—I didn't know. Shall we leave then?"

"No, judging by my nose, I'd say the food's pretty good. And if they're pacifists, there's no problem. But I feel a strange sort of tension in the air."

I was about to say, "Look—it says 'Indian food' right here on the menu," but when I carefully examined its front and back covers, and all the pages inside, it didn't say "India" anywhere. All I saw were sketches of a laughing elephant with its trunk raised, scattered throughout. How could I have been so simpleminded as to assume that elephants must mean India?

Akash changed the subject to the guy he was staying with in Copenhagen. A native of Akash's hometown Pune, he had studied philosophy as a young man but was now selling used cars. Seeing how lithe and slender he was, and that he definitely looked Indian, customers were sometimes more interested in learning yoga from him than buying a car. He found it odd that no matter how suspicious people are of used-car salesmen, they never consider the possibility of being sold defective yoga.

"You have so many friends to stay with," I said. "I bet you had fun talking to them in the evenings, when we were in Arles and Oslo."

"Yes, we did, and that's why I feel sorry for Hiruko. There's no one here who knows about her childhood. Sharing memories of trivial things, like sweets or toys that were popular when you were little, makes you feel at home. You can retrace the past, even as it's being rubbed out. Some say there's no need to talk about your homeland if you're not going back, but that's not true. If you're never going to see it again, you need to talk about it all the more, to keep a vivid image of your childhood alive. And it's no good remembering it all by yourself. That way, your memories turn into delusions. You need someone to share them with."

Hiruko arrived the following afternoon at exactly one o'clock. The dark green clothes she was wearing set off the color of her skin.

"I guess the train was on time."

"late-arriving box equals train not."

"It's too bad that most railways can't really say that anymore. Actually, I have to tell you something even worse. We couldn't find that paper you wanted to read. We spent hours looking for it, though."

I showed her the pictures Akash had taken.

"thanks," she said.

Despite the cloudy weather in her face, the first thing out of her mouth was a word of gratitude, not anger, which made me feel all the guiltier.

"I'm really sorry. I can't believe I threw away something that important. I thought I was going to be buried alive in all that mail, so all I could think about was getting rid of it."

Hiruko then noticed the pile of dirty, dogeared paper on my desk.

"Oh, that's not the one we were looking for. It just seemed like it might be important, so I kept it." Afraid she'd think I'd let myself get distracted, rather than seriously looking for the paper she'd wanted to see, I quickly added, "Sorry. It just happened to catch my eye."

"content?"

"It's about some guy who thought he heard a message from outer space in his baby's babbling, followed its instructions, and disappeared. A while ago they found him. He's living in Rome under a false identity. He was suspected of being a terrorist, but they found out who he really was while they were interrogating him. He'd gotten a job under false pretenses, which made his employer angry, and he was criticized on moral grounds for leaving his wife and baby son, but he wasn't a terrorist, so they had to let him go. Fortunately, the media never got hold of the story, but his insomnia was so bad that he consulted a psychiatrist, who got very interested in his case and, with his permission, wrote up his conclusions in this paper."

Seeing Hiruko's eyes grow bright as she listened, I heaved a sigh of relief.

"I promised to make you one of my special hotdogs, didn't I?"

I put a bun in the oven, some oil in the frying pan, fished a dill pickle out the jar with my fingers, and cut it into paper-thin slices. I had some crisp, fried onion rings in the refrigerator. Along with my usual bottles of ketchup and mustard.

"These days lots of people think the hotdogs they sell at 7-Eleven taste really good. But the one I'm making for you now is traditional home cooking."

"at hokuetsu 7-Eleven *oden* sold."

"Odin? So, the boss man of the Norse gods was in charge of a lot more territory than I thought."

"odin not. *oden*."

Like two kids playing in the sandbox, we watched our hotdogs fry, spread mustard on the buns when they came out of the oven, rolled the hotdogs into the buns, making sure they didn't fall out, then sprinkled them with fried onions, put some ketchup on while licking our fingers, and finally, nibbled at the pickles we were lining up on top.

If I were to say that all my rendezvous took place at a hospital, people would think I was a tragic hero. Going to visit a lover with some fatal illness, or maybe accompanying my girlfriend on visits

to her sick mother. Our case is a little different, though. We use
the word "rendezvous" because there's nothing else to call it when
we've agreed to meet ahead of time. And there's always a special
sense of anticipation that makes it more like seeing a lover than a
friend. But I didn't think of Hiruko as a lover. Lovers always seem
to eventually fight and break up, and I never wanted to lose her.

"Rendezvous" is now officially included in the vocabulary of
Panska, Hiruko's homemade language. She created it by blending the Scandinavian languages in her own way, with words from
other languages mixed in. For instance, Hiruko calls jackets of all
kinds "anorak." To her, parka, windbreaker, blouson, and motorcycle jacket are all "mall language," but she loves the sound of the
Greenlandic word anorak. "Mall words," according to Hiruko,
stimulate the desire of people who wander around malls, looking for clothes they can buy at cut-rate prices because they're
going out of fashion.

"We'd better get going," I said. "Put on your anorak—it's rendezvous time!"

Maybe she thought I was teasing her, using Panska words that
way, because she slapped me on the arm, then linked her own in
mine and leaned against me.

"anorak equals beautiful word. *happi* i also like."

"Happy?"

"*happi* equals happy upper body."

"Which includes the head, with mouth and ears—that's what
makes it happy."

"susanoo to speak desires?"

"Probably so. Wanting to talk is only human."

"with who?"

"For now, I'd guess he wants to talk to us. You, me, Akash,
Nora, and Nanook, I mean. Friendship is a special kind of dashi
he'd forgotten the taste of until he met us. A small group of
friends, always hanging around together, does seem like high

school, though. That closeness is a luxury you lose when you grow up."

"susanoo with us desires to speak. with me, not."

"What makes you think so?"

"on his face is written."

"Are you sure?"

"person you desire to speak not?"

"No one I can think of. Oh, maybe one."

I made an M with the fingers of both hands, but realizing it looked more like boobs I quickly put them down.

"your mother? son with his mother desires to speak not? i equal Susanoo's mother?"

"Maybe you look like her."

Hiruko looked shocked, so I raised my eyebrows, as a sort of footnote to show I was joking.

"i susanoo's mother possibly resemble. susanoo with mother desires to speak not. instead of shouting, silence, or strange language speaking. hamlet."

Now it was my turn to be shocked. Hiruko must have noticed, because she looked worried.

"hamlet equals electric shock?"

"You could say that ... definitely."

"why?"

"Because my mother sometimes says I'm like Hamlet."

"praise?"

"Just the opposite."

As we talked, we strolled into the hospital, registered at the front desk, and got into the elevator. It was so old and creaky it felt like we might see a ghost on the way up. Hiruko's face clouded over again.

"susanoo with me desires to speak not."

"He hasn't spoken to anyone yet. So it's not just you he doesn't want to talk to."

"susanoo. to him many words i threw. like baseball pitcher. my catcher he was not."

"Pitcher? What's that? Sorry, but here in Europe hardly anyone knows about baseball."

"like izanagi to izanami peach-words i threw."

"That's a sport I know even less about."

"sport called myth. running, jumping, back and forth balls throwing."

"Myth—now that's something I'm interested in. But peaches are really expensive in Scandinavia. Throw three and you'll go broke. That's why Odin and the Valkyrie never throw peaches."

Our words fluttered through the air like butterflies until they bumped into a white door. Hospital doors are scary, because you never know what sort of strange new dimension is waiting for you on the other side.

CHAPTER 8   *Hiruko Speaks*

When we opened the door, the room seemed oddly dark. Near the back, Susanoo and Nanook were sitting face to face, like a patient and his doctor. Nanook swung around to look at us. I saw a shiny dark blue silk tie peeking out from the collar of his gleaming white coat — trying to look cool. You're just a kid, hanging around outside the university gate, acting like the kind of hotshot doctor people all over the world look up to. Nanook, this isn't the real you. Are you trying to be someone else? Or just playing doctor?

But a room like this wouldn't let you play, or even laugh. Even the air was much too serious. Places like this always make me want to run away. Secret organizations. The worship services of some religious cult. Has someone brainwashed you, Nanook? Knut must have felt as uncomfortable as I did, because he waved his hands as if fanning a bad smell away as he strode into the middle of the room, and when he spoke, I could tell he was trying to be funny.

"Sorry," he said, "I figured I'd be making a nuisance of myself, breaking in on you this way, but I've always been a nuisance — seems I can't be anything else."

"I wouldn't call your visit a nuisance," said Nanook with the tired, sarcastic smile of a much older man. "In fact, I'm quite grateful, because Susanoo needs aid from a countryman. Friends aren't nearly as useful as you hope they'll be, but countrymen can be, from time to time."

Knut seemed miffed at that remark about friends, but decided to keep on playing the clown. "Is that so?" he said, "Then I'd be happy to receive a word of praise for bringing Hiruko, who is Susanoo's countryman." Knut bowed like a butler in the movies.

I'd been staring at Susanoo's expressionless face, but thought that might be making him nervous, and turned away. That's when I saw Munch's painting on the wall. It was a poster for an exhibition. Three young women lined up along a handrail, viewed at an angle from behind. You can't see their faces. Looking at the soft folds of their long dresses, off-white, reddish orange, and green, I felt the cool Scandinavian summer caress my skin. The water they peer into, elbows on the handrail, is dark. Is it a river, or part of a lake? The land opposite, and the lush, heavy-looking tree standing there, are reflected in the dark water. In this water mirror, everything looks sad, shadowy. The handrail stretches out perpendicular to the land, but maybe due to perspective or something, the angle grows sharper as it recedes into the distance, the water piercing the girls' breasts like a knife as it nears the vanishing point. In summer, night is a long time coming. Look closely, and you can see a small yellow moon in the background. Deferring to the sun who doesn't want to set, the moon stays low behind the tree, waiting.

My back still turned, I heard Nanook's voice, speaking in English to Susanoo, from behind.

"Since Hiruko is here, we'll do a different kind of experiment today. Her native language is the same as yours."

"But Nanook," Knut teased, "you speak that language too, don't you? You don't really need Hiruko."

Clearing his throat, Nanook declared pompously, "Of course, I myself am capable of speaking their language. It's an ability I achieved through natural talent and hard work, yet still, it's a foreign language I learned as an adult. I am not indigenous. Hiruko, on the other hand, is a native, so the flavors and smells of the past contained in her speech are more likely to stimulate her countryman's memory."

Nanook, using words like "indigenous" and "native." Acting like I'm some kind of savage, about whose language he's delivering a paper in English at some international conference. I wanted to casually drop a pointed comment to make him see that, but I had more important things to do. I had to talk to Susanoo. I had to help him get back his ability to speak.

I took two or three deep breaths and opened my mouth. But there was a *kibi dango* caught in my throat, and I couldn't make a sound. Ridiculous! I'd never eaten a millet dumpling, so how could one have gotten into my throat? I never even *wanted* a millet dumpling. I have vague memories of a voice saying, "Come with me and I'll give you *kibi dango*." Some kids with matching rising-sun headbands of their motorcycle gang were trying to recruit new members, so they could invade another gang's territory. I screamed, "You're a dum-dum! I don't want your dumb dumplings!" and turned away. But before I knew it my friends were all happily chewing on the *kibi dango* they'd gotten. That was a dream I'd had long ago.

My back still turned to Susanoo, I swallowed hard, over and over, waiting for the *kibi dango* illusion to fade. When the dumpling was finally gone, the voice that came from the back of my throat was surprisingly loud.

"Who am I? That's the first thing I ask myself when I wake up in the morning. Which languages do I speak? Not that I've lost my memory, but my mind shuts down while I'm asleep, so I sort of drift off, then meet myself again when I wake up. Early morning—the time of day when you can't quite remember who you are. Who was I planning to talk to today? Lots of questions like that come bubbling up. But when I say, 'Good morning!' out loud, I feel relieved. Good morning! As a child, that was the only thing I knew to say. I said it right after I got up. I'd splash some water on my face, put mint-flavored paste on my tooth brush, brush my teeth, and say 'Good morning' to my mother and father— I'm sure you did, too. You said it to friends you met on the way to school, too. Or maybe you were too shy, and made do with a 'Hey!' When you were all together in the classroom, you said to your teacher in unison, 'Good morning.' When you start the day with 'Good morning,' you know you're all sharing the same time."

I still had my back turned, but I felt warmth moving through the air, and figured it must be Knut. Just as I'd thought, right behind my earlobe I heard his voice.

"What did you say just now?"

"good morning."

"Seems awfully long. How many syllables does it have?"

"good morning only not. environment also. good morning scenes. good morning memories."

"I've got a few of my own. I used to bite into a piece of bread, then suddenly remember to say good morning. My mother was always scolding me for talking with my mouth full. When I was in a hurry I'd jump on my bike with a pastry in my mouth, then look back and yell 'Good Morning,' except it came out more like 'Ooo.' Were you late for school, too? Did you bike there?"

"bicycle forbidden."

"So did your parents drive you to school?"

"parents' cars also forbidden."

"Why?"

"upper-class pretension forbidden."

"So, your country didn't have an upper class?"

"very high class we had. the sun. power of the sun."

"You mean solar energy!?" Knut sounded flabbergasted. I heard Susanoo chuckle. Or so I thought. Couldn't be. But the trace of laughter that grazed my ears like a slight breeze was neither Nanook's voice nor Knut's. I almost turned around but stopped myself. I'd go on talking this way, without looking at him. I felt like I was onto something. The image of the sun might be the key. That single word, *taiyō*, might not be enough, though. I'd take my time and see if I could smoke out whatever was hidden in Susanoo's mind. I began by listing everything I could think of that had to do with the sun.

"The spherical goddess who shows her round face above the horizon, over water, over land, over the mountains, shining the color of an orange or a pomegranate, to awaken the sleeping birds, to bring green back to the leaves that were black in the night, to return reds, blues, and yellows to the flowers, to warm the earth, to coax people outside."

"What did you just say?" Knut asked, very eager to know.

"long name for the sun."

"Does it really have such a long name?"

"different. my invention."

Nanook, the know-it-all, broke in.

"There's a goddess in Japanese myth with a long name," he said, "I remember reading about her. Starts with Ama, Ama ... what was it?"

"Amaterasu-Omikami."

"That's right. The *ama* at the beginning means 'rain,' right? As in *ama-kasa*—umbrella."

"No."

"Mild flavor, then? As in *amakuchi* curry?"

"No."

"Like the *ama* in the name of that island, Amami-Oshima?"

"No."

"*Ama* the word for nun?"

"No."

While finding Nanook's vocabulary genuinely impressive, I was starting to get irritated. He was so intelligent, yet rather than studying here he was, playing doctor, so self-satisfied, looking down on us—what a waste.

"*Ama* means the sky," I snapped, "Above all the other gods. And that god is a woman."

"Well, what do you know," he replied in a mocking tone: "A woman in the highest position. Sounds like that religion should be called feminism."

Nanook was perfectly fluent in both English and Danish. I had never once thought of imitating upper-class speech, or trying to sound elite. While traveling from one country to another, I picked up words I needed and discarded the rest to create Panska, my own homemade language. Always changing on the way, Panska came along with me. It was a language on the move, my perfect companion. But as I listened to Nanook speak English and Danish, I couldn't help wondering if people weren't looking down on my beloved Panska, seeing it as just one more "immigrant's broken speech." My voice wilted at the thought.

"Not feminism, but Shintō."

"The island of Shin?"

"*Tō* is not island, but a path. An autobahn for the gods. A highway with lots of head-on collisions. I want to make it safer."

"So, you're going to protect everyone. What are you, a traffic cop?"

"No, I'm the Sun Goddess."

As I said these words, I looked behind me. Susanoo was still in the same position, motionless.

An image of a demon suddenly turning his head to look behind him flashed through my mind. There was a game we used to play, called Somebody Fell Down. The demon was an essential role. You couldn't manage without one. That's why this demon couldn't be killed off like the ones in old stories. But you couldn't ignore him, either. Even if Susanoo was a demon, I'd have to face him. I spoke to him, imagining he was an old friend I'd just run into, and we were talking in a coffee shop.

"Remember that game, Somebody Fell Down? The demon

would put his hands over his eyes and say, very slowly, 'Some-body Fell Down.' While he was speaking, the other kids were allowed to move. But the minute he turned around, they had to stop. It was fun to see everybody freeze like a video image when someone presses PAUSE. Maybe you'd be caught with one foot in midair. All the kids who moved, or even wobbled a little to keep their balance, were taken hostage by the demon. They lined up beside him, holding hands, waiting to be rescued. The other kids would gradually edge nearer, and when they saw the demon look away for a moment, someone who was close enough would bring his hand down like a karate chop to 'cut the chain,' and the hostages would let go of each other's hands. That meant they were free. You remember that game, don't you?"

Back then, we thought only of rescuing the hostages. Not that we'd be rewarded for it—in fact, you could get caught your-self—but even so, we were willing to take the risk. No one had to coax us into it with millet dumplings. And nobody said, "It's your own fault you got caught," and went home, leaving their friends in the demon's lair.

Speaking of hostages, I remember an incident from before I came to study in Scandinavia. One of my classmates got a job with a local newspaper after high school. The major papers were losing readers because all their articles were irritatingly vague and hard to grasp, like bits of gristle caught between your mo-lars. On the other hand, there were so many newspapers online that it was hard to find one you could trust. As soon as one got a reputation for being reliable a fake one with the same name would pop up to get in the way. News junkies turned their at-tention to print newspapers in rural areas, and even city dwellers started subscribing to them. Around this time, my classmate got a job with *Hokuetsu Pravda,* a local paper that now had readers nationwide. As an investigative reporter, he drove his jeep back and forth between Russia and the Middle East, until finally, he was captured by a terrorist organization. They demanded his government pay a heavy ransom. "He knew how dangerous it was," said many among the general public, "but he went anyway. Why should our taxes be wasted on such an irresponsible, un-patriotic young man, who writes for a newspaper that criticizes his own government?" The government issued an official state-ment: "As we understand that recently hostages are often killed when the ransom is paid, for safety's sake, we have decided not to pay." This breathtakingly logical statement, utterly free of con-tradiction, must have renewed the public's confidence in their government, for not only was the ransom not paid, but there were no antigovernment demonstrations. And yet the hostage was not killed. From some unknown location, he hacked into a government site to send a bold message: "I have no regrets about leaving a country that does nothing to save me. I plan to work as a translator, providing information to this terrorist organization. I am not a spy. I simply want to make sure that accurate reporting flows in many directions." In response to a government official who called him a despicable traitor who had sold out his coun-try, he replied, "I sell neither my country nor chestnuts. All I'm doing is peddling a few pistachios on the open market." At the time, the word "pistachio" sounded so funny that I laughed until I cried ...

"Somebody Fell Down," I chanted.

Susanoo still sat there, expressionless, so I tried again, but this time, it seemed to me that the Somebody in the title might actually have been Daruma. Bodhi-Daruma, so not somebody, but some-bodhi.

"What's that? What are you saying?" Eager to know, Knut enclosed my elbow with his hand and gently shook it back and forth. A fragrance gradually spread through my nasal membrane. Knut smelled like cedar, lavender, and freshly baked bread, all mixed together.

"children's game," I said, not even trying to hide my smile. "somebody fell down. or maybe daruma fell down. some-bodhi-daruma."

"Who is Daruma?"

"for many years zazen sat. legs and arms fell off. he who reaches. he who polishes. bodhi-daruma."

I often picture Chinese characters in my mind as I speak. The 達 (daru) and 磨 (ma) of Daruma, for instance, which mean, respectively, "reach" and "polish." But Knut was different. He gave voice only to letters of the alphabet. Not 達磨, but Daruma. Not 鮨, but sushi. He probably didn't know what I was thinking about when he said, "I once went to a restaurant called Daruma. I had ark shell sushi there. But anyway, does Daruma have anything to do with karma?"

"both from india come."

"India?"

Suddenly, we heard a whoop from an unexpected direction. The door was open, and standing just outside it was Akash in his red sari. Nanook, struggling to look serious yet barely suppressing a smile, motioned for him to come in quickly and close the door. Akash was red. So are Daruma folk dolls, although the darker, warmer shade they're painted in is different from the bright crimson of Akash's sari. Daruma's round, squat shape, too, is just the opposite of Akash. I would have liked to ask Akash if he knew Daruma, since they're both from India. I'd have to speak English, though, which would take my mind off Susanoo, so I just nodded a greeting to him.

"I was surprised to find out that Daruma was Indian," I said to Susanoo. "I didn't think he was from so far away. When I was a child, curry was my favorite food. And not just me—everybody liked it. Was it your favorite too? It seems strange that Daruma and curry, a person and food that've been around since we were little, should both be Indian. Maybe when people travel to faraway places, they're really trying to get back to their childhood."

No matter what I said to Susanoo, his face didn't move at all. Knut or Akash would have reacted immediately, their eyes brightening. They were a lot more fun to talk to. But I'd just have to keep slogging on with sullen Susanoo. Stubborn old cuss, who'd never open his mouth, or do anything else for that matter, unless he wanted to. I was his daughter-in-law, the housewife charged with keeping the family together, so angry I was throwing plates against the wall in my head. Was I now stuck in this housewife role? We'd been treating Susanoo like a friend our own age, but what if he was much older? I mean, *really* old. And if he had trouble making conversation when he was young, it would be all the harder for him now to join in with a comment here and there, or laugh when everyone else did. He looked like a lonely young man, but what if he wasn't—what if he's just an old geezer?

"I hope you don't mind my asking, but how old are you? You look awfully young, but I wonder if you might not actually be older than we are. Is talking to younger people too much trouble?"

I tried to imagine Susanoo looking relieved, admitting that he was actually in his fifties. Or sixties, maybe, or even seventies or eighties. That would never happen. A teacher I had in elementary school encouraged us to talk to stubborn old men. "Of course, it's more fun to talk to kids your own age," she said. "Just say the name of a singer you both like, and you feel like you understand each other. But if you try speaking to a grumpy old man whose voice you've never heard, something nice might happen." "What sort of thing?" someone asked. "Well, it's hard to say, but you could find a whole crop of persimmons on a tree you thought was dead, and then get lots of really cool visitors, and after that, a sick relative might suddenly get well—a sort of chain of happy events." "But Miss, that's what happens in folktales after someone does a good deed." Memories echoed through my head. That teacher always told us to be kind to "the old folks," but I never knew who she was talking about. Did she mean someone like Susanoo, who had no distinguishing characteristics other than being taciturn, obstinate, and generally hard to get along with?

Akash whispered something to Knut, perhaps because he didn't want to intrude while I was talking to Susanoo. I leaned in their direction, all the more anxious to hear. Smiling over at me, Knut told Akash, "Hiruko is a storehouse full of words. She's like a shaman—once she starts talking, she can't stop. I couldn't possibly teach you all the words that come streaming out of her mouth."

"One would be enough."

"Okay, how about *ohayō*."

"*Ohayō*?"

"The word you use more than any other. You've been saying it every morning since you were a child."

"Not much meaning to it, though. Or regional flavor, either. Say *Ohayō* in any language and it feels like it's your own."

He had a point. Wasn't there some word that would bring back memories neither a Scandinavian nor an Indian would have, with a fragrance peculiar to our part of the world? A Chinese character, perhaps?

"The character for morning has a moon in it," I said to Susanoo. "Morning, but the moon's there, on the right side. Didn't that ever seem strange to you?"

He said nothing.

"I asked my teacher about that once, and she said 月 isn't always the moon. Sometimes it's a simpler form of 肉, which means meat. But moon and meat make an odd combination, don't you think? Would you want to eat a moon steak?"

Susanoo seemed to be on the opposite side of an invisible wall where my voice couldn't reach him, not even as a slight trembling in the air.

"Sometimes the moon is still in the sky when the sun comes up. A white moon that looks like paper."

As usual, silence.

"When morning begins, night isn't over yet. Morning is when day and night overlap. That's why the moon is still there. Morning is dark. Bright, and yet dark. Are you the moon?"

For the first time, I saw Susanoo's shoulder twitch. A tiny movement that started deep in his gut, so I could feel it reverberating in my own body. I'd asked him if he was the moon without thinking, but maybe that was exactly what I needed to do — just let the words come out. To stop holding back, but keep on talking as if I were running blindfolded.

"You are the moon, aren't you. Just as I thought. Tsukio, or Tsukitarō — Moon Man. Bet there were no kids in your class at school with names like that. But there was always an Asako — Morning Child. Without an Asako, morning never comes. Such a bright, refreshing name. Bet there wasn't anyone named Noon Child — Hiruko — in your class, either. But why not? After all, noon is when things slow down, and you can relax. Hiruko's my name, too, but the Hiru part means leech, not noon. Too bad. Leeches are bloodsuckers. Slimy, too. Does my name put you off?"

Though I was sure he didn't understand, Knut looked as if he was breathing in every single word.

"Slugs, worms, sea cucumbers. Slippery, slimy, clammy, gooey. Creatures with skin that looks like it would dissolve in water. Leeches have soft bodies, too, but at least they have a shape. And speaking of shapes, how about *magatama*? You remember — those curved beads from prehistoric times. Like unborn children, curled up inside their mothers. I was curled up in a tiny space, too, before I was born, like a *magatama*. Then suddenly one day I was pushed out, and when that fleshy wall around me disappeared, there was nothing to hold me — I went all shapeless and floppy. The outside air stung my skin but did nothing to support me. And no matter how long they waited, I never took on a clear shape. That's why they threw me away, set me adrift on the water."

The moment I said, "threw me away," all the strength went out of my body, and I crumpled down onto the floor. Knut squatted beside me and put his hand on my shoulder.

"Are you all right?" he asked comfortingly.

I finally managed to pull myself up, and sat down on the chair Nanook offered me. Staring straight at me, he said solemnly, "So you were the one they got rid of."

"I was abandoned?"

"That's right."

"What're you saying?" asked Knut. I had never heard him sound so angry.

"When there are several children in a family, there's always one who's cast aside. The one that didn't turn out right. There was something wrong with Hiruko, so they threw her into the sea to drift, and finally, she reached Denmark. Isn't that so?"

"What're you talking about, Nanook? You know nothing of Hiruko's past."

"There was one in our family, too. The first child, whose arms and legs never worked right. She fell into the sea and drowned. When my father took her fishing one day, she crawled up over the edge of the boat and fell in. She was like a slug—never learned to walk but got very good at crawling."

There was a question in Knut's eyes. Though my head was a blank, I felt I had to answer it, so slowly, carefully, I began to speak.

"abandonment i remember not. house-supporting pillar i was. in mother's womb, the first, most precious child i was. my parent's treasure. two brothers after me were born. one slow as a turtle, one violent as a typhoon. mother cried."

Though I'd said them myself, these words upset me. For this was not my own story. It wasn't me who was abandoned, nor was I the one with two younger brothers. I was telling someone else's story. I'd never had a brother. So why did this story slip out so easily? At that moment, something entirely unexpected happened. Susanoo's face softened like a cube of sugar dropped in hot tea. His dark lips parted to show his white teeth.

"Finally, you're telling me your story."

That was definitely Susanoo, speaking directly to me. His voice, though hardly quiet, sounded as if it was coming from a speaker planted somewhere in the furniture.

"It's you who don't talk—not me. Sure, you've said a lot of words to me. But you haven't told me anything you didn't want to say."

My lips were clenched together so I couldn't open my mouth. My cheeks and neck felt cold and numb. Only my eyes moved, darting here and there. I was like a broken robot. Knut and Akash stared at me, open-mouthed. Nanook, in his white coat, was licking his lips. I kept seeing his red tongue, off to the side. Susanoo's voice was cool and quiet, not at all like what I'd been expecting.

"You were the eldest daughter, were you not?"

"Yes, I was the first born," I replied, adopting his oddly formal way of speaking, "cherished and loved by my parents."

"You were the young mistress in a household with servants—three, in fact. Unfortunately, your hair was thin and wispy, and the silks and brocades girls of your class wore did not suit you. What's more, you didn't know how to bend adults to your will with a charming smile. In short, you were not a sweet little girl."

I remembered how much I'd hated proper, feminine clothes. Even so, until I was about eight or so, I'd worn dresses, posing uncomfortably for photographs, my lips twisted into a smile. On weekends when I was in junior high, I'd dress in big, baggy overalls like house painters wear, with rubber boots even when it wasn't raining. I could never manage an ingratiating smile. Even when I thought I was smiling, my parents would ask me why I was so angry.

"As you did well at school, and came from a wealthy family, you surely have no memories of being bullied. Still, you were abandoned by your parents, were you not? You were never cute—more like a leech than a little girl—so they threw you into the sea."

"That can't be. If I were actually abandoned, that would mean the parents who raised me weren't my bird parents."

I must have been very upset, because I blurted out "bird parents" when I'd meant to say "birth parents." Susanoo suddenly fell silent, thinking hard. An uneasy feeling spread through me.

Of course, I wasn't abandoned. My parents bought me whatever I asked for, like an expensive collection of "Insects from the Last Century" or a very fine astronomical telescope. I don't remember them ever yelling at me. While I was studying, my mother would bring me sweets from a famous confectioner, or a plate neatly piled with freshly peeled peaches or plums. My father was in the oil business, and my mother was a licensed instructor of ikebana. I can't remember which school, though. Yet when they looked at me, I sometimes detected a hint of despair in their eyes. That I definitely remember. As a child, I didn't understand the reason, and while I was absorbed in my books, or insects, or the stars, I forgot all about it. Until one Sunday just after I started junior high school, when a family of three—old friends of my father's, it seemed—came over for a visit. The woman's taste was similar to my mother's. Her slender frame was decked out in a silk dress casually decorated with small, shiny pieces of jewelry. She talked like my mother, and they used the same makeup, too. Yet though the mothers obviously had a lot in common, the daughters were shockingly different. The other girl was perfectly turned out, her voluminous hair tied in a pony tail to reveal the already sensuous nape of her neck. The arms below the sleeves of a simple dress that set off her youth seemed to glow from within, right down to her perfectly trimmed nails. Every inch of her was polished, like an expensive bauble on display. Her refined way of talking, punctuated by the occasional trill of laughter, the way her eyes narrowed as she gently leaned against her mother or father, gazing fondly up at them — she looked exactly like the privileged daughters you see in the movies. The satisfaction in her father's eyes as he looked down on her. The mother, from time to time anxiously surveying the girl for signs of imperfection, then always looking relieved. I knew my parents were quietly observing this trio. I saw the envy in their eyes. This was the kind of daughter they'd wanted — not an awkward girl who looked more like a spindly young boy. Afraid I'd start to cry, I rushed out of the room, stepped down into the garden in my stocking feet, and jumped into the pond. An impulsive suicide. Muddy water splashed up, staining my T-shirt. The water only came halfway up my thighs. My jeans, heavy with moisture, pulled my hips down into the water. The carp darting around me in surprise were undoubtedly far more valuable than I was. Since coming to Europe, I had forgotten all about that day. So, this had been my "abandonment." It was a pond, though, not the ocean.

"I did actually spend some time in the water. But not because I was thrown in, and I pulled myself out. When my brothers were born, I fulfilled my role as their older sister. One did poorly at school, and the other was violent. No one else could do anything with them, but I loved them, and took care of them."

Susanoo burst out laughing. It was dry, unpleasant laughter.

"You were shocked when they were born. You discovered that your parents had old-fashioned ideas about boys being more important than girls. That was such an unpleasant surprise that it made you want to leave the country, did it not?"

I was feeling more and more uneasy. Then, a knock on the door interrupted my thoughts. In a deep, dignified voice, Nanook said, "Come in," and when the door slowly opened, in walked Nora. I was relieved, just to have another woman in the room. I wanted to talk to her. About when my brothers were born. Surely she'd understand how I felt. But she didn't even seem to see me.

"Is this true?"

Her first question was directed at Nanook. I caught her meaning even though she was speaking German. She delivered her line without even bothering to say 'Hello.' A bold performance. All her entrances reminded me of a diva on an opera stage. As soon as he heard her voice, Nanook shrank down like a turtle into the collar of his white coat and started mumbling a response. Her chin thrust out, Nora bombarded him with words. Nanook knitted his brow, pursed his lips like a rebellious teenager and raised his voice. Their verbal fencing match had begun. Knut and Akash listened, nodding in an "Oh, so that's it" sort of way. After a while, Knut realized that I was being left out, and gave me a brief summary.

"Nanook apparently switched personalities with Dr. Velmer. They originally decided on a time limit, but now they both want to extend the transfer indefinitely. Nora's dead set against it."

Is it possible to switch personalities? Well, I had just told someone else's story as a memory from my own childhood, so two people must be able to exchange what's inside of them.

Susanoo then flung his arms out and said, "You are a wolf in sheep's clothing," to Nanook in English.

Though she looked shocked to hear Susanoo speak, Nora said nothing. Nanook, on the other hand, seemed offended at this sudden criticism from a man he had been treating as a patient up to now. In the most affected English he could manage, he gave a credible-sounding counterargument.

"You call me a wolf, but that certainly can't be said of Velmer. Yet now that I think of it, perhaps that's exactly what he is. It all depends on your point of view. The real problem is that because human beings misunderstand wolves, they label them dangerous. Wolves are not inherently vicious. It's just that they make no attempt to appeal to people, or make themselves likeable the way dogs do. In short, they say exactly what they think. Do you find that problematic?"

"And can you tell Nora exactly what you think?"

There was another knock on the door. Who could it be? We were all here, weren't we? A mist of confusion clouded our faces.

CHAPTER 9   *Susanoo Speaks*

That was Velmer knocking on the door. No one said, "Come in," but he opened the door anyway, waltzed right into the middle of the room and looked around, beaming.

"I see you're all here. Welcome to Paradise." (He must have meant "hospital.") "Friends really are a treasure, aren't they?" he said, not noticing how tense the atmosphere was, or maybe just pretending. "No matter how far away or how busy they are, they'll drop everything to come visit you when you're sick."

Vapid nonsense, not like Velmer at all. But wait—this was Nanook's personality talking. It was still Velmer's face, but even when he was spouting sentimental drivel, he looked so pure, so naïve, that it was hard to attack him.

Just when I had everyone where I wanted them, afraid to hear what I'd say next, Velmer comes in and all my hard work goes *poof*. I'd have to give him a jab—nah, better to really stab him:

"Dr. Velmer, aren't you ashamed of yourself?"

I could tell he was shocked. I've got him, I thought, but then he came out with, "You've recovered? You can talk now?"

It was hearing me speak for the first time that surprised him, not what I'd said.

If I let things go on this way, I'd be forced back into that old doctor-patient routine. I cleared my throat to buy myself an extra three seconds, then relaxed and let him have it:

"We'll talk about my loss of speech later. Being a doctor, you see everyone as a patient. A sort of occupational disease, you might say, ha, ha. I'm sure you've heard of Doctor Faust, who sold his soul to the Devil to get his youth back. Is that why you made that bargain with Nanook—because you wanted to be young again?"

I skip the trailer and show them the main feature: their weaknesses full-size on the big screen—it rattles them, and unscrews the locks and hinges on the door to what's called the soul. Then, when all the spirits hovering outside come blasting in, the soul's original landlord gets so mixed up she can't tell the difference between herself and the invaders, and ends up tossing everything into the same pot—other people's life stories, bits of myth, her own memories—which she stirs as she starts to speak. The mechanism that tells her what to keep secret, or how much to hold back, is disabled.

My method worked very well with Hiruko. Though she doesn't seem malleable, she was probably so eager to talk to someone in her native tongue that she forgot to protect herself. This time, Velmer, crafty as a shape-shifter from the old stories, was the calm vessel, but he was also filled with Nanook's plump, frisky, sea otter of a soul, so shaking him up enough to get a confession out of him wouldn't be easy. Using force wouldn't get me anywhere, but I also couldn't let go of the reins or he'd get away and I'd have to start all over again. Making sure my shoulders stayed nice and loose, I narrowed my eyes and continued my assault.

"Aren't you ashamed, selling your soul to the Devil that way?"

I thought I saw Velmer's pupils dilate. I was sure he'd be furious, but he laughed out loud.

"The Devil? No one tries to keep the Devil away in this day and age. That's because we know how much fun life can be with a devil inside us. Lust, greed, ambition. These are the devils of modern man, but if he's rational enough to keep them under control, the stronger his desires the better. Successful people of both sexes keep their devils on a leash, like pets. Only members of some weird cult are still afraid of the Devil."

This talk about cults put me on edge. Not that I belonged to one, but I felt like he'd seen something I wanted to hide, which worried me. He must have seen me flinch, because now he seemed to be hitting his stride.

"To be perfectly honest, my reason has failed me from time to time. When my desires get the better of me, I do foolish things."

"Like what?" I fired back.

"When I was a boy, there was a minicar I absolutely had to have, so I stole it."

"Is that all? Pretty puny devil if you ask me."

"And as an intern, I stole some morphine from the hospital. But as soon as I was found out, I apologized, and that was that. Here, one's sins are all forgiven. That's European culture for you. Isn't that why you came here?"

This was veering off in a bad direction. He'd taken me for a refugee from a country where if I sinned I'd have to cut my belly open, or slice a joint off my little finger, or be put to death. He'd got it all wrong. There was a death penalty back in the homeland. But that had nothing to do with me. I'd never set foot anywhere near crime or criminals. At least I don't think so.

"But you really mustn't worry," Velmer added, kindly wrinkles forming around his eyes. "There's nothing dangerous, or devilish, about this bargain I've made with Nanook. It's simply a roleplaying game between a young man who wants to improve his position in society, and a middle-aged man who'd like to revitalize himself, body and mind, so that he can fall in love again."

"Taking someone else's youth like medicine—isn't that doping? Aren't you ashamed?"

"Doping ... An interesting way to put it. But love is hardly the Olympics. No chemical enhancement is involved. Nor have I had an operation. After all, brain transplants are a medical impossibility. I've merely analyzed Nanook's personality in order to imitate it, which is acting, not medicine. What I'm doing is just like an actor studying the role of Hamlet, who then rehearses it so that he can perform in front of an audience."

For some reason, Hiruko looked over at Knut and whispered, "Hamlet." He shook his head hard, like he was trying to get rid of that name, then broke into the conversation:

"Susanoo, you used violent mind games to break into Hiruko's heart. Dr. Velmer's your next victim—you're treating him the same way."

I'd been expecting something like this from Knut, so I knew just what to say.

"You're wrong about that. I never attacked Hiruko with words. She'd been acting like some kind of shaman, trying to get to some memory we had in common. All I did was listen. You should know that—you were watching the whole time. She poured words down on my head like a kettle of boiling water, trying get into my memories. That's a kind of brainwashing."

The word "brainwashing" put him on the defensive.

"Now you're the one who's got it wrong. All she did was talk about anything she could think of, to help you get your speech back. And since you didn't answer, she had to keep on, all by herself."

"So, if a guy doesn't say anything, does that make it all right to pour boiling words over his head?"

"No, it doesn't. I'm sorry—that's not what I meant. I apologize for Hiruko. But if it bothered you that much, why didn't you protest? When all this time you could talk..."

"I wanted her to start talking about something important. I'd been watching her, waiting till she got through all the mythical stuff, and all the happy childhood memories, and came closer to something that really hurt."

"Why would you want that?"

I almost blurted out a line from *Because I Control the Night*, a manga I liked as a kid, but decided not to, and instead said, "I hate small talk. I want people to speak from their souls. But since I can't force them, I use the power of suggestion."

"You mean hypnosis?"

"No, that's a specialized skill—I don't have that training. I just sit there, listening. And when they hit on something important, I point it out."

"By 'something important,' I assume you mean something you can use to delve into a person's weaknesses. When you find it, you react, but the rest of the time, you act as if they aren't even there. That's what I mean by psychological violence."

"But what about you—when you're talking to Hiruko, all you think about is how much fun you're having."

"I choose topics we're both interested in. We're in love with language. Words, words, and more words."

"So, you're just two kids, playing with words instead of toys?"

"What sort of weighty topic would you like to hear us talk about?"

"Well, sex for instance. You can't bear the idea of your mother having sexual desire. Have you discussed that with Hiruko?"

That shut him up for a while but he soon rallied and threw back the curveball.

"There are two types of vicious rumors," he said: "One you can buy cheap in a supermarket, and the other you make yourself. You've just started one of the homemade kind."

"Thanks for the recognition. Actually, it's not so much a rumor as my personal theory. I've only heard you and your mother talk once, but that was plenty."

"You mean that time in Arles? Forget about that."

"It was a very interesting mother-son conversation."

"My mother has preconceived ideas, but she really doesn't know anything about me—what I'm thinking, or what I do every day. That's only natural, since I don't tell her. I don't know anything about her, either, and frankly, I don't care."

"You care all right. But you're afraid if you heard her going on about her love life, you'd remember the past, and that's too painful."

"There's no way my mother could have a new lover. And even if she did, I wouldn't care. Do you really think I'd be jealous of my mother's boyfriend? That's ridiculous."

"I'm not saying you're jealous. But you hate the idea of her having sex: you don't want to see women as sexual beings. That's why you're with Hiruko—she's from a country where sexual desire has disappeared."

Knut's pale cheeks were now peach pink. He clammed up completely. And if he didn't start talking again, I couldn't get at him, so I decided to drop Hiruko for a while, and try a different angle.

"You know, Knut, you're a very nice young man. You're laid back, and women like that. You weren't born that way, though. It's a pose you put on, to keep from being like your mother's lovers, all greasy with lust and greed."

"You may have a point there."

He conceded so easily my attack lost its bite. I'd have to crank up the nastiness, put on the pressure, see if I could get him to pop.

"A boy only thinks his father's a hero until the age of five or so. You're stuck there, aren't you? Your ideal was still intact when he left. So, you think of him as intelligent, sensitive, reserved . . ."

"I don't remember my father at all. I don't even know why he disappeared."

"You have your suspicions though—you just don't want to face them. He joined some religious cult, or was lured away by a terrorist organization, or fell in love with another woman, and chased after her to a faraway country. Whatever it was, something outside was far more attractive than his little boy at home."

If Knut had been as skilled at this as I am, he would have fired back, "You've got plenty to say about me, but you cried every day after your mother disappeared." After Mom left, I didn't study or play, either, for a long time. All I remember from those days was this dream I kept having, over and over again. My mother's vanity table was always cluttered with brushes and cans of hairspray, so in the dream, I'm shocked to see nothing on it. Even the mirror is covered with a black velvet cloth. I know something's wrong, so I run to my big sister's house, wondering the whole way why I suddenly have a sister. When I get there and bang on the door, she comes out dressed like a man, with fake whiskers and thick eyebrows drawn on. Before I can open my mouth, she screams, "You think the oldest son still inherits everything, don't you? You stupid fossil!" And she slaps me hard on the cheek. Though it doesn't really hurt, knowing my own sister doesn't trust me makes me so sad I cry all the way down a dark alley until I get to the very end, where I see a sign for the cabaret "Kingdom of Night." That's where my mother works. I climb down a moldy-smelling staircase. At the back is a room lit with red light, where Mom's sitting on an old sofa. Yellow foam rubber bulges out of cracks in the upholstery. The sofa smells like a dog left out in the rain. I'm relieved to see Mom alive. But she ignores all my questions. Doesn't even look at me. The odor turns sour, like rotting fish. Then it hits me—maybe the stench isn't coming from the sofa, but from human flesh. Terrified, I run back up the stairs, bawling all the way, and when I come out into the bright light, I wake up. There were small changes depending on the night, but it was basically the same dream. Around that time, I always kept my head down at school so the other kids would leave me alone. I hardly talked to my father, either. I couldn't tell him about rancid nightmares while he's quietly working on his robots. I'd collected so much pain inside I was sure pus must be leaking out through my skin, making me smell bad. Why else would the girls in my class keep giving me strange looks? I'd suddenly look up to catch the one who was staring at me, only to find that no one was. But I couldn't get rid of the feeling that people were watching me, laughing at me. I had one girl in particular in my sights. She always took big steps when she walked by my seat, to show off as much of her thigh as she could. She did it all the time, to tempt me, and I couldn't let her get away with it. I got so mad I ambushed her one day after school. I can't remember exactly what happened, but it must have been awful. If Knut were to mention that now, I'd throw up my hands and run out of the room. Fortunately, he doesn't know how to get at my weaknesses, though god knows I have plenty. Anyway, this was no time to be getting lost in my childhood memories. I hurried back to Knut's.

"You tell yourself you were so young when he left that you know nothing about him, but you remember him all right."

He looked surprised, but didn't object.

"Are you sure about that?" he said, sounding very humble. "You may know more about him than I do, so why don't you tell me?"

"It's not my place. Try talking about him yourself. Start with a lie if you like—if you say it as if you believe it, you'll get to the truth when you're least expecting to."

"What do you mean?"

"Make something up. I'm always cooking up stories in my head about what I did before I got here, then erasing them and starting over again. A total lie is fine. How about this? When you were little, your mother fell in love with another man. He was a sly, sneaky bastard, who tricked your father into leaving home."

"What sort of trick would make a man desert his family?"

"Use your imagination. Say he talked your dad into joining some organization. A group that … let's see … started out with a noble purpose but then got radicalized and went off the rails—how's that? Let's say they were working for world peace, protesting against arms manufacturers. But when nobody listened to their appeals about how destructive bombs are, they got more and more irritated. Finally, they started sending pictures through the mail, directly addressed to all the employees of a certain munitions plant. One photo every day, of children covered with blood, injured when their homes were bombed."

"That sounds scary. My father would never go after people in such a creepy way."

"Maybe not. So, how about this? There was civil war in a certain country, and your father was asked to go there, to help the kids whose parents were killed. He suddenly remembered that he'd always wanted to help people, and off he went."

"My father wasn't an idealist, and had no interest in politics, either."

"See—you *do* remember him. You convinced yourself that you didn't, but that's not possible."

"You're right. Some memories are definitely coming back now. Strange, isn't it?"

"Or how's this? Your father was refined, liberal—a real intellectual, who fed you, changed you, and always did his share of the housework. He hardly ever argued with his wife. Yet every morning, he woke up with an empty hole in his heart, as big as a full moon. One night, he dropped in at a bar for a drink, and started talking to the man next to him. They really saw eye to eye, and the conversation continued late into the night. When the man suggested they go traveling together, he left and never came back."

Just then, a grating sound gave me such a jolt that I nearly jumped out of my seat. With those skinny arms of his, Akash was pulling a chair over for Nora. Then, he sat down next to her. So that's all it was—a chair scraping across the floor. Don't scare me like that. I thought it was a ghost. Akash seemed ready for a fun afternoon, watching the rest of the play. I couldn't have him so cheerful and relaxed. Because this was an utterly dark drama. Besides, there were too many people in the room. I perform best when pitted against a single person. I couldn't very well ask Knut to stay and order everyone else out of the room, though. Knut stood there in a daze, gently swaying back and forth like a tall tree in a storm. Nanook and Velmer had their arms confidently folded across their chests, while Hiruko leaned back into the sofa behind them, looking very small. She seemed to be resting, after using up all her energy, but don't let scrawny little women like that fool you. They can be near death any number of times then spring back again, stronger than before. If I wasn't careful, she'd be treating me like her little brother. Knut opened his eyes, gawked around at everyone, and apologized.

"Sorry—I've been talking too much about myself. There's no sense talking about my father at a time like this."

"I don't mind at all," said Akash in that clear voice that carried so well. "I want to know everything about you." That was what I wanted to hear. With a thankful nod, Knut went on.

"I think I remember seeing my father's back. He'd be washing the dishes, or taking clean clothes out of the dryer, helping with the housework. And I'd watch him from behind. When I spoke to him, he never answered. He'd finish with the housework, then go out, looking really happy. I always wished he'd stay and play with me."

"One time you went after him, didn't you?"

"I was still pretty small, so I usually didn't go out by myself."

"But one time your dad said he'd take you someplace fun, and you were overjoyed, weren't you?"

"Maybe so. It was a Sunday afternoon, but for some reason my mother was sleeping in her bedroom. My dad took me somewhere on a bus."

"The town square was crowded with grownups, and on the table where people registered there were pamphlets, and juice they were passing out for free, along with flags and balloons floating in the sky, and music playing, and small as you were, watching your father talk to everyone there as if they were all old friends seemed odd somehow."

"Now that you mention it, I do remember something like that."

"One woman was especially nice to you, and so friendly with your father that she seemed like family, and that made you feel like you'd seen something you shouldn't have, didn't it?"

"Yes, that's right."

"Be careful, Knut, don't let him brainwash you."

That was Nora's voice. I can't stand people who interrupt my work. All this time I'd been cool and collected, but now I was so angry I marched straight toward her, raising my fist in the air. Akash got to his feet and stood in front of me, blocking my way.

"Don't do anything rash," he said. "Haven't you learned to control your anger?"

I couldn't let him have the upper hand.

"What's this? One minute you're turning into a woman, and now you're suddenly Superman?"

"Just a while ago you mentioned a country where sexual desire's disappeared—that's your country, isn't it?"

"What of it?"

"It hasn't disappeared in your case, but simply undergone a chemical reaction, and changed into the desire to control everyone around you."

"And what about you, in love with that body of yours, dressed in women's clothes."

Nora, who had a much heftier build than Akash, stood up and started lecturing me in German. I used to be pretty good at German, but now I couldn't catch her meaning. She had a steady voice, though, rather low for a woman—a voice I could trust. Like one I heard long ago, so different from my mother's cheery, seductive way of talking. And I remembered too suddenly getting serious about my studies and turning over a new leaf, you could say. That's right—it was that young German woman who came to teach us English. Her voice, like a big, sturdy cargo boat, had carried me all the way to Europe. If I'd stayed in my home town, I probably would have been a teacher, attracting girls with a few sweet words, giving them advice that sounded sincere enough, skillfully using words, first to hurt, then to comfort them until they'd do what I wanted, and without even touching them, I'd feel satisfied. But no teaching career materialized: instead, the German woman with the deep voice gave me a boat so I could leave the country. Then I got myself a normal girlfriend, and we dated in the usual way. But how could an English teacher from Germany have gotten me a boat? There was something wrong with this memory, too.

"I'm so glad you can talk now, really I am": this time, I understood what Nora was saying. She sounded concerned, like a big sister.

"We're all so happy to finally hear your voice, Susanoo."

And that was Hiruko, from her corner of the room. A while before, she'd been too tired to even open her mouth, but hearing Nora must have bucked her up, and now she was fine again. But wait—Hiruko doesn't know German, does she? Yet now the two of them were joined together so tight there was no chance they'd misunderstand each other. It was like having *two* older sisters, too depressing to bear. Nora's so tall I can't look down on her, but if I turn my face up it makes me feel a little bigger. I flared my nostrils at her, and felt like I'd got my own back, just a little.

"You came in late, Nora: you don't know what's going on. It wasn't me that couldn't speak—it was you guys. Oh, you were talking, all right. But you were just opening and closing your mouths, without saying anything important. That's true of you, too, Nora. What's most important to you? Your relationship with Nanook. And he took off to get away from you. Doesn't that make you sad?"

"Is that true, Nanook?" she asked, ignoring me, turning to him. "Are you running away from me?" She sounded serious.

"No, not really," he calmly replied. "I just stepped outside for a breath of fresh air. When I was cooped up in your place, I felt so useless I could hardly breathe. Now that I'm enjoying life, I don't really need a lover. I have money, and a position here in the hospital."

"Not a job you earned yourself, though."

"Play a role long enough, and it fits like your favorite sweater."

"Sure, but do you remember that story about the man arrested for fraud? He'd never studied medicine, but worked for years as a doctor in a hospital. I'm sure the role fit him like his favorite sweater—how else could he have gotten away with it? But Nanook, do you want to live like that, as a con man?"

Velmer let out a strangely flat laugh.

"What she's asked you is an awfully weighty question," said Akash from his seat in the audience, "so you'd better take your time answering it. In the meantime, I'd like to hear more about Knut."

As the director of this play, I couldn't allow him to take charge: "How about it, Knut? If you feel like I'm brainwashing you, you don't have to say anything more."

"No, I'm all right. That place my father took me when I was little wasn't at all like a secret meeting, not dark or gloomy. The sun was shining, lots of red helium balloons flew overhead, and all the people—men and women—were talking like friends, or comrades."

Nora's face softened as she listened; she was enjoying herself enough to forget about Nanook for a while.

"That sounds like a labor union rally," she said. "Lots of people used to bring their kids, so that might be where your father took you when you were a little boy."

"So, you're interested in the labor movement?" Akash commented from the side.

"Yes, I am. Union culture almost died out for a while, but then it came back again. I used to go to rallies all the time. May Day, Women's Day, the Summer Festival, the Christmas Bazaar."

I shot an arrow in the dark.

"But your real reason for going was to meet some man."

I said the first thing that popped into my head. I didn't know anything about Nora, and there was nothing to give me even a hint, so I had to rely on instinct.

"Now that you mention it, there may have been someone."

"Kind of depressing don't you think, having to go to political gatherings to see the man you love."

Nora looked a little sad. I'd touched a nerve, and that was my opening: I couldn't let things get too bright and sunny, or I'd lose control. I take charge when the moon's out, not the sun. Nora took in a deep breath, the air whistling between her teeth like a snake slithering through the grass.

"You might be right—there was a man I always looked forward to seeing back then."

"But he had no interest in you as a woman."

"No, I'd shown him how I felt, and he didn't seem the least bit interested. In fact, he even started avoiding me."

"You thought you could attract men by working on your personality, by having the right attitude. He, on the other hand, wanted a woman who was sexy enough to keep him excited, and could tell at a glance whether to move in on her. He wasn't interested in personality, or lifestyle. He'd just compare a woman to himself, and if she seemed dreary, not as cool as he was, he'd stay away."

"What a dreadful thing to say."

"Easy to understand, though, if you think of sex as a drug."

"So, you're saying he was like an addict," Akash protested, "who'd do anything to get money to buy drugs—someone who doesn't care about anything."

"All men are like that, more or less."

Though I didn't really believe that, I wanted to see how Akash would react.

"If that's true, no wonder people want to quit being men."

That cool self-irony of his didn't leave any cracks I could slip a knife into. But seeing Nora wilt apparently made Nanook uncomfortable.

"You're a really wonderful person," he said, trying to comfort her. "You're honest, straightforward, and everyone depends on you."

I never thought I'd hear him talk like that. Velmer must be giving him some middle-aged tips on handling women. His soothing words had no effect, though. Nora looked sadder than ever.

"Nanook," she pleaded, "who are you, anyway? I know you got your position and personality from Dr. Velmer. But does that mean you love the woman he loves, too?"

Nanook laughed and shook his head.

"If I did, I wouldn't let him borrow my youth. He does have a lover, but I don't love anyone."

"Is romantic love interesting?" Hiruko quietly asked from the sofa. That startled everyone, but I made a point of ignoring her, and turned to Knut.

"Do you know who Dr. Velmer's in love with?" I asked roughly.

Shaking his head, he looked confused for a moment.

"No, and I couldn't care less," he said, now perfectly calm. "I would like to know why my father disappeared, though. If you know anything, won't you tell me?"

He'd asked me for information. Nice. If you want to control someone, a good way to start is helping him out.

"I might be able to give you a hint or two."

"He's trying to hypnotize you," warned Akash. "He probably knows nothing about it, so he wants you to tell him. Are you okay with that?" He looked awfully worried. But of course—he's in love with Knut. There's no other explanation.

"Knut," I said. "If Akash asked you to spend the night with him, what would you do? Refuse? Accept?"

I went straight to something no one wanted to talk about. Knut apparently didn't notice, and came back with something really weird.

"Once my mother said my father would look good in drag. It seemed like such a strange thing to say that I've never forgotten it."

"Knut, Susanoo isn't really having a conversation with you," said Akash, looking very serious. "He just wants to pull our strings, like marionettes."

"Ha ha," I laughed. "So, you have something to hide, too, do you?"

"Susanoo, we tracked you down, and tried our hardest to get you to talk for Hiruko's sake. To help her find her homeland, a country she's lost touch with, that's disappeared from the map of the world. We're not here to let you put rings in our noses and drag us into your barn like cattle. That barn of yours is awfully small, and much too dark."

"But did you ever once ask me if I wanted to go back to that homeland, if I missed it, or wanted to get in touch with people there, to talk to them again? No, you assumed I must, because it's only natural, so you all barged in—I call that nationalism."

Akash's jaw dropped. He probably can't imagine life here in Europe without his network of Indian friends. It took him a while to recover.

"I always thought," he finally said, "you only feel nationalistic in your own country."

"Well, you're wrong."

"But this isn't nationalism. It's personal desire. Wouldn't you like to contact your family, or old friends?"

"No. People from the past drag you down. Why do you guys want to help Hiruko, anyway? OK, so her country's disappeared—what's it to you?"

No one said anything.

"We're all inhabitants of this earth," Akash finally stated: "That's why we care." He didn't sound very sure of himself, though. I heaved a sigh of relief and went on.

"Akash, you should worry more about yourself. You say you're moving to another sex, but do you want to spend the rest of your life in a moving van? Nobody's going to want to share it with you. Knut, how would you feel about staying in a moving van with Akash?"

"What's that? A moving van? That might be kind of cool. A little cramped, maybe. When I was a kid I thought it would be fun to sneak into the back of a truck and go somewhere faraway. That gives me an idea—how about renting an RV we can all travel in together? It's been rough so far, with everyone having to find their own transport and places to stay."

Knut was pulling things way off course.

"Or wait!" He was getting more and more exited. "Maybe a boat would be better. Our next destination won't be someplace like Rome, somewhere we can drive to. Why not try to reach Hiruko's country by boat? We could go places where airplanes can't land. From here we could go south, cross the Mediterranean, go through the Suez Canal, navigate around Akash's homeland, floating to Southeast Asia, and then we can see what's happening beyond there for ourselves."

I had to pour a bucket of cold water over his enthusiasm: "What're you talking about? You're like your father after all. He must have set out on a trip on the spur of the moment with people he hardly knew, with no idea where he was going. And he never came back. Sad to say, a certain percentage of the population has genes that make them do that sort of thing."

"That's not true of me. Or wait, maybe it is …"

"Knut, you don't have any children to leave behind," said Akash. "Now is the best time for you to set out on a long journey." Knut's dream of traveling by boat was like a balloon he was blowing up, and I had to find a pin to prick it.

"On one of those luxury liners? What a drag. The pool on the deck, the store selling expensive jewelry, and every night you have to put on a tuxedo."

"No, no, it doesn't have to be like that," Akash protested. "We can take a freighter to India. Then we can transfer at Mumbai for one bound for Singapore."

"They'll have you earn your fare by washing dishes every day below deck. You'll be seasick, struggling not to puke the whole time."

"I don't think hard labor is required. Actually, friends have asked me a number of times if I didn't want to take a freighter with them."

Akash seemed to have one foot on deck already, and oddly enough, Nanook was the first one to catch his enthusiasm.

"The sea … Makes me homesick. Working inside the hospital every day I forget how close the ocean is. When I was a kid I used to watch sea otters from a rowboat, rocked by the waves. Grandpa taught me how to fish. This trip sounds really good to me right now."

I was about to warn him that once he left the hospital he couldn't keep acting like a bigshot, but saying that might make him dig in all the more, so I tried a different tack.

"It's the North Sea you're homesick for. The sea off Greenland, you know, with ice floes. You'll just get farther away from it if you head for India. That lukewarm Pacific water is sickening."

"Can we really divide the sea into 'mine' and 'theirs'?" asked Nanook. "As a kid, I didn't know anyplace except Greenland. Getting to Copenhagen made me want to go further. In Trier, I stepped into the Roman Empire, which doesn't even exist now. I never got a bigger view of Europe than that."

Akash then broke in with some completely irrelevant nonsense: "And now you're back in Copenhagen. Is that all you want, Nanook? This is a nice city to live in all right. But is that all you were looking for—an easy life?"

I shut him down before Nanook had a chance to reply.

"What's wrong with an easy life? Being cooped up in a tiny cabin with the floor pitching from side to side can make you sick."

"It's true you don't have a lot of room on a freighter," Akash said, looking straight at me. "But what is an ocean voyage if not being confined to a small space while going far, far away?"

Suddenly, Dr. Velmer joined the conversation.

"Hang on there, Nanook. You can't just run away with my personality. If you're going somewhere, I'm coming with you."

He was the last person I expected to get roped into this.

"You'd get awfully tired on a long trip with a bunch of baby birds cheeping the whole way, Doctor. Young people are idiots," I told him. "Best not to get involved with them."

"I can't agree with you there. I myself am thoroughly enjoying being young again. Take me with you, Knut. And by the way, can I bring my girlfriend?"

"No way," I said. "Couples are prohibited on this trip."

"Prohibited? Why?" asked Knut, who had no idea who Velmer was talking about. "You can bring anyone you like."

"Are you sure about that? Even if it's your mother?" I said pointedly. Knut thought I was joking.

"I'd rather keep family members out of it," he laughed, adding, "Couples are okay, though."

He's so out of it—he'll be sorry when he gets on board and sees who it is, but why should I care?

"The ocean. Time off from work. The wind. The boat. The

waves. And above us, the sun," Nora said, her eyes half-closed, her face turned up, like she was trying to see the sun through the ceiling.

"How can you call a journey you might not come back from 'time off'?" I scolded, but Nora ignored me and turned to Akash:

"I've just been through a real adventure, so no matter what kind of trouble we have on this trip, I'm ready for it. And besides, boat travel's best for the environment."

If you ask me, that last bit was entirely beside the point. Meanwhile, thinking about this boat trip must have taken Hiruko very far away, because she started singing softly, in the language only we could understand, "We are children of the sea/On the white, white waves."

"What's that song?" asked Knut, his eyes shining.

"ocean song. 'wind in the pines/that line the shore.'"

"A children's song?"

"yes. at school we sang. 'smoke drifts o'er/that rude thatched hut/my dearest childhood home.'"

"Is that a folk song?"

Ignoring Knut's question, she turned to me and said, "The lyrics were written by a man who translated the works of Knut Hamsun. Doesn't it seem like this song is calling us to Scandinavia?"

Without really knowing why, I strongly objected: "Not at all. No one knows who wrote the words. They're based on somebody's mistranslation of an old Scottish song."

She must have started to doubt herself, because Hiruko didn't say anything more. I didn't know what I was talking about, either, but at least I'd stopped her from carrying everyone off to the sea that surrounds our homeland.

"Boats are humanity's ruin. In the middle of the ocean there's no place to run, so people stick together, but not out of mutual affection. Community by force—that's all a boat is."

I tried desperately to put a stop to this nonsense. But I already sensed that I didn't stand a chance, pitted against the whole group. My body stiffened, and my hands and feet got cold. And then, I felt a hand on my shoulder from behind. A warm, heavy hand. I turned around to see that boy standing there.

CHAPTER 10   *Munun Speaks*

Things people leave behind are so lonely. They don't know where their owners are, or if they can go home again. And usually they don't have legs, so they can't walk home. Like this little penknife. I wonder why my brother always carried it around with him.

"Knives-drives are scary," Vita said when she saw it. "Whose is it?"

"My brother-other's."

"You have a brother-other?"

"He's been here a while-pile. His name is Susanoo."

"I remember now-pow! Susa susa NO! NO! NO! But is he really your brother-other?"

"Dunno-go. But I wish he was-buzz."

"Why does Susanoo have a knife-life?"

"For the dragons he fights-kites."

"This knife is too small for that-cat."

"I bet it can peel an apple, though-pro."

"I eat my apples peel and all-tall"

"Why's that-cat?"

"Eating the peel makes me prettier than I am now-pow."

The knife in my hand laughed at what Vita said. It's so lonely I was sure it was crying. I was really surprised to hear it laugh.

"I'm gonna take it back to my brother-other."

"I'll go too-boo."

"No, you can't-pant."

"Why-guy?"

"Because you have to stay here-tear!"

I took the elevator up to the third floor, and hurried down the corridor so fast the white doors lining both sides melted into ice cream. So did the nurses' shiny white uniforms.

"You're really busy today," one said, smiling as she passed the other way. I headed for Room 357. Or was it 375? I forget the number, but remember the place. That's where my brother plays a word game with Dr. Velmer and Nanook. It's fun. They look at stuffed animals, or dolls, and then say words from lots of different countries. When I opened the door, the first thing I saw was Susanoo's back. Hard as a board, and sad somehow. My poor brother. Looks like everyone's attacking him head on. Just him against a whole bunch of people. He's the outsider, the one everybody bullies. Like someone I know, when he was a little kid. I gently put my hand on Susanoo's shoulder from behind. Like Vita does sometimes, when I'm sad. It makes me feel like I'm glowing inside, so I wanted to do the same for him. Susanoo shivered at first, like my hand was ice, and turned his head. When he saw it was me he relaxed, and smiled. Then the rest of him turned around, too.

"Oh, it's you," he said. "What're you doing here, Munun? Are you looking for something?"

"You forgot this," I said, and handed him the knife.

He opened his eyes wide and whispered, "My *tsurugi* sword." Then, he took it carefully in his hands. Tsurugi? What's that? The other people weren't really bullying Susanoo after all. In fact, they looked kind of confused. Doctor Velmer. That fake doctor Nanook. And a man and a woman who were here before. Knut and Hiruko, they're called. There was another woman today, too. Real tall, with yellow hair—golden, sticking out all around her head. And there's someone else, wearing nice red clothes. Depending on your point of view, this one could be a woman or a man. I wonder which. When someone looks this pretty, maybe it doesn't matter. But why are they all here, anyway? It doesn't seem like they're having a party. Or a meeting, either. Susanoo and the knife stared at each other a while. Then his face got serious, he stood up right next to me, and held the knife out in front of him like a warrior in a movie. "Hope nothing bad happens," the window whispered. It wasn't dark outside yet, but the sun was starting down the stairs.

The door opened and there was Vita, breathing hard. I'd told her to stay in the basement, but she followed me anyway. She was holding our old radio in one hand.

"Munun, the radio's broken-token."

"I'll fix it later. I'm busy now-pow."

"Busy doing what-putt?"

A hard question for anyone. Even me. Vita got tired of waiting for an answer.

"Munun, the radio's broken-token. So fix it, won't you-boo? Look, I turn it on but it doesn't say anything."

Vita put the radio on the floor, and pushed the button with the star seal on it. No sound came out. It always plays music from Vita's favorite station. Or if it's not tuned in right, you hear a hissing, buzzing sound, but now, nothing. Did this ever happen before? I was trying to remember when suddenly a big wave came up inside the radio, and music came on. I quickly turned it to OFF, but no matter how many times I pushed the OFF button again, the music didn't stop. What a mess. But what to do? It was accordion music, the kind you hear at traveling carnivals when it's starting to get cold, cheerful but a little sad, too.

"Nice song!" Vita was so excited about the music she didn't notice how upset I was. She was swinging her hips, about to start dancing. I was going to take Vita and the radio and leave the room, but before I knew it I was moving in time to the music, too. I remembered that time at summer camp when we all

practiced dancing in a circle. That was fun. Sparks were dancing
around the campfire, too. Let's do that again. For some reason,
the words I always used to say at that camp popped right out of
my mouth:

"Everybody take the person next to you by the hand!"

Vita, who got the message before I did, grabbed my right
hand and Susanoo's left, and started lifting her legs in time to
the music.

"Vita, what are you doing?"

"We're all gonna dance together, aren't we?"

Vita likes dancing even more than ice cream, so whenever she
hears music with a strong beat she starts bouncing around like
a ball. She was like a crazy little kid who does what she wants
no matter what. Everybody was watching her with their mouths
open, like they were about to laugh.

"Hurry up, come on you guys, join hands!"

Nobody can say no to Vita. Hiruko couldn't either, so she
shyly took Susanoo's right hand. He turned away, but held her
hand anyway. When she lifted her free hand, Knut quickly
moved in to take it in his. These two always fly together, like the
wings of a butterfly. You can't really call them a couple, though.
It's hard to explain why, but anyway, I don't think they're having
sex. The one in pretty red clothes slowly squeezed Knut's free
hand—his right. Then the tall woman took the pretty one's right
hand. "Akash," she said, so that must be his or her name. Akash
then turned to her and said, "Nora," so I guess that's her name.
Akash and Nora seem to get along well together, but not at all
like a married couple. In fact, they're so different from a married couple I'm not sure what to call them. Nora looked over at
Nanook like she was trying to figure out what he was thinking,
and seemed almost afraid to take his hand. Nanook frowned
as if dancing was the last thing he wanted to do, but he didn't
shake off Nora's hand. These two don't get along—somehow

they seem more like a married couple. The only one left was Velmer. He quickly took Nanook's and my hands. Now we were all one big circle.

"Does everybody know how to do the circle dance?" I asked, but the only one who yelled, "I do!" was Vita. She knows how, all right, but in her own way. She started kicking her legs in the air, yanking on our hands so me and my brother almost fell over.

"Cool it, Vita," I said, "Let me show them." I let go of the hands I was holding and walked into the middle of the circle. Three steps to the left, and stop a beat. Then three more steps to the left, and stop again. Stomp in place four times, then another three steps to the left, and stop a beat. That makes one set. Repeat as many times as you like.

"Do you know the song 'Sur le pont d'Avignon'? Sing it in your head while you do the steps—that makes it easier."

"You left out the kicks!" Vita yelled.

"The kicks come later. First, let's practice the steps."

Strung together like rosary beads, everybody started moving. To my right, Vita was bouncing up and down, while on my left, Velmer was stumbling because he couldn't quite get on the rhythm train. Vita right, Velmer left, and me, the bead in between. Akash twisted and turned, like he or she had lots of little extra joints between the main ones. Knut looked embarrassed. His steps were a little unsteady. With everyone moving at a different pace, the circle got all bunched up, and the dance stopped. Only the radio kept on playing.

"Can we all stick to the same steps?"

"No way," said Susanoo, sounding very sure of himself. "Our personalities are too different."

"Could we try taking tiny steps?" Hiruko suggested. Even Susanoo nodded his head like a good little boy.

"Okay, let's try it again. One, two, three!"

It seemed like Dr. Velmer worked out the rhythm as a sort

of math problem, and was now stepping in time like a robot. Whatever else is wrong with him, he's got a really good brain. Nanook was on the other side of him, so I couldn't see him from where I was standing. Nora tried so hard to keep her steps small that her long legs were pointing inwards, like a big X. It didn't look right, and I wanted to say something but couldn't find the words. Then Akash whispered something in her ear, and right after that her knees got straightened out. Soon she was floating along to the rhythm, having a good time. But then Akash missed a step, and one of his sandals almost came off. Nora held him up and carried him along so he could put his foot back in his sandal without stopping the dance. These two need each other. Knut still looked like a big teddy bear.

"Youth is an energetic machine," I heard Velmer say in a low voice. I couldn't understand why he thinks youth is a machine and not a person, but that's okay, because he was dancing along with everyone else now.

"Even without a director we're all keeping to the same beat," said Nora, her cheeks flushed. "We're really a circle now."

"There are many different kinds of circles," said Velmer. "We've moved on from 'Sur le pont d'Avignon' and are now dancing to the Wedding March, ha, ha, ha. Perhaps there's some-one besides me here who's planning to marry in the near future, ha, ha, ha." Now he was sure enough of the steps to make jokes.

"You know, you look kind of like the Nutcracker," Nora teased. "Without the beard of course." She wasn't being nasty, though, and Velmer didn't get mad at all.

"The Nutcracker?" he said cheerfully. "Do you like Tchaikovsky? Now that you mention it, there's something like a circle dance in that ballet," he added, spreading out his cultural tablecloth.

Bored with this simple rhythm, Akash's arms and legs started fluttering up, down, and around between beats. He or she stretched out his or her neck, too, moving it like a snake. Knut looked more like he was walking in time than dancing, but he seemed to be enjoying himself.

"This is fun," he said. "Let's get together on deck every night and dance." As soon as those words reached my brain, my heart did a back flip.

"Are you going somewhere on a boat?" I asked.

"We've been talking about it, yes. Since we're going to look for an island that may have disappeared, traveling by ship would be best. Planes aren't flying there anymore anyway."

"Is it far away?"

"Yes, very far away."

I squeezed Vita's hand hard. She'll stay with me no matter what. Even so, I'll be lonely if all these people go away. Especially Susanoo. I finally found my brother, and now I have to go back to being an only child? My eyes went all blurry so I couldn't tell who was who. My feet were still dancing, but my chest had a heavy stone inside, and tears ran down my cheeks. Vita looked over at me.

"What's wrong-bong? Are you sad-bad?"

"Susanoo's going far away, on a boat-coat."

Now they were all looking at me. One by one their feet stopped, they let go of the hand of the person next to them, and stood there like pillars of ice. Only the music went on ahead. In this frozen world, Susanoo was the first to melt. He came and gave me a hug.

"I want to stay, too, little brother," he said. "I don't want to get on a boat with these people. I'd much rather be here, with you. But I've got to go."

Vita was so angry her voice sounded strange.

"Susanoo, why are you going away? Look how sad you made Munun. Aren't you sorry? Where are you going, and why? For work?"

"Not for work," said Susanoo, his eyelashes full of kindness. "Through sheer meanness I pried open all these people's doors. So now I'm responsible for them."

"But you'll come back soon, won't you?" That was my question, but Vita asked it for me.

Susanoo took Vita's right hand, lifted it up, and then, looking at Hiruko as if he was a little afraid of her, took her left hand and said, "The answer is in the dance. So let's dance a little more."

The radio had already gone on to the next song, which sounded a little bluer than the one before, but still matched the steps we'd practiced. It was like our feet were all breathing together. Kind of strange. Nora looked like an oak, Akash like a willow, and Knut like a teddy bear. Their bodies were so different, but they were all dancing together to the same tune like a long snake. The snake was a big circle, with its tail in its mouth. As the circle went round and round, the things I saw changed, little by little. The window, the desk, the chair, the wall, the door. The door was partly open, and beyond it, two little guys were looking in. So small they hardly came up to my knees. They weren't children, though. The one on the right was a robot, and the one on the left was a shabby brown teddy bear. Without lifting its feet, the robot walked into the room, went over to the radio, bent at the waist, and suddenly turned the radio off. The music stopped. The robot had a shiny blue metal rucksack on his back.

"That robot!" shouted Nanook. The robot didn't let him say anything else.

"Enough dancing," it said, sounding just like a robot. "Now it is time to prepare for your trip. As you will be traveling by boat, each person is allowed a hundred pounds of luggage. The sun will be strong on the deck, so be sure to bring a hat. For the cold nights, remember to pack sweaters."

"You'll be leaving this coming Sunday," added the teddy bear from the doorway where he was standing: "Everybody meet in the waiting room for international ferries at Copenhagen Port, at six in the evening." He sounded like the talking animals in puppet shows.

"Where did these toys come from?" asked Velmer. "Are they escapees from the cupboard where I keep my therapeutic equipment?"

"No," said Nanook, wiping the sweat off his forehead with the back of his hand. "A man I met on my way here asked me to carry them."

"You brought them here?"

"Not all the way. Only as far as Hamburg."

"A different boy carried us from Hamburg to Copenhagen," the robot said in Nanook's place. So, to this robot, Nanook is just a boy, like me. Then, some squarish stiff paper tongues came shooting out of the metal rucksack on the robot's back.

"These are your tickets for the ship to Cape Town. When you arrive there, go to the Gandhi Travel Office and buy tickets for India. The destinations are Chennai and Mumbai. Explain that you intend to go further east, and ask which Indian port is better." The robot was now giving orders like a ship's captain.

"We're in the middle of a dream," Nora said softly.

"So we're all having the same dream?" asked Akash. "Or am I merely a character who appears in your dream?"

Velmer bent over to pick up the tickets that were scattered on the floor. He'd always told me he had lumbago, but now he was moving as lightly as a young man.

"Your names are on them," he said as he passed them out. "Nanook, here's yours. This one's for Nora ..."

"Just think," said Nanook as he took his ticket, "all countries, close by or far away, are connected by the sea. Both the North and South Poles are parts of the same sphere. The sea water around Scandinavia may even flow all the way down to the South Pacific."

Nora looked over at Nanook and said, "Everyone's looking

forward to this trip." Then she suddenly got very serious and added, "But ocean liners spill oil, and leave carpets of garbage on the water."

"Here's your ticket, Akash."

"I haven't been in India for such a long time. It'll be fun, going back."

"But this will only get us as far as Cape Town," Nora said. "We'll be counting on you when we have to find that Gandhi Travel Office and buy tickets to India."

"Are you really going with them?" asked Velmer as he handed Knut his ticket. "Shouldn't you be concentrating on your research?"

"A ship's a good place to study linguistics," he said, looking far off in the distance. "Actually, through an odd series of circumstances, I was about to take on the role of a young man starting a new publishing company, but I'll have to put that plan on hold for a while. I guess I'm destined to keep looking for Hiruko's homeland."

Hiruko watched him as she took her ticket from Velmer, but didn't seem so sure about all this. To cheer her up, Akash said, "I'm sure we'll find your home country. Even places that seem to have disappeared can't escape from the sea."

"My home country?" she asked quietly. "What country? Is there any meaning in looking for it, or not?" I couldn't tell who she was talking to.

"This last one is for Susanoo," said Velmer. "Wait a minute— mine seems to be missing. I must have given it to someone by mistake. Could you all check to see if my ticket's hiding under yours?" Everyone shook their heads. Susanoo was staring down at the picture of the ship on his ticket, looking scared. He noticed that Knut was watching him.

"There's no sense searching for a country that's disappeared. Why don't we take a trip to look for your father instead?" Susanoo's such a nice guy, but when he talks to Knut, there's a sharp thorn in his voice. Velmer's eyes were mopping the floor, trying to find a ticket with his name on it. Vita and I didn't have tickets either, but getting on a ship seemed like a lot of trouble, so I didn't say anything.

"There's no ticket for me!" Vita cried. That made her really mad.

"There's none for me, either," I said to calm her down, "so why don't we just stay here?"

I guess she must have cared more about that boat than me, though, because she kept on making a fuss.

"I wanna go on the boat!" she yelled.

"Even if you have to say goodbye to me forever?" I asked, and that finally shut her up.

Then the stuffed bear walked out to the middle of the floor, his round body swaying from side to side. He had a rucksack, too, a little denim one. It was open, so when the bear bowed, three tickets came flying out and landed on the floor. They were green, with a pretty gold pattern on them. Velmer reached down and grabbed them.

"What's this?" Velmer said, blinking as he reached for his reading glasses. "Invitation to the Exile Film Studio. This is a ticket to a dinner party, not a boat voyage. But it has my name on it. And the other two are for Munun and Vita. This is really something—we'll be having dinner with the most famous film director in Scandinavia. He's throwing the dinner party to show his thanks to everyone who cooperated with his latest movie. I don't remember anything like a film, but what the heck, I must have helped him out without realizing it. But why are Munun and Vita invited along with me? Definitely a strange combination. I guess it doesn't really matter, though. To tell the truth, this is better than a long voyage. The furnishings in my cabin would probably not meet my standards, and I'd hate to leave *her* behind, but were I to take her along, it'd do me serious financial damage. But wait—the dinner's tonight. At eight o'clock. There's no time to lose. I'll have to hurry home and change. I don't keep my tuxedo here at the hospital."

He rushed out of the room, but turning around, just as he was about to shut the door, Velmer first shot me and Vita a look as if we were a real bother to him, and yet then suddenly he smiled, making little wrinkles at the corners of his eyes. "I'll come and pick you up in my car at a quarter to eight, so make sure you're all dressed up." This time he was really gone, like a ghost or something. Dr. Velmer really is a nice man.

Vita made up a little song, "Directors make me happy, studios make me glad, movies never ever make me sad!" As she sang, she started to dance again, hands on her hips, her feet making figure eights. I guess she'd forgotten all about that boat she couldn't ride on.

It was getting dark outside, and the room was full of that "let's-go-home-or-back-to-the-hotel" kind of feeling. I wanted to stop time somehow, so I blurted out, "I have presents for everyone, so please stop by at my place before you go."

"A birthday present?" asked Susanoo, gently touching my arm.

"Is today someone's birthday?" asked Knut as if that was strange somehow.

"No, but setting out on a long journey is like starting a new life," Susanoo explained for me. "So today's everybody's second birthday." I don't really know if that was what I was thinking or not. But I was glad to hear Susanoo say it anyway. He really is my big brother.

"So, you see," I said, "giving presents to people who are starting out on a long trip is the right thing to do."

"Not so much a present as a talisman," Nanook said as if this was something everybody knew, "to protect the travelers from evil spirits."

"*Sobetsukai* present," said Hiruko. I wonder what a *sobetsukai* is. Doesn't really matter, I guess. I led everyone to our half basement. As we walked down the corridor in a line, the nurses passing by gave us funny looks. When we got in the elevator, I started hearing the stars moan, somewhere far away. Vita says the stars don't moan, but I think they do. This elevator always goes right where it's supposed to when it's going up, but doesn't know when to stop on the way down, so sometimes I get a chilly feeling, as if a ghost's pulling the strings.

There's a place where we wash dishes in the half basement. Behind all the gleaming silver machines and shiny white plates is our living room and bedroom. I turned on the light, and threw all the clothes scattered over the floor onto the bed so everyone would have room to stand.

"Come in," I said, "right this way."

Knut hunched over as he walked in. Our ceiling isn't all that low, and there's plenty of room for him to get through the door, but he's so big I guess our place looked small to him. Nora gawked around like she'd never seen such interesting rooms. Hiruko and Susanoo marched right in like kids coming to see a sister or brother. Akash found my star chart on the wall, and ran his fingers over it.

"So this is where you live," he whispered. "It's very nice. I wonder what our presents will be."

I closed the curtain and switched off the light. Light from the streetlamp outside came in through the holes I'd made with a hole puncher, and they started to shine like stars.

"Oh, I see," shouted Akash: "You've got your own homemade planetarium!"

"That's right," I said, "and now I'm going to give each one of you a star. Please take it with you, to protect you on your journey."

I followed the lines I'd drawn on the curtain with yellow crayon until I came to the star Regulus.

"Nanook, this is your star. It's called Regulus. It means lion's heart."

"A star that makes people happy, isn't it?" Nora said, maybe because she was hoping someone would make her happy. Maybe Nanook? But I've never heard of a lion's heart making anyone happy.

"Nora, your star is Arcturus."

"I thought it might be. Thank you, Munun."

"You chase the Great Bear, always going to the North."

"I wonder who the bear is. And if I catch that bear, do I marry him?"

"Arcturus is actually made up of two stars, husband and wife. So they're married from the start." These sentences are from a book I read, about fortune telling. It was so hard I didn't want to go over it again and again, so I memorized it the first time. Nora was surprised when I told her that, and looked through the Arcturus hole in the curtain from all angles. Unfortunately, it's just a hole, so I don't think it looked at all like husband-and-wife stars.

"Are you studying the constellations, Munun?" asked Akash. "I really respect that."

"I've got a red star for you," I said, feeling happy he'd praised me that way.

"Really? What's it called?"

"Betelgeuse."

"Is it far away?"

"Pretty far. But lots of people look up at it, so it's never lonely. That's true of Knut's star, too."

"Which one's mine?"

"This one," I said, pointing to one of the bigger holes in the curtain. "It's bright because it's close, and that makes it easy to find."

"You mean Sirius?" asked Nora.

"Yes. Oh, and remember, everyone—the farther you are from the sun the darker you are, so try not to get too far away."

"The sun—that's Hiruko, isn't it?" asked Susanoo.

"No, Hiruko is Capella. If the sun were a star, and much farther away, it would look almost exactly like Capella."

"Stars stay far away out of kindness," said Hiruko, looking like she was thinking hard: "There's danger if the sun gets too close."

"Without the sun's rays," said Akash, "every living creature would die." He sounded kind of mad.

"But if it moved a little closer to us, even a distance too small for the universe to notice, we'd all burn to death." Hiruko looked really gloomy, as if she was imagining killing us all by coming closer. I knew I had to say something.

"Capella doesn't kill anyone. Capella is lonely, so she stays far away from everyone."

That didn't lift any clouds from Hiruko's face.

"You're a star made up of several different parts," said Nora. "Two pairs of stars come together to form Capella." She seemed to like the stars as much as I do.

"Nora, you're a Doctor of Stars," I said.

"No, not really," she said. "Once I fell in love with a man from Syria, and followed him all the way to Aleppo. I never found him, but ended up spending a month in the desert. The nights were lonely and cold, but the stars shone so brightly they looked like jewels, so close I thought I could reach up to the sky and touch them. I couldn't, of course."

"I'll bet you can see them clearly onboard ship," said Knut. He sounded like he was already there in his mind. I spoke to Susanoo, using words from one of my favorite anime.

"Beloved brother Altair, Soar through the sky like a big, bold bird!" As I said those words, my eyes got blurry with tears. "Since you're going by boat, I thought maybe Susanoo should be Canopus, the guide. But that's not so good, because with Susanoo for a guide, the boat would sink. So I want Susanoo to be a bird. That way, even if the boat sinks, he won't drown." While I was talking, two tears rolled down my cheeks.

"Hikoboshi," Hiruko whispered.

"Who's that?" asked Knut. He's interested in everything she says.

"Hikoboshi is looking for a woman, a weaver. Her name is Orihime."

Then Susanoo hung his head and said, "I did something terrible to Orihime. I'll have to find her, and talk to her about it." That sounded mysterious. Orihime. That's a star I've never heard of.

"Well, I think we'd better go home and start planning our trip," said Knut. "Besides, Munun and Vita have a dinner to get ready for, so we shouldn't be hanging around." That was the sign for everybody's hearts to leave the stars behind. I went as far as the elevator to see them off, and decided to say goodbye there.

"Have a good trip. No hugs today." And with that, I turned around and went to my room without looking back. I found Vita sobbing in the bedroom.

"Why are you crying so much-touch?"

"Because you're sad-bad, I'm crying instead-bed."

"How much longer are you going to cry-pie?"

"About seven minutes more, or maybe nine-pine."

I always see people's feet as they leave the building from our half-basement window. I'll bet they don't know I'm watching them, though. I pressed my nose to the glass and waited until I saw Knut's shoes step lightly out. The ocher-colored leather looked like a fox I wanted to touch. Knut stopped to wait for Hiruko, and the two of them walked toward the gate, side by side. Hiruko's ankles were thin, and so was the leather that covered them. I could see the shape of her ankle bones. I think climbing boots would be better for a long trip than pumps. We all have to protect our feet. Next came Akash's sandals, chasing after Hiruko. Those sneakers taking big steps must be Nanook. Nora came after him, planting her feet firmly on the ground. Since Susanoo's staying in the hospital, he probably went out a different door.

A tired feeling came over me in waves. I'd have to wipe away Vita's tears with a towel, talk her into putting her party dress on, and look for something to wear myself. After all, we're invited to dinner tonight. There's not much time until Velmer comes to pick us up in his car. Still, I wanted to sleep for five minutes. Just a little would be enough. My eyelids were getting heavy. I saw Susanoo with his shirt off, sitting on top of a sea turtle. So . . . that boat they said they were going on was really a turtle? It looks like fun, riding a turtle, but there's nothing to hold on to, and you might fall off. But where was everybody else? Maybe they all ran away because I said that if Susanoo was the guide the boat would sink. Poor Susanoo—I shouldn't have said that. He got off the turtle and started swimming in the sea—the crawl stroke—toward me. But seaweed was wrapped around his arms, making it hard to swim. I could see through the seaweed, and it had supermarket logos printed on it, like Aldi, Netto, Bilka. Susanoo tried to get it off his arms as he swam toward me. When he got to a shallow place, he stood up. Why was his body covered with scales? He was wearing only white shorts, and his feet, stomach, chest, and arms were all scaley like a snake's. He squatted down, looking for something. What he finally found was a little black shellfish. He bit down on it with his back teeth, trying to open it. He must have been really hungry. But a shell that won't open is dead, so you mustn't eat it, I wanted to warn him, but I lost my voice. That's right—I didn't come on this trip. That means I'm not where he is. The wind blew, bringing a bad smell that made me want to throw up. I looked and saw a fishing boat that had washed up on the beach, with some gray, gooey stuff stuck to its side. It looked like rotten plastic. But does plastic rot? Susanoo gave up eating that shell, and walked unsteadily away from the sea. There was a fishing village, but not like the ones in picture books—just a line of square houses with steel walls. They didn't have windows or doors. The sunlight was so strong it reflected off the road, so bright you couldn't see anything. I'd hurt my eyes if I kept on looking at it. That's how it seemed to me, anyway. I could see through the trunks of the trees lined up along the road. The leaves had fallen, and were all crinkled up on the ground, the color of dog shit. I saw some tall buildings in the distance, but they'd burnt up; they were all black with soot. Susanoo went around to the back of one of the houses. I followed him and found a zipper, like on a dress. Susanoo pulled it down and went in. Inside it was all white, like a hospital room, and in the middle of it was a loom. Hiruko was sitting at it, weaving. Flowing from her fingertips, she was turning into the thread that she was weaving into cloth, so her head was already gone, and her shoulders were going. I saw Hiruko's face in the pattern on the cloth she was weaving. Hiruko spoke to Susanoo as she turned into cloth, but in words I didn't understand at all. I felt awfully chilly, and noticed a speaker beside me, but what came out of it was cold air instead of music. I wish I had a big, warm sweater, I was thinking, just before I woke up.

The window had opened, all by itself. The moon had taken charge, sending cold air into the room. My heart was beating hard. That's when I saw Vita, her tears all gone, wearing her best dress, walking toward me.

New Directions Paperbooks—a partial listing

Adonis, Songs of Mihyar the Damascene
César Aira, Ghosts
   An Episode in the Life of a Landscape Painter
Ryanosuke Akutagawa, Kappa
Will Alexander, Refractive Africa
Osama Alomar, The Teeth of the Comb
Guillaume Apollinaire, Selected Writings
Jessica Au, Cold Enough for Snow
Paul Auster, The Red Notebook
Ingeborg Bachmann, Malina
Honoré de Balzac, Colonel Chabert
Djuna Barnes, Nightwood
Charles Baudelaire, The Flowers of Evil*
Bei Dao, City Gate, Open Up
Yevgenia Belorusets, Lucky Breaks
Mei-Mei Berssenbrugge, Empathy
Max Blecher, Adventures in Immediate Irreality
Jorge Luis Borges, Labyrinths
   Seven Nights
Coral Bracho, Firefly Under the Tongue*
Kamau Brathwaite, Ancestors
Anne Carson, Glass, Irony & God
   Wrong Norma
Horacio Castellanos Moya, Senselessness
Camilo José Cela, Mazurka for Two Dead Men
Louis-Ferdinand Céline
   Death on the Installment Plan
   Journey to the End of the Night
Inger Christensen, alphabet
Julio Cortázar, Cronopios and Famas
Jonathan Creasy (ed.), Black Mountain Poems
Robert Creeley, If I Were Writing This
H.D., Selected Poems
Guy Davenport, 7 Greeks
Amparo Davila, The Houseguest
Osamu Dazai, The Flowers of Buffoonery
   No Longer Human
   The Setting Sun
Anne de Marcken
   It Lasts Forever and Then It's Over
Helen DeWitt, The Last Samurai
   Some Trick
José Donoso, The Obscene Bird of Night
Robert Duncan, Selected Poems
Eça de Queirós, The Maias
Juan Emar, Yesterday
William Empson, 7 Types of Ambiguity

Mathias Énard, Compass
Shusaku Endo, Deep River
Jenny Erpenbeck, Go, Went, Gone
   Kairos
Lawrence Ferlinghetti
   A Coney Island of the Mind
Thalia Field, Personhood
F. Scott Fitzgerald, The Crack-Up
Rivka Galchen, Little Labors
Forrest Gander, Be With
Romain Gary, The Kites
Natalia Ginzburg, The Dry Heart
Henry Green, Concluding
Marlen Haushofer, The Wall
Victor Heringer, The Love of Singular Men
Felisberto Hernández, Piano Stories
Hermann Hesse, Siddhartha
Takashi Hiraide, The Guest Cat
Yoel Hoffmann, Moods
Susan Howe, My Emily Dickinson
   Concordance
Bohumil Hrabal, I Served the King of England
Qurratulain Hyder, River of Fire
Sonallah Ibrahim, That Smell
Rachel Ingalls, Mrs. Caliban
Christopher Isherwood, The Berlin Stories
Fleur Jaeggy, Sweet Days of Discipline
Alfred Jarry, Ubu Roi
B.S. Johnson, House Mother Normal
James Joyce, Stephen Hero
Franz Kafka, Amerika: The Man Who Disappeared
Yasunari Kawabata, Dandelions
John Keene, Counternarratives
Kim Hyesoon, Autobiography of Death
Heinrich von Kleist, Michael Kohlhaas
Taeko Kono, Toddler-Hunting
László Krasznahorkai, Satantango
   Seiobo There Below
Ágota Kristóf, The Illiterate
Eka Kurniawan, Beauty Is a Wound
Mme. de Lafayette, The Princess of Clèves
Lautréamont, Maldoror
Siegfried Lenz, The German Lesson
Alexander Lernet-Holenia, Count Luna
Denise Levertov, Selected Poems
Li Po, Selected Poems

Clarice Lispector, An Apprenticeship
  The Hour of the Star
  The Passion According to G. H.
Federico García Lorca, Selected Poems*
Nathaniel Mackey, Splay Anthem
Xavier de Maistre, Voyage Around My Room
Stéphane Mallarmé, Selected Poetry and Prose*
Javier Marías, Your Face Tomorrow (3 volumes)
Bernadette Mayer, Midwinter Day
Carson McCullers, The Member of the Wedding
Fernando Melchor, Hurricane Season
  Paradais
Thomas Merton, New Seeds of Contemplation
  The Way of Chuang Tzu
Henri Michaux, A Barbarian in Asia
Henry Miller, The Colossus of Maroussi
  Big Sur & the Oranges of Hieronymus Bosch
Yukio Mishima, Confessions of a Mask
  Death in Midsummer
Eugenio Montale, Selected Poems*
Vladimir Nabokov, Laughter in the Dark
Pablo Neruda, The Captain's Verses*
  Love Poems*
Charles Olson, Selected Writings
George Oppen, New Collected Poems
Wilfred Owen, Collected Poems
Hiroko Oyamada, The Hole
José Emilio Pacheco, Battles in the Desert
Michael Palmer, Little Elegies for Sister Satan
Nicanor Parra, Antipoems*
Boris Pasternak, Safe Conduct
Octavio Paz, Poems of Octavio Paz
Victor Pelevin, Omon Ra
Fernando Pessoa
  The Complete Works of Alberto Caeiro
Alejandra Pizarnik
  Extracting the Stone of Madness
Robert Plunket, My Search for Warren Harding
Ezra Pound, The Cantos
  New Selected Poems and Translations
Qian Zhongshu, Fortress Besieged
Raymond Queneau, Exercises in Style
Olga Ravn, The Employees
Herbert Read, The Green Child
Kenneth Rexroth, Selected Poems
Keith Ridgway, A Shock
Rainer Maria Rilke
  Poems from the Book of Hours

Arthur Rimbaud, Illuminations*
  A Season in Hell and The Drunken Boat*
Evelio Rosero, The Armies
Fran Ross, Oreo
Joseph Roth, The Emperor's Tomb
Raymond Roussel, Locus Solus
Ihara Saikaku, The Life of an Amorous Woman
Nathalie Sarraute, Tropisms
Jean-Paul Sartre, Nausea
Kathryn Scanlan, Kick the Latch
Delmore Schwartz
  In Dreams Begin Responsibilities
W. G. Sebald, The Emigrants
  The Rings of Saturn
Anne Serre, The Governesses
Patti Smith, Woolgathering
Stevie Smith, Best Poems
  Novel on Yellow Paper
Gary Snyder, Turtle Island
Muriel Spark, The Driver's Seat
  The Public Image
Maria Stepanova, In Memory of Memory
Wislawa Szymborska, How to Start Writing
Antonio Tabucchi, Pereira Maintains
Junichiro Tanizaki, The Maids
Yoko Tawada, The Emissary
  Memoirs of a Polar Bear
  Scattered All over the Earth
Dylan Thomas, A Child's Christmas in Wales
  Collected Poems
Thuan, Chinatown
Rosemary Tonks, The Bloater
Tomas Tranströmer, The Great Enigma
Leonid Tsypkin, Summer in Baden-Baden
Tu Fu, Selected Poems
Enrique Vila-Matas, Bartleby & Co.
Elio Vittorini, Conversations in Sicily
Rosmarie Waldrop, The Nick of Time
Robert Walser, The Tanners
Eliot Weinberger, An Elemental Thing
  Nineteen Ways of Looking at Wang Wei
Nathanael West, The Day of the Locust
  Miss Lonelyhearts
Tennessee Williams, The Glass Menagerie
  A Streetcar Named Desire
William Carlos Williams, Selected Poems
Alexis Wright, Praiseworthy
Louis Zukofsky, "A"

*BILINGUAL EDITION

For a complete listing, request a free catalog from New Directions, 80 8th Avenue, New York, NY 10011
or visit us online at ndbooks.com